Praise for the Malin Fors series

'Kallentoft's novels always run at a high emotional temperature.' *Sunday Times*

'[An] atmospheric series.' *Independent*

'One of the best-realised female heroines I've read by a male writer.' *Guardian*

'Kallentoft's books have been called beautiful, exquisite and original. I can see why.' *Literary Review*

'The highest suspense.' Camilla Lackberg

'The strengths of this complex and excellent novel include realistic dialogue, thorough characterisation and concern for social issues.' *New Zealand Listener*

'Meditative. Dark. Really, really cold . . . This is a worthy successor to Larsson's Millennium trilogy.' *Booklist* (Starred Review)

'Malin Fors is an intriguing and complex heroine . . . Kallentoft is an outstanding writer.' *Nordic Bookblog*

'It is Kallentoft's characterisation and distinctive, often poetic style which make his crime-writing more memorable than most . . . It is compelling reading. The atmosphere of oppressive heat creates the sense of a hell on earth, where evil thrives. It is a powerful and disturbing vision.' *Canberra Times*

## About the Author

Mons Kallentoft grew up in the provincial town of Linköping, Sweden, where the Malin Fors series is set. The series is a massive European bestseller and has been translated into over twenty languages. Before becoming a novelist, Mons worked in journalism; he is also a renowned food critic. His debut novel, Pesetas, was awarded the Swedish equivalent of the Costa Book Award.

Mons has been married to Karolina for over twenty years, and they live in Stockholm with their daughter and son.

*Also by Mons Kallentoft*
*and published by Hodder & Stoughton*

Midwinter Sacrifice
Summertime Death
Autumn Killing
Savage Spring
The Fifth Season
Water Angels
Souls of Air

Visit Mons' website at www.monskallentoft.se and his Facebook page at www.facebook.com/MonsKallentoft and follow him on Twitter @Kallentoft

# Earth Storm

## Mons Kallentoft

Translated from the Swedish by
Neil Smith

HODDER

Originally published in Swedish in 2014
as *Jordstorm* by Bokförlaget Forum

First published in Great-Britain in 2018 by Hodder & Stoughton
An Hachette UK company

This paperback edition first published in 2018

2

A CIP catalogue record for this title is
available from the British Library

Paperback ISBN 978 1 444 77642 3
eBook ISBN 978 1 444 77644 7

Typeset in Plantin Light 10.75/13.5 pt by
Palimpsest Book Production Limited, Falkirk, Stirlingshire

Printed and bound in Great Britain by Clays Ltd, Elcograf S.p.A.

Hodder & Stoughton policy is to use papers that are natural,
renewable and recyclable products and made from wood grown
in sustainable forests. The logging and manufacturing processes
are expected to conform to the environmental regulations of
the country of origin.

Hodder & Stoughton Ltd
Carmelite House
50 Victoria Embankment
London EC4Y 0DZ

www.hodder.co.uk

# Prologue

[In silence]

The worms are slithering around me. I try to move my
arms, but the wood stops them. It is wood, isn't it?

I don't remember how I ended up here.

My head has stopped aching. But it was aching when
I woke up. And the skin around my nose and mouth
stung.

I can breathe, and I can scream. The air could run out
at any moment.

I've been here for many hours now, but how long? A
day? Twenty-four hours? Probably no longer. A second
feels like an hour, which feels like a day.

I'm trying not to be frightened, because this must be
a dream.

There's a smell of earth, of damp earth drying.

I'm lying stretched out, no other position is possible.

The planks get in my way if I try to raise my head.
Splinters catch in my forehead when I move it from side
to side. I'm not naked, though. Trousers, a top, cloth against
my skin.

Unless it is actually my skin, and I just think it's cloth?

My body stings, and there's blood running down my
cheeks, making my hair sticky under my head. I've got
cuts on my body. Did somebody hurt me?

I fall asleep and wake up. Make an effort not to panic.

The first time I woke up I did that. I strained, kicked,
and screamed, and scraped with my fingernails until my
fingertips were raw. I screamed until I couldn't breathe.

But my screams bounced back into me, and when I stretched my legs I felt my feet hit a barrier.

There are barriers on all sides. And I hit them and push at them, but don't get anywhere. I know that now.

I'm tired, I want to sleep.

Maybe I'm already dead?

I've got something to drink, there's a cold plastic tube above my mouth. If I suck it I get water, and I drink, which must mean I'm not dead, because the dead don't drink. Do they?

Sometimes I imagine I can hear footsteps from above, and think I can hear voices.

But now everything is black and silent, like deaf and blind people's lives must be. As if someone had hollowed out my eye sockets and inner ears and filled them with earth.

I have to get out of here.

Someone has to find me.

Because the water will run out. The air.

Hunger is making me nauseous. Dissolving my thoughts before they take shape.

Ticking. What's that ticking sound I can hear? I'm not wearing a watch.

I move, push once again, and scream, but get nowhere, and I yell: 'Rescue me! Rescue me!'

Who the hell put me here? How did I get here?

Blood from my forehead mixes with my tears.

Someone has to help me.

I close my eyes, and in my thoughts I am carried up, up across the fields, away towards a city in darkness.

# PART I

# A love of longing

# I

Malin Fors is sitting at the kitchen table in her flat on Ågatan, looking out at the tower of St Lars Church. The black spire, topped with a cross, is lit up against the encroaching night. The ground around the church has been dug up, and it looks as if the entire building is slowly sinking into its own grave. The rain earlier in the spring crept into the foundations, and now the water needs to be drained.

Not many people about. Linköping has been as quiet as usual for a Sunday evening.

The digital clock above the new Ikea table says 23.14. The red numbers glow in the darkness as she feels the evening's events linger inside her.

She was working the evening shift. Just after seven o'clock they received a report about a domestic in a flat in Skäggetorp. When they got there they found a woman in her fifties, so drunk she could barely stand, brandishing a knife. Her husband was lying in the floor in a pool of blood. The woman was so out of it that she didn't know what she'd done.

Yet another drunk shipped off to hospital with severe injuries, and another one to Hinseberg Prison.

Alcohol, wreaking havoc again.

And Malin can't help thinking it could have been her in that flat, if she hadn't joined the police, and if it hadn't been for the people who had tried to guide her in the right direction over the years.

She runs her hands over her face, feels her taut skin, then lets her fingertips play across the deepening wrinkles around her eyes.

She sees those wrinkles in the mirror every morning. She likes them, knows there's no point fighting the lines that time wants to engrave on your face.

No grey hair yet, and she can still keep her body in shape.

She exercises, exercises, exercises. Runs, swims, lifts weights, and she fucks. More than she's done for years.

She thinks about what she and Daniel do in bed.

They don't make love, they fuck. The former would be far too dangerous.

Daniel.

The man who's moved in and out of her life.

She'd like to be gentler with him, take things nice and slowly, but what they do in bed, on the kitchen table, in the car, and plenty of other places, isn't making love.

The pattern of their behaviour is purely physical. At first Daniel wanted to be more tender, but that didn't work. It was as if they were holding back, retreating before the attack had even started.

So they set all gentleness aside.

And now we're like animals, Malin thinks, even though what we do has absolutely nothing to do with reproduction. He knows she can't have any more children, and it doesn't seem to bother him. Doesn't seem to want any of his own, even if she has trouble believing that.

She sees Daniel's face before her, his brown eyes, sharp nose, and the laughter lines that have become more prominent.

As if he were happy.

As if we were happy.

Are we happy?

I'm fine with the way things are, she thinks, with the two of us keeping our separate flats. But Daniel lives here almost all the time. He works a lot, like tonight, working the night shift on the paper. He works hard in the newsroom at the *Östgöta Correspondent*, they've got far too few staff after years of financial crisis, and they're buying in more and more material from freelancers.

And he doesn't drink much either. Even if he's in no way teetotal. It's as if he understands when she's in a vulnerable state, when she's thirsty as hell and can't bear to see anyone else drink, and then he abstains.

She wants a drink now.

There's a bottle in a cubbyhole under the rubbish bin. Drink.

And she longs for him, more than she really dares to, longs for Tove, who's so far away, and that longing saves her, because there's something solid in the emotion.

Malin sits down on the sofa in the living room, reaches for the remote on the table, and turns the television on. Zaps through the channels.

Celebrities. A load of rubbish.

She thinks about the Eurovision Song Contest. The final took place the previous weekend. Every single newspaper had led with Eurovision news.

And she hated it.

People on television talked about pop songs as though they were the most important thing in the world, and she felt ashamed when she heard them. Is this what we choose to do with our wealth and freedom of speech?

She and Daniel sat on the sofa watching the spectacle.

'General education,' he said. 'Current affairs. This is Sweden now, whether you like it or not.'

'The world's totally fucked, and all we're doing is singing?'

'Chill out, Malin.'

She felt like smashing him in the head with the bowl of crisps, then realised that he was right.

Why get worked up?

There was no point fighting against it.

Like her wrinkles.

She switches the television off.

Thinks: You make me chill out, Daniel. You calm me down, make me less restless, but you also make me feel more alone.

She wishes he were there with her. Would like to feel his arm around her shoulders, his hand on her cheek. And then they'd fuck. Maybe tenderness and sexuality should be kept separate. Maybe that's how you make a relationship work.

He usually leaves little messages for her. Hidden in places where she's bound to find them sooner or later. Most recently a note under the coffee maker. 'I love you,' it said.

And reading it made her happy, she believed it, and felt like calling him, but held back. Whispered in his ear that evening: 'I found the note this morning.'

Nothing more.

She stifles a yawn and switches the television on again.

The late news.

A report of heavy fighting in Damascus, where a young Swede from Karlstad has died a martyr's death. Some young men from Linköping have also been killed there, lured by manipulative radicals and their own ennui. The news presenter goes on to talk about a bomb in Egypt, the liberals being tortured in Libya, and the international success of a new Swedish computer war game.

Renewed fighting has broken out in the east of the Democratic Republic of Congo, and she feels her stomach tighten.

Tove.

In western Congo. Doing voluntary work in a home for children whose parents have died or disappeared.

Hell on earth.

As you wrote in one of your emails.

But also paradise.

Everything all at once, you wrote, Tove. The jungle, beauty, love. Sickness, violence, hatred.

Tove had already spent several months in Rwanda, following in her dad Janne's footsteps, but had found Rwanda too 'organised', and moved to Congo with the same relief agency.

Malin had protested, but knew there was no point, Tove did as she liked anyway. And Janne had backed her up, telling Malin on the phone: 'She'll realise what it means to be human once she sees what she's going to see there.'

'She doesn't need that level of insight.'

Felt like saying: Look at how it changed you, Janne.

How had his time in Bosnia and Rwanda changed her ex-husband? He became more guarded. Resigned. As if he'd lost faith in what might be possible in this world.

Women assaulted.

Children eaten alive by ravenous dogs.

Children dying from curable infections.

Rendered mute by terror and loneliness.

And those are the things he wants Tove to experience.

There are thousands of kilometres between the east and west of Congo. Impenetrable jungle.

It's a country where women are raped as a tool of war. And why should Tove be spared simply because she distributes a bit of medicine and food?

She wishes Tove were here with her. Would like to hear her talk, breathe, see her walk through the living room on her way to the kitchen to make a cup of tea.

She wants to be disturbed by Tove's noise.

Yet Tove is nothing but silence now.

Sometimes she thinks that Tove might never come home again. That she'll stay in Africa for good.

Malin is lying in bed. The white cotton sheets are cool against her skin.

Pleasantly cool. But the pillow could be thicker, and when Daniel is here she often lies with her head on his chest.

She's pulled the blind down, shutting out the light of the stars in the cloud-studded sky. She wants to sleep. But longing is keeping her awake.

She considers trying to read, maybe switching the radio on, but she never does that when she's trying to sleep, and why would it work this time? She looks up at the ceiling, a dark ochre colour in the gloom.

Tove. Janne. Daniel.

All the people who come and go and sometimes linger in my life.

I don't want to feel anything, she thinks.

Something is moving in Linköping tonight, and she knows that it's going to have some sort of effect on her.

She lets herself become her longing. Pure longing, a feeling that makes her more tired than tired, and just after half past midnight, Malin Fors falls asleep.

She dreams about children left speechless with terror, human bodies coming together like animals, hands gently caressing cheeks.

Then her dreams end and she sleeps in total darkness.

# 2

The street lamps glow above the young man as he makes his way along Repslagaregatan, not far from the *Correspondent*'s offices, and only a few blocks from Malin Fors's flat. The street is deserted, one of the few real backstreets in the centre of Linköping. The buildings are a mixture of two and three storeys tall. A brown-fronted office building, a sand-coloured block of flats, with a porcelain cat gazing out from one window.

Peder Åkerlund is tired. He's dragging his feet. He's drunk too much beer, but his head is still full of thoughts, ideas, and opinions.

You have to be smart. Say what people want to hear, but do the opposite.

They have to go.

They're not like us.

They're ruining Sweden.

Give Mother Svea back to us and send the rabble back to where they belong: Somalia, Iraq, Turkey, Bangladesh, Syria. Who cares where: they need to go, one way or the other. No means prohibited, any alliance permitted.

That's what people are thinking. Far more of them than you'd imagine, Peder Åkerlund thinks, as he walks home. But you're not allowed to say that.

Sometimes you have to side with the devil, he thinks.

He imagines he can hear footsteps behind him. Stops, turns around, but there's no one there.

He walks on. The effect of the beer is getting worse, and he's weaving badly now. Ahead of him one of the street lamps is broken, and where there ought to be a cone of light he can see a square black shape, a van, by the looks of it.

He carries on walking.

He's never been scared of the dark, that sort of thing's for poofs.

Get rid of them as well.

The Pride Festival makes him feel sick.

Something about the street, the van, the broken lamp, unsettles Peder Åkerlund, and he crosses the road, doesn't want to go too close to the vehicle. Can't put his finger on why.

A few streets away he can hear two people talking too loudly, obviously drunk. On their way home, like him.

He's opposite the van now. It looks like it's been painted by hand, with matt black paint. He speeds up, and is already past it when he hears one of the side doors open, then a voice: 'You've got to help me.'

A terrible sound from his lungs.

'I can't breathe.'

It sounds like the man in the van is being asphyxiated by some invisible force, and Peder Åkerlund wants to carry on walking. But he also wants to help.

'My asthma inhaler. It's in that bag, over in the corner. Can you get it for me? I can't reach it myself.'

Not an immigrant. Unless he's learned to speak perfect Swedish.

This is someone in trouble. And you have to help your fellow man.

If not, you're no better than an animal, a poof. A Muslim.

He steps over the body lying on the ridged metal floor of the van, can just make out the bag in the corner, and he digs around inside it, finds a plastic object. He can feel that it's an inhaler, but it's too dark for him to see what state the van is in.

Dirty or clean?

It smells of iron.

Blood?

No.

Yes. And urine. Excrement.

And Peder Åkerlund thinks that he shouldn't be here, he should have carried on walking when he heard the weak voice, but it touched something deep inside him, and he had to help.

Be a hero, maybe.

Like those nutters in Syria. The guys from Ryd who blew themselves to pieces, voluntarily. At least we're rid of them here now.

Be like them. Only in reverse. Save this man and end up in the paper for a reason everyone can agree is good. Mum and Dad as well.

Peder Åkerlund turns around. Bends over the gasping man, holds out the inhaler.

'Here you are.'

The man holds out his hand.

Grasps the inhaler and puts it to his mouth.

Takes a deep breath.

Then another.

And then Peder Åkerlund sees the man quickly and with unexpected agility and force turn the inhaler towards his own face and let it off like it is a fire extinguisher. He hears a different hissing sound, and his eyes flare with pain. His mouth fills with fuggy air, and against his will he breathes it in, feels himself being shoved backwards hard, and he hits the back door of the van with full force.

The metal doesn't give way.

His eyes are stinging now. Burning, as if he were going to be blind for ever.

His lungs are smarting, and he tries to stand up, knows he has to stand up, but he can't, the man is on top of him, pressing him down, and Peder Åkerlund screams silently because his eyes are burning, and then he feels something cold and chemical against his nose and mouth and tries to flail with his arms.

But his arms won't move.

His thoughts fade.

He hears laughter and shouting.

Sees his mother's face in front of him.

Then a sharp pain in one temple. And his eyes stop burning. Everything seems to stop.

How much time has passed?

Peder Åkerlund is lying on the cold metal floor, he realises where he is, feels the van moving.

Bouncing. Are they heading into the forest, or down some rough gravel track somewhere else?

He can feel tape around his wrists. Over his mouth.

His eyes are stinging rather than burning, and in spite of the darkness he knows he isn't blind.

He's lying on his stomach and his chin is bouncing on the floor, his nose too, and it starts to bleed, the metallic smell is his own blood now.

He can't move his legs. They must be taped as well. He tries to free himself, but it's impossible.

His trousers are wet and sticky. Those smells are also his now. His whole body has contracted with fear, first cramping, then into a jellyfish softness.

His head is thudding.

Have the coloureds got him? Those Muslim cunts? The gay pride wankers?

Fuck them.

His thoughts scare him. What if they can hear me thinking, if they hit me and ram my nose into the floor and break it? And he feels like screaming.

But he can't scream.

The tightest piece of tape is the one covering his mouth.

# 3

Something forces its way into Malin's brain.

Into her sleep. Beyond the dream of evil creatures in dense jungle. An alien sound, a tone she recognises, and she rubs her legs and stomach, the sound is her phone, and she sees an opportunity to escape. She reaches for the bedside table. The phone lies there in sleep and wakefulness alike, and now she's holding it in her hand.

She sits up. Opens her eyes and yells, and she sweats as she hears the ringtone, and it goes on ringing.

The white sheet is damp now.

There's a light flickering outside the window. There must be something wrong with the street lamps.

She presses to take the call. Hopes it's Daniel. But why would he be calling now?

Then the dream outside the dream: it's Tove. She's got hold of a satellite link and has decided to call even though it's the middle of the night. Knows she has to call whenever she gets the chance.

'Are you awake, Mum?'

And the longing forms itself into sound now.

'Tove?'

'I got a link. Just for a few minutes. How are you?'

'I should be asking you that.'

Malin hears Tove take a deep breath.

'It's hot here. And humid.'

'Has there been any sign of trouble there?'

'No. But there are rumours.'

'What sort of rumours?'

Malin can hear crackling on the line, but she imagines she can also hear the jungle in the background. The sound of living things in motion.

'That the rebels have gathered a force near here.'

'Are you going to be evacuated?'

'It's just rumours.'

Malin's wide awake now, feels like yelling at Tove and demanding that she jump on the first helicopter away from the camp and the children's home.

'We're heading out tomorrow,' Tove says. 'We're taking medicine and food to some villages in the mountains.'

'Is that wise?'

'It's not dangerous. We're the good guys, that's how they see us.'

Naïve.

You're naïve, Tove.

'It has to be done, Mum. There are children with cholera up there, and they'll die if we don't do something.'

Nothing naïve in those words.

You're better than me.

'Are you scared?'

'There's no point being scared.'

'Be careful.'

The connection breaks, and Malin doesn't know if Tove had time to hear her plea.

She looks at the alarm clock on the desk next to the computer.

04.33.

She'll never get back to sleep now.

The alarm clock is over on the desk, so she has to get out of bed to switch it off. Up until ten months ago she never had any trouble getting up, but something's changed, a first sign of old age in her body.

Tove.

Thinking about her is like a form of sickness now. Longing replaced by poisonous anxiety.

She gets out of bed.

Looks out at the courtyard at the back of the building. The dark windows of the office block, and the flashing, which must be coming from Repslagaregatan. She can just make out her reflection in the glass, imagines she can see Tove behind her. Seven years old, sitting on the living-room floor playing with the cut-out dolls she found at her grandparents'. Lost in play, making the world harmless and comprehensible at the same time.

Malin turns around.

Tove's there. Small and beautiful, tentatively conjuring up her own world, making it her own.

That little girl is gone now. She's a different person, somewhere else. She's an anxiety, a sickness, a different sort of love.

You had to run when you were younger, Malin thinks. You're heading towards something now, not away from it.

And that's a blessing.

# 4

Malin has a new game to make her run even faster. To forget her body's protests and keep moving.

She plays the thinking-about-her-workmates game.

She runs along beside the Stångå River, past the overblown villas of Tannefors, under the dense foliage of the old birch trees, feeling her heart pump as the soles of her shoes pound the ground fast, first tarmac, then grit, and she glances at the watch on her wrist.

06.20.

Has anything happened in the city overnight? Will they finally have something to do? They haven't had a big case since March, when a gay man was beaten to death late one night in Berga. His brother was responsible, egged on by their father.

They didn't like his sexual orientation, wanted him to keep it to himself. So as not to bring dishonour on his family. But he wanted to come out, seeing as that, thankfully, is perfectly acceptable in this rainbow nation.

It was Sven Sjöman's last case.

He's retired now, and, as far as Malin knows, right now he's in the basement of his house standing at his lathe, carving something beautiful to sell at the market. He'll have had one of his crispbread sandwiches with strong, low-fat cheese.

It took Sven a long time to take the decision to retire, but now that he's done it he seems relieved. Didn't appear to be remotely upset when they celebrated his retirement with strawberry cake and Henkell Trocken.

Right up to the last minute he nagged her to take over from him, but she refused. Didn't want to be in charge. He tried to imply that she was being cowardly, but that wasn't it. She prefers only having to take responsibility for herself. At least at work, anyway. And she likes being out in the field. If she had taken Sven's job, she'd have had to spend far more time behind a desk.

Malin can feel her heart beating in her chest.

Working hard instead of longing.

An external appointment was made. A Göran Möller.

He started a month or so ago, and Malin took an immediate liking to the blunt, art-loving fifty-five-year-old. But he's no Sven Sjöman. He doesn't fill the vacuum left after her previous thoughtful, sharp boss, who used his wealth of experience to steer them in the right direction in all their investigations.

Göran Möller is single. His wife walked out on him and the children when they were small, and got married to a German from Berlin.

A week or so after he started, Göran Möller took her to lunch. They went to the City Hotel, where they sat in the glazed veranda facing the square, and he told her he had spoken to Sven and had realised that she, Malin, was the key member of the Violent Crime Unit. And that he was happy for that to continue to be the case. In most places he had worked, one strong, competent detective had set the tone. And that almost always produced results.

'But,' he had said, 'you need to bear in mind that I'm the boss.'

Malin swallowed a serious flash of anger and took a forkful of her steak, then looked into her new boss's green eyes and asked: 'What else did Sven tell you?'

'About what?'

'About all the nonsense.'

'I think he told me most of it,' Göran Möller said. 'But you're better now, according to what he told me.'

Göran Möller paused.

'So what have you heard about my nonsense?'

Göran Möller's reputation went before him. He had been forced to leave Landskrona after some ill-advised remarks about immigrants during the riots in Malmö in the spring of 2010. He had said that it wasn't OK to set fire to cars even if your name was Mustafa and you'd experienced traumatic things in Iraq. That people had to pull themselves together. Then, after he was transferred to Helsingborg, he had defended a police officer who had shouted 'fucking niggers' over police radio when some thugs had thrown a Molotov cocktail at their patrol car.

After that his position in Skåne became untenable. You couldn't defend colleagues who expressed racist views without some sort of punishment.

'I don't care about that,' Malin had said. 'As far as I understand it, you're about as far from racist as anyone can be. People can come out with all sorts of things in certain situations without meaning anything by it. And as police officers, we need to understand that. Whether it concerns us or other people.'

Göran Möller smiled.

'You should probably have taken the job,' he said. 'You can bear to see people for what they are.'

When he smiled he looked younger than his fifty-five years. But usually his cheeks sagged a little, making him look a bit like a boxer puppy, and his nose was disproportionately long and pointed.

Göran Möller has got character, she thought. And you can't help listening to what he has to say. But as she sat there at the table, she couldn't help feeling that there was something missing, without quite being able to put her finger on what.

'Well,' Göran Möller said in conclusion, 'you won't get any more chances from me. Not like you did with Sven.'

To her surprise, Malin didn't get angry. His words merely frightened her.

Shit, she thinks now. One of her shoelaces has come undone.

She has to stop, doesn't want to trip over.

You need a few constants in life, Göran Möller thinks, turning up the heat in the shower.

He likes hot showers. They wake him up better than cold ones.

His constant is art. Classical painting.

He's happy to have been given the job in Linköping. He spent a long time in quarantine after the debacle in Helsingborg, and for a while he thought he'd spend the rest of his career compiling statistics.

But Sven, an old acquaintance, came to his rescue in the end.

Hot water runs down his back. The taste of his morning coffee lingers in his mouth, and he thinks: I know I'm a good police officer. I'm not a racist. But sometimes it isn't easy to determine whether your thoughts and feelings are racist even if that isn't the intention.

Better to stay quiet.

Learn to keep your mouth shut.

Göran Möller turns the water off. Wraps a towel around his body and stands in front of the mirror.

He likes the team in the Violent Crime Unit.

Börje, Waldemar, Johan, Elin, Zeke, and Malin. He's never been in charge of a better group of detectives.

Sven warned him about Malin, about her alcoholism, but also said: 'You won't find a better detective. Give her plenty of room to manoeuvre.'

Göran noticed Malin's talent immediately. But also her

need for boundaries. He wasn't planning on being the surrogate dad that Sven had evidently been to her.

Sven also warned him about Waldemar Ekenberg's tendency towards violence.

'But it can be useful sometimes.'

Violence is useful, from time to time, Göran Möller thinks, as he puts on a white shirt. But violence always leads to more violence, and where it ends is never easy to predict.

He hasn't seen any trace of Waldemar Ekenberg's violence. But the battered old detective has stopped smoking, without even using nicotine patches, and has been in a filthy mood.

The others in the group don't seem to care. People say things, do things. Sometimes they mean well, but things turn out badly. And sometimes the other way around. Like when his wife left him and the children. They were better off without her, and the kids had turned into decent human beings.

Göran Möller is happy on his own. He's seen a lot of terrible things in his career, and he doesn't want to share that with anyone.

Push it to the limit, Malin. Burst your heart.

She reaches the sluices at Braskens bridge. She speeded up for five hundred metres and now she can feel her body tugging her towards the benches on the little island in the middle of the river.

But she resists. Feels her knees creak, and finds herself thinking about Johan Jakobsson.

Six months ago his daughter started to suffer severe pain in her body. One knee swelled up and some nights she would cry out in pain. The doctors at the University Hospital confirmed that she had an aggressive form of juvenile rheumatoid arthritis. They pumped her full of cortisone, which made her body puff up, and she got so depressed that she stopped going to school.

Malin can see how much Johan is suffering when he talks about his daughter. How unhappy he is because she isn't happy, as if he'd like to make her suffering his own but knows there's no way he can do that.

In the depths of our pain we are all alone.

Chief of Police Karim Akbar, and prosecutor Vivianne Södergran have had a son. Karim is on paternity leave and paid them a visit not long ago. The buggy was from Louis Vuitton and must have cost a fortune, but there was no denying that it matched Karim's pin-striped suit perfectly.

Malin runs back towards the centre of the city.

Increases her pace still further, feels that she is capable of it, that her body can deal with anything today.

But the body's energy is finite. It's good that Sven left while there was still time.

Her partner, Zeke Martinsson, is more balanced than she has ever seen him. He seems to be happy with Karin, and to have no regrets about getting divorced.

Elin Sand has become a more integrated member of the group, but revealed a few days ago that she had broken off the relationship she had been having with a doctor.

'We were too different.'

And maybe you just didn't fuck that much any more? Malin thought. She felt the cynical thought run through her whole body. When did I get like that?

Elin went on: 'She wants children, but I don't. And the sex had got really rubbish.'

Malin breathes air into her lungs, tries to force the pain out of muscles full of lactic acid, and she keeps running, sees the world as a tunnel of bushes, leaves, grit that turns into tarmac, the sky half-covered by cloud above her.

She tries to think about Börje Svärd.

He can have five hundred metres.

But all she has time to think about is his dogs. His two Alsatians, and the rumours of his affairs. His smart clothes, with his long, Marlboro-man coat and broad-brimmed hat, very sexy and elegant, according to the ladies of Linköping.

Her vision starts to go black.

I can't take another step.

Yes, I can.

Malin runs past the sports hall, then up to Hamngatan, and she races past McDonald's, down towards the church, and she sees the sign outside the pub, the windows of her flat, and stumbles, but manages to stay upright.

She slumps in front of the door to her building. Feels her stomach tighten, happy that she didn't eat anything before she set off.

Even so, she can't help it. Her stomach cramps and she vomits yellow bile onto the pavement.

'You need to stop doing that,' a voice says. 'You're far too beautiful to make yourself feel that bad.'

Malin lifts her head.

Looks into Daniel's tired face, and wonders what it is that she's feeling.

# 5

Evy Kvist is up early, as usual, and is eating a bowl of plain yoghurt standing at the counter in the kitchen of her villa in the Ugglebo district of Ljungsbro, some ten kilometres outside Linköping.

Her husband is still asleep, and her thoughts turn to their children, both of whom have moved out and are studying down in Lund.

As she puts her empty bowl in the sink the family's seven-year-old boxer dog, Frida, gets up from her basket and lumbers over to the outside door. She waves her tail excitedly as Evy puts her leash on: the new neighbours are scared of dogs.

Then they head out for a walk along the banks of the Göta Canal. The morning air clears her lungs and the sun warms Evy's forehead as they walk along the path beneath the old oak trees.

The tourist season hasn't properly started yet, so the locks at Heda are deserted as she leads Frida over to the other side of the canal, stepping carefully across the narrow platform on top of the lock gate.

Eva wonders if she should go the long way around, via Hedaängen and off to Blåsvädret, or take the shorter path to Vreta Kloster and then come back the same way.

She's between jobs, so has all the time in the world, the weather's good, and Frida loves being outside, but still Evy chooses the shorter route. She wants to get home to the book she's currently reading, and wants to be back in time to say goodbye to her husband before he leaves for work.

She carries on along the western bank of the Göta Canal, looks around to see if anyone else is about, then, when she's sure she's alone, she lets Frida off her leash.

The dog gives herself a shake.

Then she sets off along the canal path as if she has an infinite supply of energy, and Evy feels envious of Frida the way you envy someone who has something you want but know you will never have.

A few hundred metres further on, a road curves to run parallel with the canal. The road is lined with tall bushes. Evy sees the dog stop by the bushes, shake herself again, and then disappear under the bushes and emerge on the other side.

Frida stops.

Throws her head back and starts to howl, then settles into a long, persistent bark.

Evy starts to run. She runs towards Frida faster than she has ever run towards anything, faster than she knew she could run.

Something's wrong.

Frida is still barking.

There's something not right.

What have you found? We should have gone the long way around.

Evy reaches her. Looks in beneath the bushes, down into the ditch beside the canal.

The dog barks.

Howls.

Evy Kvist feels her legs give way beneath her. She's never seen a dead body before.

If this is what they look like, she never wants to see one again.

# 6

The skin is bluish white, marbled, with red blood vessels on the legs and torso, the genitals hidden by one leg. The position of the body is unnatural, yet still calm in the way that only the dead can manage. As if they're surrounded by soil before they're even in the ground, Malin thinks.

White flowers have rained down from the bushes above, catching in the man's short blond hair, green leaves scratching his skin.

He's lying in the ditch by the side of the canal, beneath some vegetation. He's about twenty years old, no more, his face is contorted, the area around his nose and mouth is swollen and red.

His face is oddly familiar, but she can't place him.

The ditch is dry. The grass around the body appears untouched.

It's quiet here, Malin thinks as she takes a step towards the body.

Quiet in a completely new way.

It feels as if something has disappeared, withdrawn in order to return later, and is now lying in wait just out of reach. As if the death in front of them were worse than any other death they have seen before.

Malin, Zeke, and Elin Sand came out here as soon as they got the emergency call. A hysterical woman walking her dog had found a body, a naked man.

They realised at once that they were dealing with a murder. Men are not usually found naked and dead in these parts, or anywhere else on the planet, and now Malin is standing alone, looking down at the body and wondering: Who are you? How did you end up here?

Behind her she can hear Zeke trying to calm the woman, Evy Kvist, and her dog is still barking occasionally, as if it understands that something's wrong, and that it can't do anything about it.

An animal's despair.

Instinctive intelligence and inadequate language.

Elin Sand walks over and stands close to Malin, who can sense her breath, almost feel it against the back of her neck, but Elin's breathing is soundless, why is everything so quiet here?

'What do you make of this?' Elin asks. 'It's pretty obvious he was murdered.'

Malin nods but says nothing. Keen to keep hold of the frightening silence, trying to understand what it means. The body, its nakedness, the vulnerability of bare skin even though there's no longer any life to protect.

It's very clear that someone dumped him here, and she looks at his face again. The nose is straight. Cheekbones sharp, as though chiselled with an ice pick. She can't help feeling that she ought to recognise him, know who he is.

She racks her brain, gets close to finding something, when Elin Sand says: 'Karin's here.'

Damn.

Whatever she was close to finding vanishes at the sound of Elin's voice.

'Can't you ever keep quiet?' Malin hisses, and Elin throws her long arms out and says: 'Sorry, I didn't realise we'd imposed a ban on talking.'

Malin looks up towards the gravel path leading up to the canal from the old Motala road.

Karin parks her white Volvo estate, gets out, opens the

boot, and removes the bag containing her forensic equipment. She glances at Zeke, nods to him, and the dog barks at her. She and Zeke never display their feelings for each other at work. Malin knows they both think it unprofessional. They work with life and death, grief and violence, and there's no place for expressions of love.

Karin comes over to Malin and Elin, and looks down at the body in the ditch.

'Well he didn't get there on his own,' she says.

Then she pauses.

'You haven't touched anything?'

'Actually, we have,' Elin says. 'As much as we could. I gave him a great big hug.'

Karin snorts, then laughs.

'I didn't know you were into necrophilia, Elin.'


Tasteless.

Where does the line run? What I've just said, Karin thinks, what am I allowed to say or not say in the vicinity of the victim of a crime? How far am I allowed to go?

What I said was on the wrong side of the line, but it feels as if our boundaries have shifted, as if the members of the team have become harder, more heartless than we used to be. We're more cynical, more pessimistic, and our words have to reflect that, while gallows humour masks the impossibility of the things that have actually happened.

That will happen.

Mentioning necrophilia in the vicinity of someone who's only just died.

Get a grip, Karin.

She looks over towards Zeke, his shaved head shining in the sun. He's a handsome man, more handsome with each passing year. It's as if the contours of his head and face are becoming more chiselled over time, their lines and expressions clearer.

And he's a good dad to Tess.

Our little girl. My daughter.

Our daughter.

Malin and Elin Sand are standing over by the crime unit's blue Saab now, they've pulled back, realised they were in the way. They're talking, but Karin can't hear what they're saying.

She does her job, tries to focus on that alone. Examine the body, secure the evidence around it, footprints on the bank of the canal, tyre marks on the road. And then, when she's done all that, she goes back to the body again.

It's naked.

Alone.

And oddly free of visible damage. All she can see is a noticeable swelling around the nose and mouth, which could suggest that he was drugged by someone pressing a rag soaked in some sort of anaesthetic over his face.

There's a bruise on the back of his head.

Maybe he put up a fight before he lost consciousness.

Over by the road she managed to find tyre tracks leading up here. The tracks made by the blue Saab are the most prominent, but there are several others beneath those.

Karin crouches down beside the body. Feels her knees creak and protest.

Did someone drive you here in a vehicle?

Or did they kill you here? And then undress you?

The former seems more likely.

She walks along the edge of the ditch towards the road. Stares down at the grass. It looks too neat, as if someone had tidied it.

Where the ditch meets the road she crouches down again. The stems of some small flowers have been snapped, and there are faint drag marks in the grit on the road that could have been made by the man's heels.

She goes back to the body. Looks at the heels, pulls a

magnifying glass from her pocket, sees the almost microscopic splinters of grit caught in the dry cracks of the heels.

That's how you got here, Karin thinks, and then she looks up at Malin and Elin, and waves them over.

Zeke stays behind with the woman and her dog.

She seems calmer now, and the dog has stopped barking.


'So, you were out walking your dog, the same route you take every morning?'

Zeke is making an effort to sound calm, and it works, because he is calm. He manages to bring Evy Kvist out of the state of near-shock she was in when they arrived.

'You talk to her,' Malin had said. 'She seems to need reassuring.'

He put an arm around her to start with, comforting her, so that she would feel that all the bad things would come to an end, and if she wanted him to, he could arrange for her to see a counsellor, but first she had to talk to him.

And now she's answering his questions.

The dog has stopped barking at last.

'I took the short route today. She likes it. Sometimes I go the long way around.'

'And it was your dog who found him first?'

Evy Kvist nods.

'I let her off the leash and she rushed off.'

'Did you see anyone else here?'

Evy Kvist thinks.

'No, I was all alone. There was no one else here.'

Apart from the man in the ditch, Zeke thinks.

'And you didn't touch anything?'

'No.'

'How about your dog?'

'No, she didn't either. She just started barking.'

He's already taken her address and phone number, and

doesn't really have any further questions right now. It's obvious that the woman had nothing to do with the murder, so when she asks if she can go, he says: 'Yes, of course.'

He watches as the woman takes her dog and starts to walk along the towpath beneath a canopy of oaks in blossom.

'Give us a ring,' he calls after her. 'If you need someone to talk to.'

Malin is standing at the edge of the ditch, looking down at Karin. Elin Sand is rocking gently beside her, and Malin can feel her breath again.

But she can't hear it this time either.

There's a muteness here, and it's as if the murdered young man is screaming to her without making any sound.

Smothered longing.

Muffled.

That's what's happened, Malin thinks. The world has been transformed into a silent scream.

# 7

Daniel Högfeldt is clutching the wheel tightly. In front of him he can see the ancient church at Vreta Kloster on the top of the ridge, off to the east the expensive villas are feeling their way up the slope, away from Lake Roxen, and a few silvery masts are swaying in the marina between the upper and lower locks.

The fields of rape are singing out, bright yellow, and the radiance of the flowers lends a buttery glow to the whole picture, as if the oil has been overpowered by butter.

He's drunk four cups of coffee. Taken two caffeine pills. But he still feels indescribably tired.

When his phone rang and he saw it was his contact in the police station he couldn't help answering. He was lying naked in Malin's bed, home from the night shift, and had just fallen asleep when the call woke him. So he tugged off his eye mask and answered.

A naked body.

Even in his sleep-addled state, he knew instinctively that this was something big.

So now he's sitting in his car, awake for more than twenty hours in a row, and he puts his foot down, passes the roundabout by the convent, and heads on towards Blåsvädret, past the white-tiled school.

It doesn't take long to reach the turning.

He pulls in. Sees Karin Johannison's white Volvo and the crime unit's blue Saab.

He sees Elin, Zeke, and Karin.

And Malin.

They're standing by some bushes, staring down the slope, and God, she's beautiful, with the wind tugging at her hair and revealing her narrow neck.

My lips on that neck.

You want me to be rough, you refuse to let me be anything else. But that will come. Things will change.

He gets out of the car, taking his camera with him. He's having to work without a photographer more and more. Only occasionally is there enough money for a professional photographer.

'What are you doing here?' Malin calls out. Daniel is walking towards them along the road, his bulky camera slung over his shoulder. She can hear that she sounds irritated, but she's actually pleased to see him, pleased that he's the first journalist on the scene.

'Shouldn't you be asleep?'

She knows he's tired, but also that his source at the police station must have called him. He refuses to say who it is, and she hasn't pushed him. It would be against the law for him to reveal his source. Sometimes she wonders if it's her. Do I talk in my sleep; do I say things about work that I forget I've said? Did I call him about this? She feels like pulling her phone out to check the list of calls, but stops herself.

I. Didn't. Call. Him.

He has dark rings under his eyes, and his skin is grey, the way only lack of sleep can make it.

Every so often she teases him about his discretion.

'Come on, who is he?'

'It could be a she.'

'Me?'

'No. We both know it isn't you.'

Do we?

He walks up to them. A tentative smile that quickly turns into a look of concern.

'Hi. What have you got?'

The others say hello, and Karin points down into the ditch. Nowadays, Malin knows they think Daniel is OK. He's not as pushy as some of the journalists from the evening tabloids can be.

'It's not a pretty sight,' Zeke says.

Daniel steps closer, looks down into the ditch, at the body of the murdered young man.

Malin sees his eyebrows rise.

Not from revulsion or fear, but genuine surprise.

'Bloody hell,' he says. 'Christ.'

'What is it?' Karin asks.

'Yes, what?' Elin adds.

'Don't you recognise him? That's Peder Åkerlund.'

# 8

Peder Åkerlund.

That's what she couldn't quite get hold of just now. She did recognise him, and now that she hears his name, Malin knows who he is.

A member of the Sweden Democrats.

Peder Åkerlund used to be on the council before he was forced to step down after saying that all Muslim men abuse women and would rape their own daughters if given the chance. A student studying journalism at the university bumped into him at the Hamlet and recorded his drunken ramblings. It was a big deal.

Daniel's voice says what she's thinking.

'The nationals made a big deal of it.'

She remembers the whole debacle. The way the media tried to get Jimmie Åkesson, the party leader, to apologise, but he merely referred them back to the party's local representatives. He dodged the question. Refused to apologise for someone else's behaviour. Or even to condemn the claims.

Peder Åkerlund.

Racist.

And now here he is, lying below us.

'He must have had plenty of enemies,' Daniel says, and Malin feels the wind against her neck, a mild wind carrying an early promise of summer.

'This is going to stir things up,' Elin says.

Zeke rubs one hand over his shaved head.

'What more do you know?' he asks Daniel.

'He ended up being expelled from the party.'

'They got rid of him?' Elin says.

'Yes, like they do with anyone who reveals their true colours. But he saw the light. Peder Åkerlund distanced himself from the party and his previous opinions. We ran a piece about it. Said he wanted to go around schools warning about the dangers of xenophobia, tell his story. About how easy it is to be led astray.'

Conversion, Malin thinks. Deathbed conversion.

'He was young,' she says.

'You mean we all say stupid things when we're young?' Karin asks.

'No, I mean that sometimes we have to pay a high price for who we are and the mistakes we make,' Malin says, just as Göran Möller arrives in a police car.

Göran Möller looks focused, and it strikes Malin that he must be feeling nervous and worried about this, a case that's bound to be linked to the reasons why he had to leave his post in Skåne.

They've walked a hundred metres towards the locks, and are holding a first meeting of the investigating team at a picnic table. Johan Jakobsson arrived with Göran, and is sitting there waiting with his laptop.

Down by the bushes Karin is still moving around the body.

They're waiting for the ambulance to arrive to take it to the pathology laboratory. There Karin will perform a post mortem, and give them a probable cause of death.

Göran Möller leans across the wooden tabletop.

'We're regarding this as murder. It's obvious he didn't end up here by himself. In all likelihood, as Karin says, he was killed somewhere else and then brought here by car.'

'What do we know about him, apart from what Daniel told us?' Zeke asks.

The others wait in silence as Johan taps at his keyboard.

'Looks like there are plenty of people who have good reason to be angry with him,' he says after a while. 'First and foremost his old opponents. Left-wing activists, Muslims. And then his former party comrades. Evidently he refused to resign, and then when he eventually did, he turned against them. I see here that he's got a website. Pretty tough reading for anyone who likes the main racist sites.'

Johan turns the screen so they can all see it.

*In defence of the niqab!*

*More immigration.*

*Integrate the WHOLE of Linköping.*

Malin reads the headings on Peder Åkerlund's website and tries to feel sympathetic towards him, towards the body lying over there, the person he was, because she knows that if she can feel something, she'll do a better job.

She goes on reading, but fails to feel anything. In spite of her best efforts.

'The media are going to have a field day with this,' Göran Möller says.

Johan shows them some other sites.

One left-wing activist, anonymous, writes that Peder Åkerlund and everyone like him deserves to die. Calls his conversion 'pointless'. Once a racist, always a racist.

Another site contains a video clip of a man wearing a kaftan. His face is hidden by white fabric, but he declares that Peder Åkerlund ought to be stoned. The post is dated before Peder Åkerlund changed his allegiance, when he was still on the council.

'So there's quite a bit to go on,' Göran Möller says, his voice factual and calm. He isn't at all anxious or upset, Malin thinks, and he smiles towards her.

'We need to establish a timeline,' he says. 'What was Peder Åkerlund doing yesterday? Who was the last person to see him alive? And we need to inform his family. Right away, before the news gets out.'

'His relatives are going to have to identify him,' Malin says.

Göran Möller looks at her.

'I was just coming to that. They'll need to be questioned as well.'

A white van from TV4 arrives, and an ambulance pulls up behind it. Two paramedics get out, neither of them is Janne, thank goodness. They take out a trolley from the back.

Karin waves at them from down in the ditch.

You'll soon be leaving, Peder Åkerlund, Malin thinks.

'There are no serious injuries to the body,' she says. 'And nothing of a sexual nature either, according to Karin.'

'So we can probably assume that this isn't a sexually motivated crime,' Göran Möller says. 'Despite the fact that the body is naked. Violent sex offenders aren't usually content with nothing more explicit than nakedness. But we can't rule anything out until after the post mortem.'

Then Göran Möller falls silent, and Malin and the others wait in vain for him to take command properly, the way Sven always did, except towards the end when exhaustion got the better of him.

But nothing happens.

'We'll need to organise door-to-door enquiries,' Zeke says instead.

Göran Möller nods.

'I'll sort that out.'

And then Elin Sand asks: 'Should we talk to the imam at the local mosque? Radical left-wingers? Anti-Fascist Action and so on?'

No one answers her questions, and the detectives

exchange a hasty glance: they are all aware that this case is a potential minefield. Göran Möller slowly exhales used-up air.

'Not yet. But Johan, try to identify the people behind the websites and the other things you've just shown us, and carry on digging. We need to look at Peder Åkerlund's flat. Examine his computer. Who knows, there may even be a mobile phone there.'

'Why naked?' Malin says. 'If there's no sexual motive?'

'To humiliate him,' Elin says. 'If the murderer hated Peder Åkerlund, maybe it seemed perfectly natural to expose him to the world, completely defenceless and pathetic.'

'Or maybe just to remove any evidence? Make sure we couldn't find any DNA on his clothes?' Zeke says.

'The perpetrator seems to have tried to use the grass to cover any tracks. Whilst simultaneously wanting the body to be discovered,' Göran Möller points out. 'Otherwise you wouldn't leave the body so exposed, surely?'

'It's as if the killer is trying to send a message,' Malin says. 'But without getting caught.'

She approves of Göran Möller's plan to feel his way forward.

'What message?' Elin Sand asks.

'No idea. He was probably confused, or else he wants to confuse us.'

'Or she,' Elin adds.

'Or she.'

A sparrow lands at the end of the table, pecks at something, then flies off when it realises there's nothing to eat. A large motor cruiser has just entered the furthest lock, a German flag fluttering from the top of its radio antenna.

The invasion is starting, Malin thinks.

'It seems to be premeditated,' Göran Möller says. 'If Åkerlund was drugged like Karin thinks. Anaesthetic isn't the sort of thing you usually go around with, or keep at home.'

'And who has access to anaesthetic, anyway?' Elin says. 'Doctors?'

'Anyone,' Göran says. 'You can get hold of anything online.'

Malin sees embarrassment hit Elin Sand. Her blushes. But it wasn't a silly question. At the start of an investigation everything needs to be considered, examined from every angle, and the only thing they can be sure of is that they're bound to miss something.

Malin has never been involved in a faultless investigation.

'His parents live in Sturefors,' Johan says. 'They seem to be his next of kin.'

'Malin,' Göran Möller says. 'I want you and Zeke to inform the parents. Take a priest with you if you want.'

Malin nods.

Doesn't want to go to Sturefors.

She hates having to inform next of kin, but knows that she and Zeke do it as well as anyone can. That their factual approach can actually be a source of support at an incredibly hard time. And maybe by giving her this unpleasant job, Göran is keen to show that he's in charge.

'We'll do that,' Zeke says.

'He lived in Johannelund,' Johan says.

'I'll call Waldemar,' Göran says. 'Elin, you go and look at the flat with him.'

A reporter from TV4 is heading towards them, followed by a cameraman, and now Malin can see several other vehicles pulling up over on the road. More reporters. They're flocking around the trolley with the yellow body bag as it is pushed inside the ambulance.

Karin gets out of the ditch. Brushes herself off. Her work here is done.

Daniel's car is weaving backwards between the newly-arrived vehicles.

Go home and get some sleep, Malin thinks. Otherwise you won't have the energy to deal with this case.

'What's the parents' address?' she asks.

'Älgvägen 34.'

Malin feels her heart lurch.

Älgvägen.

One of the roads that run parallel to the horrible road where she grew up, the only road in the whole world that she can honestly say that she hates.

# 9

I can still hear the clock ticking.

Or am I imagining things?

The tube is cold and disgusting in my mouth, but the water is good, my lips are so dry, my mouth a hole full of dry earth, that's how it feels.

I've worn the skin off my elbows. Splinters of wood are trying to eat their way into me. So are the worms.

I scream at them to stop. But there's no reply.

Am I awake or dreaming, or am I dead?

When does a person die?

I hit my knees against the lid of the coffin, but the only sounds are muffled thuds.

I'm getting air from somewhere. Someone must have fixed it so that I get air in my coffin, but it could run out at any moment.

I couldn't hold back any longer. I gave in, and now everything down there is sticky. At first it stank, and I screamed and cried, but now I don't notice the smell, just the stickiness against my thighs, my behind and back.

I have to get out now.

Out, to breathe real air. I can't breathe here, not the way I want to. In through one nostril, out through the other.

Someone has to help me.

Who buried me alive?

# 10

The apple trees will soon be in bloom.

Malin closes her eyes as the car rolls into the villa-lined streets where she grew up. Doesn't want to see the little brick houses, older now, and much smaller than in her memory. But you can never escape from yourself. She knows that.

Her mum's face.

Those embittered expressions, and the desire to be better than other people that tainted her whole life. All their lives. Cheap imitation rugs on the floor. Prints of third-rate artists on the walls. Her insistence that Malin's father should wear his suit at home and when he went out in the city at weekends. Malin always had to wear a pink dress.

She remembers those dresses. She must have suppressed the memory up to now. She was never allowed to go to the playground, to prevent those pink tulle dresses getting messed up. She can still feel the shame in her whole body, the way the other children laughed at her.

She wanted to hide away in a cupboard, and she can still feel the slap. Her mother hitting her when she tore one of the dresses.

Malin is running barefoot across muddy ground.

No, the dress isn't torn. It's muddy, and I'm six or seven years old, and she wants to make me an extra in my own life.

Fuck you, Mum.

'You're shaking,' Zeke says. 'Are you feeling ill?'

'No.' But she keeps her eyes closed. Forces her body to be still.

Malin recognises herself as a little girl. She wanted to play, that's all, but her mother had other ambitions. Her mother wanted to be anything but what she actually was.

Which turned her into a liar, a liar worth hating.

And then she died.

But Stefan's OK now. At the new home he's in, in Ljusdal. The people who work there have their hearts in the right place, and the home's owners don't put profit above everything else. They seem to understand him, even though he can't speak, and appears unaware of the world around him.

Her dad.

Who abandoned Stefan. Kept her brother's existence secret from her.

Evidently he's got married to his rich German woman down in Tenerife. Tove saw it on the bitch's Facebook page.

He didn't tell us, and certainly didn't invite us. He's written us off, and we've done the same with him.

Malin is holding back the shakes. Thinks that her father must be the most cowardly person in the world. He must have seen how much I hated those pink dresses. And he just left Stefan to his fate – and me too, in a way.

Malin opens her eyes again. Sees the houses. Neatly kept flowerbeds and perfectly pruned apple trees.

'Don't go down this one,' she says when they reach her road. 'Go around the block instead.'

Zeke doesn't reply, just goes the other way, and soon they reach Älgvägen. They pull up in front of a two-storey, red-brick house.

They get out. Her legs feel stiff as she starts to walk.

They're good at this, her and Zeke.

Used to it.

How sick is that? Malin thinks as she rings the doorbell.

Footsteps behind the door. Then it opens.

A man of Malin's age holds it ajar and she can't help thinking that he's attractive, blond, keeps himself in shape. In the background she hears a woman's voice: 'Who is it, Anders?'

Peder Åkerlund's mother. Rebecka, according to Johan.

'The police!'

Anders Åkerlund has worked out who they are without them having to say anything, but judging by the look in his eyes he hasn't guessed why they're there.

'Is Peder in trouble?' he says, gesturing them into the hall. 'He hasn't done anything silly, has he?'

'Malin Fors,' Malin says. 'Linköping Police. This is my colleague, Zacharias Martinsson.'

They shake hands.

'There's no need to take your shoes off.'

They follow Anders Åkerlund into the house, and he leads them into a living room furnished with a mixture of things from Ikea and inherited heirlooms: a large lime-washed chest of drawers dominates the room.

In a red armchair sits a woman who could be Malin. She's around forty, blonde hair cut in a bob with a fringe, she looks fit, but next to the armchair is a wheelchair, and the legs in the woman's jeans look wasted.

'Rebecka.' Her handshake is firm, and she adjusts her position in the armchair. Seems to want to get out of it. It looks as if her upper body is going through the motions to stand up, but she doesn't move.

Anders Åkerlund is standing motionless. Something bordering on understanding has crept up on him.

'It's probably best if you sit down,' Zeke says, and at that moment the reason why the police are there finally dawns on Peder Åkerlund's parents, and with almost perfect synchronisation their faces contort, and Rebecka Åkerlund whispers: 'Say it isn't true, say it isn't true.'

Anders Åkerlund sinks onto the blue sofa, and Malin sits down beside him, puts an arm around him, and she hears Zeke say: 'I'm afraid we have to inform you that your son Peder was found murdered this morning.'

'How can you be sure it's him?' Rebecka says.

Malin sees the resistance in her eyes. And sees it fade.

Half an hour of exclamations, of wondering how and why, denials, tears and cursing, and then the realisation that this room, these people, this message, is here and now, this is reality, this is the start of the future.

What does it consist of?

Grief.

Practical matters.

Peder Åkerlund's parents know their lives have changed for ever, that they have to live with a pain that will change character but never end. In her armchair Rebecka Åkerlund rocks back and forth, clutching her paralysed legs.

'Obviously we were surprised and upset about the views he held at first. We don't think like that, not at all. We tried to talk some sense into him, but it was impossible. He refused to listen. But later on he changed his mind.'

'He was persistent,' Anders Åkerlund adds. 'To start with, schools kept refusing to let him come and tell his story. But he persuaded them. He was supposed to be visiting a lot more schools this autumn. And you've probably already seen his anti-racism website?'

'He's a sensible boy,' Rebecka Åkerlund says.

'How did he get caught up in right-wing extremism?' Malin asks.

And Rebecka Åkerlund goes on: 'He met a girl when he was fifteen. Nancy. He fell in love with her, and they were together for a year. But then she met a black lad. And broke up with Peder.'

She looks at her husband.

'He didn't take it very well.'

Her gaze slips across to Zeke. They both know not to ask questions now, to let Anders and Rebecka speak. The parents are the voices of the investigation at the moment.

Let their words flow from their shock.

Their vulnerability.

'He started to hate all immigrants,' Rebecka continues. 'Said that if they weren't here, he'd still have had Nancy.'

'And then he started to get involved in politics,' Anders interjects.

'In the Sweden Democrats, their youth movement. When they needed people after the last election. And it turned out the way that it did.'

The couple fall silent.

Then Rebecka begins to move to her wheelchair. Shifts her body first, with a great effort, then her legs.

You've done that thousands of times, Malin thinks. Does it ever feel straightforward?

'Did he have any enemies in the party?' she asks.

Both parents shake their heads.

'They weren't pleased when he refused to resign. But enemies? I got the impression that they all stuck together,' Rebecka says. 'Even if they didn't like the fact that he switched sides, I think he kept in touch with some of them. As friends.'

'You're leaving one thing out,' Anders Åkerlund says. His voice is tight, authoritarian.

Rebecka rolls her wheelchair out of the room towards the kitchen.

'What isn't she telling us?'

'I know he received a threatening letter from someone in the party.'

'Who?' Malin asks.

'He didn't want to say.'

'Did you see the letter?'

'No, but he told us about it.'

'Do you have any idea who it might have been?'

Anders Åkerlund bites his tongue. Behind the grief in his eyes Malin can see his shame at his son's attitudes, and she understands why Rebecka doesn't want to talk about the letter. She wants to protect her son's memory.

'You might want to talk to Max Friman,' Anders says.

Malin makes a note of the name on her phone.

'Do you know where we could find him?'

Anders Åkerlund shakes his head as his wife returns. In her lap she has a tray that she keeps carefully balanced as she pushes the wheels in turn.

A jug of pale red juice.

Four glasses.

'I thought you might be thirsty.'

Once she's put the tray down on the coffee table she turns towards Malin.

'We were very young when Peder was born, but then I had my accident and we didn't have any more children.'

No more children.

Malin can understand that sorrow, and perhaps Rebecka can tell, because the next moment she rolls over to Malin, takes her hand and whispers: 'He was my only child.'

Then she starts to cry, and Anders Åkerlund looks as if he wants to get up from the sofa to comfort his wife, but his muscles won't obey him.

'My only child. And now you're here to tell me that he's been murdered.'

She lets go of Malin's hand, rolls backwards, and with a sweeping gesture knocks the jug of juice from the table.

'How dare you? How dare you do a thing like that? How DARE you?'

# 11

Being alone is bittersweet, Elin Sand thinks. The best thing about it is the silence. Not having to listen to anyone else shuffling about, not having to hear someone open their mouth without actually having anything to say, without thinking first.

Her girlfriend, or former girlfriend, the doctor, was just like that. An opinion machine, as it turned out.

Women's rights.

Equality.

Feminism.

Elin has never had much time for all that. Not the rhetoric, anyway. Her entire life has been a feminist act, proving by her actions that she as a woman is just as good as a man.

That's the only way.

She looks around the sparsely furnished room.

This is a single man's home, she thinks.

She and Waldemar Ekenberg have entered Peder Åkerlund's flat together with a forensics officer. The flat is on the seventh floor of one of the tall yellow blocks of rented flats in Johannelund. You're close to the sky up here, Elin thinks, and outside the weather has got even hotter, and over on the horizon, the world becomes bluer and bluer the more you stare at the various shades.

The world feels infinite.

Then it disappears.

They've opened the balcony door to air the stagnant

flat. The forensics officer is busy in the kitchen, God knows what he's looking for. He's already packed Peder Åkerlund's computer away.

The little one-room flat is neat and clean, despite being rather spartan. No signs of a struggle. The few pieces of furniture seem to have come from flea markets, but still indicate a degree of taste, all of it matching shades of brown. On the walls hang reproductions of paintings Elin recognises. Produced by that failed artist who became a dictator.

Adolf Hitler.

If you can't paint, you might as well murder millions of people.

If you can't get acceptance, you might as well fight.

It's odd that Peder Åkerlund still has them on his walls after becoming a fervent anti-racist, she thinks, then looks away from the pictures and goes out onto the balcony.

Looks out across Linköping.

She's lived here almost two years now, but knows she'll never feel at home among all the self-important academics and civil servants. There's something off-puttingly smug about the city. A lot of people here think they're so fucking special without having any good grounds for doing so. Even the shop assistants are supercilious. A load of young girls who really think they're something.

Elin realises the way her thoughts sound, and she doesn't want to be like that. Doesn't want to be a bitter bitch, and thinks to herself that she needs to get away from here.

In a way, there's less racism here than in other cities. It feels as if people from other cultures are let in without too much fuss. As if the inhabitants understand that immigrants are needed.

This goes hand in hand with a certain highbrow attitude. The majority of Linköping's residents think too highly of themselves to look down on anyone because they come from somewhere else or have a different coloured skin. But their judgement of those of their own who show signs of eccentricity is all the harsher.

She goes back inside.

Waldemar snorts and rubs his brown trousers, making a rough, almost crackling sound. Elin can see how badly he wants a cigarette, how alone he seems to be without nicotine. She can't help smiling at him.

'Stop grinning, for fuck's sake.'

He used to behave in a terribly sexist way towards her. But he's almost stopped that now, even if sometimes he can't help commenting on her long legs.

She likes him. Likes the fact that he can be rough.

She doesn't have any time for people who don't realise that force is sometimes necessary, even for the good guys. Only weedy left-wing intellectuals would come up with an idea like that. People who've never experienced violence, or been faced with its consequences.

'Tidy,' Elin says, carefully opening a desk drawer. She doesn't want to mess anything up for the forensics officer.

'External order, internal chaos. Even if he had a point to start with. There are too many coloureds in the city.'

'Come off it, Waldemar,' Elin says. 'Don't start all that again. I thought you'd moved on from that sort of talk?'

'How many coloureds do you think there are living in this building? Thirty per cent? Forty? Hardly surprising that he ended up a racist.'

Elin shakes her head and goes through the rest of the desk.

Nothing but bills, blank white paper.

She looks inside the only wardrobe.

Clothes, a few bits of sports equipment. In the bookcase she finds some leaflets from the Sweden Democrats. The usual patriotic nonsense. She also finds some books about Nelson Mandela.

There's a chest of drawers in the small hallway. Elin pulls out the top drawer.

Underpants. Socks.

The second drawer.

T-shirts.

The third drawer.

Empty, apart from a few letters.

Elin takes them out carefully.

Peder Åkerlund's name on the front of the envelopes.

No address, no sender's name.

She opens one of the letters. Pulls the sheet of paper from the envelope and unfolds it, and finds herself looking at a photoshopped picture of Peder Åkerlund. His head has been chopped off, and under the picture is a mass of Arabic writing that Elin can't decipher.

'Can you read Arabic?' she calls to Waldemar.

He snorts.

'I'd rather go gay than learn Arabic.'

Then she calls to the forensics officer: 'Simon, you need to take these letters.'

# 12

An open, freshly-ploughed field to the right, ridges of soil like curling snakes between the deep furrows. To the left thin pine forest.

Malin toys with her phone as they head along Brokindsleden towards the city centre.

She hears a howl behind the car, then beside her, and sees a motorcycle disappear towards the horizon.

Someone with the cheek to blast past them at what must be at least one hundred and fifty kilometres an hour. Black leather. A ghost-rider, playing his way towards death.

They don't take up the chase. More important things to be getting on with.

It feels good to have the conversation with the Åkerlunds out of the way. Good to get out of Sturefors. She doesn't want to have to go out there again, but as long as she lives in Linköping it's inevitably going to happen from time to time.

Google.

Max Friman.

Who's supposed to have threatened Peder Åkerlund. Because that was what Anders Åkerlund was implying, wasn't it?

'What have you found?' Zeke asks as they pull up at a red light outside Ekholmen Shopping Centre.

Linköping, in miniature. On one side the flashy doctors' villas of Hjulsbro. On the other the mass housing project of Ekholmen. Satellite dishes on the balconies, women in niqabs with pushchairs.

The car park a mixture of rusting wrecks and shiny Mercedes. A collision of worlds, yet somehow not.

Max Friman.

Leader of the five Sweden Democrats on the council, took over when Peder Åkerlund resigned. He's twenty-two years old. A well-groomed lad who evidently sells computers at the I-Centre in Tornby. In all the pictures of the council Malin has been able to find he's wearing a suit and tie, his gaze is focused and challenging, his face unremarkable. He has the same sort of military hairstyle as Peder Åkerlund, just slightly longer.

'Head for Tornby,' Malin says. 'We're going to talk to Max Friman.'

The building in Tornby that houses the I-Centre has seen better days. The red-brown cladding is stained with mould, and the low white roof needs repainting.

The car park is almost full, and the harshly lit showroom glows with some fifty or so computer screens. The room is hot, and the smell of sweat very noticeable.

There's an urge to buy in people's eyes, the adverts have worked, desire has been stoked.

You can't live without me.

I'm your new best friend.

It's as if the computers dangle those promises, Malin thinks, fulfilling the dreams of the empty advertising slogans.

They go over to the information desk. A man in his thirties, dressing in a red shirt and blue tie, greets them far too familiarly.

Zeke holds out his police ID.

'We're looking for a Max Friman.'

The man gets nervous, fiddles with the bundle of receipts in his hand, and says: 'What's he done?'

Then he pulls himself together, aware that he's not going to get an answer to his question.

'Max is standing over there with some customers.'

He points towards the back of the showroom, at a thickset man with his back to them. A similar shirt, presumably a similar tie. The man is talking to some very attentive customers, it looks as if he's got them hooked.

'We'll wait until he's finished,' Zeke says, but Malin isn't so sure. It could take a long time; salesmen often seem to have verbal diarrhoea.

Sure enough.

Five minutes pass.

Seven.

That's enough.

Malin goes over to the corner where Max Friman is standing with his customers, taps him on the shoulder, and holds up her police ID.

He turns around. Sees the ID.

What's your face showing? Malin wonders, staring at his thin features.

Fear, shame, guilt?

No, surprise, anxiety. That's it, isn't it?

'Malin Fors, police. We'd like to talk to you.'

He doesn't appear to know what's happened.

'I'm busy with customers at the moment. Can you wait ten minutes?'

The customers, two men and a woman, all dressed in suits, take a few steps back, and one of the men says: 'We can come back another time.'

They walk off.

'Thanks a lot,' Max Friman says. 'A sale worth a hundred thousand just walked out of the door.'

The windows of the staffroom look out onto two shipping containers on the loading bay. A truck has pulled up, and the driver and another red-shirt are unloading boxes of computers.

They've explained about Peder Åkerlund, about him being found dead, probably murdered.

Max Friman lost it when he heard the news. Picked up the cup of coffee in front of him. Drained it as if it was full of water, and his body reacted instinctively when great gulps of uncomfortably hot liquid entered his mouth. But he did at least manage to turn his head, and sprayed coffee across the shabby, cork-tiled floor rather than the table.

As he wiped it up, he kept repeating: 'That's not possible. Who'd want to do a thing like that?'

And now he's sitting opposite them, fighting back tears.

'Did you know each other well?' Malin asks.

'We were good friends. I should say straight away that he was around mine last night. We had a few beers and talked until half past one. Then he went home. A school night and everything.'

'Where do you live?' Malin asks.

'On Ladugatan, down by Åhlén's.'

'So you still socialised even though he'd changed his political opinions?'

Max Friman looks expressionlessly at Malin. Then he smiles.

'We've been friends for a long time.'

'So, good friends?'

Max Friman nods.

You met up yesterday. So you could be the last person to see him alive, Malin thinks.

So you could be the person who killed him.

'How did you find him? What happened?'

'We can't go into that,' Zeke says. 'Did you often drink together?'

'Once a week or so. So you're saying that Peder was murdered on his way home from mine?'

Neither Malin nor Zeke replies.

'You weren't angry with him about his new views?' Malin goes on.

'You don't think that I . . . ? That I've got anything to do with this?'

If you did, you probably wouldn't volunteer the fact that he'd been around at your flat before saying anything else, Malin thinks. But, on the other hand, you don't seem particularly bright.

'We don't think anything,' Zeke says. 'We're trying to uncover the facts.'

'We heard that you threatened him,' Malin says. 'Sent him threatening letters.'

Max Friman holds his hands up in front of him, palms out, as if to protect himself.

'I've heard the rumours as well.'

So there were rumours. That's what Anders Åkerlund meant when he mentioned Max Friman's name.

'And?'

'They're completely wrong.'

Perhaps you didn't send any letters, Malin thinks. Perhaps those rumours spread because of the other letters? The ones Elin and Waldemar found. Elin called her a while ago to tell her.

But stick with it, for now.

'You didn't think he'd become a problem after he was expelled from the party?'

'What do you mean, a problem?'

'When he changed his opinions. Wanted to go to schools and give talks?'

'No, like I said,' Max Friman says, 'that wasn't a problem. He probably felt the party had let him down.'

Malin sees Max Friman's pupils contract. He isn't lying, but he could well be hiding something.

Then he leans back, and the fact that his friend is dead,

gone for good, seems to sink in, and he gets angry. He slams his fist down on the table, making the coffee cups jump.

'It's the fucking Muslims who've done this. Or left-wing bastards. They made threats against him, no one can deny that. They didn't give a damn about his conversion.'

'You mean the letters showing him with his head cut off? The ones written in Arabic?'

Max Friman looks at them in surprise.

Unmasked.

But he says: 'I don't know anything about any letters. None at all.'

'But you just said he'd been threatened.'

'On his website. Sure. In the comments on there.'

'Have you ever received any threats yourself?' Zeke asks.

'No,' Max Friman says. 'I keep a low profile. Jimmie prefers it that way.'

Jimmie.

Jimmie Åkesson.

Holding the lunatics in his party on a short rein, as best he can.

'But you know that Peder received threats?'

'Yes. From anonymous Muslims and left-wingers. On his website. The new one as well as his old one. Maybe a few anonymous emails.'

'Do you have any names?' Malin asks.

'No, nothing definite. But you can check with the mosque, and the Revolutionary Front here in the city. That's where you'll find the dregs of humanity.'

Malin tries to control her rising anger, but only half succeeds.

'It's probably best to keep that sort of talk to yourself. I could take you in for that.'

'Hardly,' Max Friman says. 'We live in a country with freedom of speech, and what I just said doesn't count as incitement to hatred. It's just the truth. And I want you to be very clear about one thing: Peder was seriously fucking smart. A thousand times better than you'll ever be.'

'You were drinking beer last night,' Zeke says. 'Did you argue about anything?'

Max Friman shakes his head.

'How many beers did you drink?'

'Six each, maybe.'

'And you didn't disagree about anything?'

'No.'

'What did you talk about?' Malin asks.

'We talked about the state of the police,' Max Friman grins. 'About how bad the cops in this city are at protecting its citizens from the scum. And how they waste loads of time harassing innocent people when they ought to be trying to solve crimes instead.'

Max Friman pauses. Looks Malin straight in the eye with barely concealed contempt.

'That's what we talked about. Happy now?'

## 13

Books that rhyme. Books with nothing but pictures, books that are too long, books that are too short.

All books burn. Linköping found that out on the night of 20 September 1996, when the old library burned down.

Thousands of books were destroyed. Some of them were the last copies in existence, and are now gone for good.

Buried by the world.

By the flames.

Börje Svärd never reads books. Unless they're about guns or dogs. He tried with military history, but not even that managed to spark his interest. His wife Anna used to read several books a week until her MS began to affect her optical nerves and made it impossible for her to read without getting a splitting headache. Then she switched to listening to audiobooks.

Börje Svärd walks through the vast space of the new library, his long coat slung nonchalantly over his shoulder. He left his hat at home today. It's just past one o'clock, and he can almost feel his thoughts taking flight, up towards the bare wooden beams in the roof.

How many books are there here?

Young people and pensioners are sitting reading in the egg-shaped chairs by the windows facing the park. They're not in direct sun, so the temperature by the glass is probably very agreeable now.

He's here to meet Nancy Hårdstål and Javier Riva. Peder Åkerlund's former girlfriend, and the dark-skinned man whose success in love is supposed to have driven Peder towards right-wing extremism.

He managed to get hold of Nancy Hårdstål's number and gave her a call. She said they were both at the library, revising for an economics exam. He'd find them downstairs, so where the hell is the staircase?

Börje suddenly feels smothered by all the books. Their passivity.

What sort of activity is reading books? Or writing them? When you could be hunting or grooming dogs or making love? Having sex. That's far better. Reading books is what you do when you're too ill to do anything else. There has to be something abnormal about trying to escape the world by reading, or, even worse, thinking you could capture the world and the people in it with words.

Over there.

The staircase.

Let's see what these two are like, Börje thinks, and quickens his pace. Sees a dark-skinned guy with dreadlocks and large eyes sitting next to a red-haired girl with defined features. She's wearing a tight T-shirt that fits her curvaceous figure perfectly.

Nancy Hårdstål looks at the detective who called earlier. What an idiot. But presumably there are women his age who like that kind of thing. Think he's a real man.

Mum would like him.

He's standing beside the fixed desk, has just introduced himself. He didn't want to say what this was about, and Nancy can see that he's nervous, as if he's just been told something unpleasant.

He fetches a chair and sits down next to them, then he looks at her and says: 'I've got some bad news.'

A burglary, Nancy thinks.

'Your ex-boyfriend, Peder Åkerlund, was found dead

this morning, probably murdered. You might have read online about a body being found out in Ljungsbro, near Heda?'

Nancy hears what he's saying. But the detective's words don't seem able to shape themselves into meaning.

She hasn't read about any bodies, she never looks at the news sites, you always find out anything you need to know sooner or later.

Then she hears Javier say: 'What the hell . . . ?'

'Peder Åkerlund has been found murdered,' the police officer, Börje, repeats, and Nancy understands what he's saying, and her first reaction makes her feel ashamed, but it's genuine and she can't help it.

She thinks and feels: Good, he's gone, I won't have to deal with him any more. Javier sits silent and contained beside her, and she needs to pretend to be sad, but how do you do that?

'That's awful, is it really true?' she says. And she tries to squeeze out a tear, but fails. 'I'm really shocked.'

'How was he murdered?' Javier asks, but the detective doesn't want to answer that, and asks instead: 'I understand that he reacted badly when you broke up with him.'

Nancy gives up trying to be sad.

So he really is dead?

Gone?

Just like that.

'He went mad when I met Javier. Turned into a racist and wouldn't leave us alone. To start with he used to call and email several times a day, then a bit less often, but still a lot. I very nearly went to the police.'

'But you didn't?' the detective asks, leaning towards her, and she can't help thinking that his moustache really is very off-putting. Why would anyone want a thing like that?

'No.'

'Why not?'

'I suppose I was a bit scared of him. Thought he and his friends might hurt Javier.'

'He was a racist,' Javier says, and she can hear the anger in his voice, a very dark anger that's only there occasionally, and which frightens her.

'There are lots of them about, sadly,' he goes on in a milder voice.

'What about his conversion?'

Javier snorts.

'I never believed a word of it.'

'How about you?' The detective turns towards Nancy.

'He seemed to have changed. But he still used to hang out with some of them.'

'Did he ever threaten you?' the police officer asks.

'No, he was just a bloody nuisance,' Nancy says. 'Has he really been murdered?'

She thinks: Murder. Here? In Linköping? Sure, it happens, but not to anyone I know. It only happens to alcoholics, and people who get in the way of nutters and sex-mad lunatics.

A young man a few desks away is trying to listen to their conversation.

Peder.

Dead.

It's not real. And suddenly she misses his awfulness, his wounded pride, the phone calls in the middle of the night.

He's never going to phone them again.

'Did you used to argue with him often?' the police officer asks, directing the question at both of them.

What's Javier going to say? she wonders. That they ended up having a fight just a few months ago? Is he going to mention that?

She looks at him. He looks back, and the expression on his face changes.

'We never really argued. But he was bothering us, and we protested.'

'Protested, how?'

'We asked him to stop.'

'And he did?'

'He hasn't bothered us at all in the last few months,' Nancy says. 'It was like he finally realised that our relationship was over, several years too late. And he was OK, really. Deep down. Just confused by the world. And he probably had changed for the better, in spite of everything.'

The truth, she thinks, is very different.

He'd started again. Worse than ever. A real stalker. But there's no need for the police to know about that. And he was never OK. He was a selfish egomaniac.

'Do you have any idea who might have murdered him? Did he have any enemies?'

'He must have had thousands of enemies,' Javier says. 'With those vile beliefs of his. They're not so easy to forget when you're on the receiving end.'

'We don't really know who, though,' Nancy says, smoothing her trousers. 'But if you look online you're bound to find a whole load of hatred.'

'From him as well as other people,' Javier adds.

She takes Javier's hand, squeezes it, and the detective asks: 'Where are you from?'

'What's that got to do with anything?'

'Nothing, probably. I'm just curious,' the police officer says, and smiles again, very patiently.

'From the West Indies. Dad's from Trinidad, Mum Venezuela.'

The detective rubs his fingers together. Looks at them steadily.

'You are telling me everything, aren't you? Everything I need to know?'

'Of course,' Nancy says.

'What were you doing yesterday evening and last night? Were you together?'

They look at each other again, and Javier squeezes her hand hard.

'We were around at mine,' he says. 'All night.'

'What were you doing?'

'We watched *Sons of Anarchy* on DVD.'

'What's that?'

'A television series about a biker gang.'

'I think I've seen it,' the detective says, then falls silent, evidently thinking. 'That's all for now,' he says eventually, but he just sits there looking at them, as if he can tell that they're lying.

The truth.

I was at home, and Javier said he was at home. And as far as I know, that's where he was.

Then the detective turns and leaves them alone with their economics.


Börje Svärd walks away from the attractive young couple, perfectly able to understand why Peder Åkerlund must have felt crushed. There aren't many girls as beautiful as that in a small city like this. He would have been at a very vulnerable age, and all hell must have broken loose in his impressionable brain.

They're lying, Börje thinks. That much is obvious.

We'll have to see if that matters. We'll find out whatever it is they're lying about. Could they have wanted to be rid of him?

Very possibly.

He makes way for a man pushing a trolley laden with books and manuscripts. The man is staring down at the floor, doesn't seem to have seen Börje, or to want to see him.

Pardon me, Börje thinks.

Then he emerges from beneath the ground, and out of the building full of books.

The fresh air feels good in his lungs.

A kilometre or so away, Malin and Zeke are each eating a hotdog with mashed potato at the Snoddas Grill, sitting on one of the benches on the grass beside the Statoil petrol station. The cars are going by on the Ryd roundabout, and there's a smell of barbeques on the breeze blowing from the allotments in Valla, even though it's still only early afternoon.

They've checked the websites of the *Correspondent* and the evening tabloids. They're running hard with the story, now that the relatives have been informed. Publishing the name of the victim.

*Former Racist Murdered!* according to *Aftonbladet.*

*Hate Crime?* thunders *Expressen.*

*Local Politician Murdered* is the headline of a more nuanced article by Daniel Högfeldt, in which he actually highlights Åkerlund's conversion.

The hotdog and mash taste good.

Karin has sent a team to Max Friman's flat. He had no objection to letting them examine the place where Peder Åkerlund is supposed to have spent his last evening alive.

They might find something in the flat.

Anaesthetic.

Signs of a fight.

But Malin doubts it. Max Friman didn't have to give them access to his flat at this stage of the investigation, and his willingness to cooperate despite his sarcasm and snide remarks seems to suggest that he wasn't involved in the murder.

But what hasn't he told them? There's something. Maybe we'll find an answer in the search of his flat.

In all likelihood Peder Åkerlund did spend the evening

drinking there, then set off home towards Johannelund, taking a long walk to sober up, and somewhere along the way encountered the perpetrator, who killed him, and then dumped his body by the canal.

Malin eats the last piece of sausage, then tosses the tray, smeared with yellow and red spattered mash, in a nearby bin.

The naked body in the ditch.

The swollen skin around the mouth.

The lips that had spoken their last words.

# 14

Tess. Tess.

Karin Johannison feels like calling out to her daughter, summon her to her by invoking her name, but it merely bounces silent and lonely inside her, then out across the pathology lab in the basement.

Karin can almost feel the earth pressing against the walls, the way it wants to pour in through the concrete. She wants to get out, go home. But she's got work that needs to be done.

How many times have I been down here on my own on an evening like this? With just a body for company?

Far too many times.

I should be with Tess, she thinks. I should be with Zeke.

The dead don't scare her, they never have. Occasionally, early on, she might feel frightened of the violence, and its effect on the human body, but now that doesn't frighten her either.

The young man on the post-mortem slab.

She's opened him up, checked all his organs, then sewn him back up. She found nothing unusual or noteworthy. She's screened the area around his mouth for traces of different substances. There were remnants of tape, traces of pepper spray, some sort of compound, and it's possible that he was sedated with ether.

Old-fashioned ether.

Using a cloth.

Whoever murdered him must have known what he

or she was doing. Ether's highly volatile. The fumes can make anyone in its vicinity drowsy, and it's easy to administer an overdose. But it wasn't the ether that killed Peder Åkerlund. If it had been, there would be signs of collapsed blood vessels in his lungs, as if someone had squeezed the air out of them, and there was nothing like that.

His death is still a mystery, and she's about to open up his skull. It'll take her another hour or so. Then her phone rings: Zeke's number on the screen.

She can't deal with him now.

But if it's something to do with Tess?

No.

This business of being able to love and miss and long for a person, yet simultaneously not be able to talk to them. The way feeling can become too tangible, too easily transformed into aggression.

They're home now, he texted an hour ago, and nothing can have happened. She clicks to reject the call. Wants to concentrate on this, so she doesn't miss anything.

She turns her back on the corpse, on what used to be Peder Åkerlund. His parents were there a few hours earlier to identify the body. Two uniforms came down with them, but Karin showed them into the room herself. She had her white coat on, aware that it muffles emotions better than a uniform in situations like that.

The woman in her wheelchair.

Fortunately, the whole building has been made accessible.

The parents beside the body. The man with his hand on the woman's shoulder, the woman rocking her upper body from side to side in her chair.

They both nodded without saying a word.

They took their time with their dead son, and Karin left them alone. Went out to the uniforms and watched through the windows in the door as the parents stroked their son's cheeks.

After fifteen minutes they were done. Emerged from the room of their own accord.

'That's Peder,' the woman said as she rolled past them, heading towards the lift.

Can you love a racist?

Should you love someone like that? Regardless of whether they've changed their views or not?

Love is the only thing we can do, Karin Johannison thinks. Meeting hate with hate only leads to violence and death. But sometimes you have to fight back. Protect the very core of your own life. But when? When do you resist? And what price must you be prepared to pay? Love, she wants to believe, is always bigger than hate, but she's well aware that this isn't always the case.

She fetches the bone saw from the cabinet under the narrow windows up by the ceiling. She takes a deep breath and becomes once again aware of how strongly the basement smells of chemicals and disinfectant. Sometimes the room feels like a grave. As if strange men were standing outside the little windows with spades in their hands, ready to shovel earth on top of her and bury her alive.

She raises the saw towards the skull. Peder Åkerlund's hair has grown slightly during the course of the day.

She starts the saw. The shrill noise forces its way into her head, and she hates it.

She stops the saw before it bites into the bone of the skull.

Looks down at it.

Hang on.

She switches the saw off, puts it down next to the body.

What am I looking at?

There's something here.

There always is, she thinks.

In a laboratory three floors up in the same building, forensics specialist Axel Nydahl is sitting hunched over his desk. He's a recent graduate, happy to have got the job, and there's no one waiting for him at home. He'd be happy to work through the night, and now he's searching for fingerprints on the envelopes and hate mail that were found in Peder Åkerlund's flat earlier.

Carefully he brushes the paper with detection solution, then powder.

Then he waits.

It always takes a few minutes before anything appears, if anything is going to appear at all.

They've had the three letters translated. A lab assistant who fled Iraq ten years ago helped them.

Similar messages in each of them. No punches pulled. The right-wing extremist was shown no mercy.

*You're a faithless dog. You shall die the death of a thousand deaths.*

*We're going to flay you alive. You most faithless of all infidels.*

*Cherish your head, because it will soon be separated from your body.*

The envelopes. The letters.

Slowly a few fingerprints are appearing.

From one – no, two people. Axel Nydahl can see that immediately. Whoever wrote these letters, he or she wasn't terribly careful.

Karin has found a pinprick in the middle of one of Peder Åkerlund's pupils. A tiny, almost microscopic red swelling that only stands out from the rest of the pupil by being slightly paler. The pinprick seems to vibrate with life even though the body is dead. She's certain it was made by the needle of a syringe.

She clears the area around the eye.

Picks up the saw again and starts to cut, cursing the noise once more.

And now the skull is open, and she looks down at the devastation in what used to be Peder Åkerlund's brain.

Burn marks. Black patches in the brain tissue. A scorched smell.

Acid.

Sulphuric or hydrochloric acid.

Someone injected corrosive acid directly into Peder Åkerlund's brain through his eye, burning up his soul from inside. If he was conscious when it happened, he must have suffered extreme pain, an intense flaring, burning sensation before everything went black and he died. But first his optical nerve would have burned out.

Blind, mute.

The brain tissue looks as if it's melted. But even so, Karin can see how far in the murderer must have pushed the needle before injecting the acid. Past the frontal lobe, deeper in, but not all the way to the base of the skull.

The murderer stopped at Broca's area.

The language centre of the brain. Where we form and understand words. From where the tongue is governed.

Mute and unable to understand language. That's what happens to someone with severe damage to their Broca's area.

But Peder Åkerlund doesn't have to worry about that.

Any doubt as to whether this was murder is dispelled now.

A pinprick to the eye.

As though someone wanted to blind you.

Acid in the Broca's area.

Someone wanted to make sure you would never speak again.

# 15

I stuck the syringe into his pupil.

Pretended to gasp for breath, pretended I couldn't get a single word out, but I never get words out, so what difference did it make?

I stuck the syringe into one of his pupils. Straight in, then up and to the side.

He screamed! And then he couldn't scream any more.

No longer two of them.

The girl may not be screaming in her grave now, but she can breathe and drink.

I see him walk along a street in Linköping, a random street, and I'm not the cat, and he's not the mouse.

That's too banal.

Unless perhaps I'm lying in a flat, watching a programme on television. Some hour-long documentary in which some idiot opens his heart and talks about the mistakes he's made in life. Or about how we must try to be good people. How we need to pick ourselves up again after catastrophes. They try to explain how everything is connected.

Where to start? I find myself thinking then. What game can I make of this?

I shall scream at the door and it will open. Make me small again, make everything that I am start again.

I shall wipe out everyone who says good things but does evil.

I see you. I know what you're doing.

Take care, or you might die.

# 16

Axel Nydahl takes the fingerprints he found on the envelopes and letters and scans them into the computer. Then
he logs into the national fingerprint database. He's already
confirmed that a number of the prints belong to the
victim.

He waits patiently while the cumbersome system loads:
it was already antiquated when it came into use years
ago.

He clicks his way through the program. Sets the searches
off to run concurrently, even though that takes a bit longer.

The word appears in a separate window on the screen.

Searching.

For a while, back when he was a teenager, he didn't
actually like immigrants himself, and was attracted by the
idea of one nation, one people, one culture. Then he spent
a summer working as a cleaner in a hospital. There he
met a woman from Somalia who wore a headscarf at work.
She had so many stories. About violence, madness, love.

A nuclear physicist from Iran.

'What do you think they wanted me for?'

The search continues.

Ten per cent complete.

Fifteen.

He became friendly with a guy from Algeria, who fled
his homeland after ending up on the government's kill-list.
During lunch breaks Axel would hear stories about human
courage that he had trouble relating to, and realised that

he himself had never come anywhere close to that sort of experience in his safe little life.

He gained respect for those people.

More than for his sluggish Swedish summer workmates.

What did they know about anything?

What did he himself know about the world?

After that summer he made up his mind: Whatever I do with my life, it must have some sort of positive goal. And that put an end to his nationalist thoughts.

Seventy-five per cent.

And now I've ended up here, he thinks. Working on the investigation into the murder of a former racist, someone who might still have been a racist. Is that good? Can that be a positive goal? Shouldn't they all just be silenced? That stuff about being ready to die for everyone's right to express their opinions is bollocks. Some things must never be said. Thought, sure, but not said.

Ninety per cent.

Bloody program.

But the last ten per cent go quickly.

One hundred per cent.

And a match appears.

Followed by a name.

Prints on all the letters.

Belonging to one and the same person.

A Julianna Raad.

Her passport photograph appears on the screen a moment later. Dark-haired, beautiful, but her eyes are full of anger.

He looks for her in the criminal records database to see why her details are in the system.

Much quicker this time.

She was arrested on 30 November two years ago in Kungsträdgården in Stockholm, at a counter-demonstration to the nationalist commemoration of Karl XII's death. She assaulted a police officer with a brick, and he lost the sight in one eye. She was sentenced to six months in prison, served four, and was released last summer.

He does a quick search for Julianna Raad on Google and soon has a pretty good picture of who she is.

A militant left-wing activist. Member of animal rights groups and Anti-Fascist Action.

Prepared to resort to violence.

Gold, Axel Nydahl thinks.

A woman on the extreme left-wing with a proven inclination to violence.

Her name. What sort of name is that? Could she be Arabic?

Threatening letters written by her, or someone else, and sent to a right-wing extremist.

A right-wing extremist who has been found murdered, naked in a ditch next to a canal.

Wait till Karin hears this.

# 17

Music is thudding from the ancient ghetto blaster. The speakers vibrate as a French singer gives voice to her pain and suffering.

Malin sees Elin Sand pump two large dumb-bells at the other end of the cramped gym in the basement of the police station, thinking: I can manage more than that.

Elin's black and pink gym clothes contrast sharply with the vomit-green walls. There's been talk of renovating the gym, and it could certainly do with it, but there's no money.

Elin puts the dumb-bells down. Smiles at Malin, who smiles back.

She's noticed that Elin Sand looks up to her, how on earth could anyone do that?

A failed, alcoholic mother and police officer.

A broken wreck.

A human being who still has the capacity to feel longing, in spite of everything.

As she carries the dumb-bells back to the rack after a set of shoulder lifts, she feels how much she wants to be with Daniel. Lie in bed beside him and feel sleep come.

The clock in the gym says it's a quarter to seven, and Karin is bound to be finished with the post-mortem soon. Maybe she can find something that can give them some answers, help them make progress.

'Can you spot me?' Elin calls.

'Sure.'

Malin goes over to the bench where Elin is lifting a bar laden with seventy kilos.

She's strong, I can only manage sixty at most. And even that makes me feel that my brain is going to explode.

Elin shrieks and grunts.

'Cunt!'

'Damn, you're pretty weak,' Malin smiles above her.

'What the fuck are you laughing at?'

Three times twelve. Silent rest between the sets, and Malin may never have met anyone as competitive as Elin Sand. Presumably that's what it takes to get as far as she did in volleyball, all the way to the national team.

After the last set of reps Elin gets up from the bench.

'That's enough,' Malin says.

They train together almost every week. Sometimes several times, but they rarely talk about anything personal. In the changing room they use lockers on opposite sides.

Malin takes her clothes off, wraps a towel around her body, and heads toward the showers. The basement stinks of damp and mould. The sealed linoleum floor has come loose in the corners, and the baby-blue walls are speckled with small black stains.

She turns the shower on and stands under the hot water with her eyes closed.

Feels the water run down her body.

Feels someone staring at her body.

And she opens her eyes, and Elin Sand is standing under the shower opposite her with her back towards her.

The water on her body.

Perfectly formed. And with a young person's shimmering, vibrant skin.

Was she looking at me just now?

She's not allowed to fucking look at me.

Malin soaps herself with jerky movements, rinses, turns the shower off. Wants to get out of there as quickly as possible.

She wasn't looking at me.

I'm so fucking ridiculous, Malin thinks. And prejudiced.

Elin Sand turns her own shower off and Malin hurries out to the changing room. Doesn't want to be there when Elin turns around again.

She throws her clothes on.

Elin walks past with her towel wrapped around her. Her brown hair is wet, and she looks ridiculously attractive. Those cheekbones. How does anyone have cheekbones like that?

'What's up with you?' she asks. 'I'm not an alien.'

Malin laughs.

'I was just thinking about something. Sorry.'

Then they hear the door to the changing room open, and they look at each other. No one else usually comes down here, and suddenly Karin Johannison is standing in front of them.

'I've got quite a bit of new information,' she says, looking simultaneously focused and restless.

Julianna Raad.

Hydrochloric acid in the Broca's area.

Speechless. Colliding ideologies.

Who cares about someone renouncing their views? There can be no forgiveness.

Karin and her colleagues have worked fast, and they've done good work.

She's left them again, and Elin and Malin are standing side by side in the changing room. Malin is the same height as Elin's breasts.

They've got an address for Julianna Raad. She lives on a small farm in the middle of the Östergötland Plain, just five kilometres from where Peder Åkerlund's body was found.

A militant left-wing activist.

Her father is from Lebanon, Arabic his mother tongue,

so it's by no means out of the question that Julianna knows Arabic.

'I think we should talk to Julianna Raad straight away,' Malin says. 'There's no good reason to wait.'

Elin Sand shrugs her shoulders.

'I've got nothing better planned.'

They fetch their service pistols from the gun cabinet in the little room next to the open-plan office on the first floor of the police station. The metal rattles as Malin hurriedly inserts the key in the lock.

She wonders if they should inform Göran Möller before they go, if they should get his permission to question Julianna Raad, but decides not to bother. Göran Möller likes it when she shows initiative, has actively encouraged her to do so. And that's what she's doing. Karin is bound to call him to tell him what they've discovered.

Time to act, Malin thinks, and looks at Elin, who seems to be thinking the same thing. She says: 'Right, let's go.'

Within minutes Malin is sitting in the passenger seat of a white Golf, and they're heading through the city, past the cemetery, past the National Bank building and the old fire station, on past Abisko, and then down towards Skäggetorp and Tornby. The big, out-of-town stores are shutting up shop for the day, and in the flats in Skäggetorp perhaps people are happy that Peder Åkerlund is dead. Or perhaps not. Few people are pleased when a young person dies. Probably only really militant opinion-machines, regardless of political persuasion.

Then they're out on the plain.

Elin puts her foot down. Malin looks out across Lake Roxen: the slowly sinking sun makes the broad expanse of water look as if it's made of brittle glass.

A few boats. Fishing for char, probably.

The car's engine rumbles and rasps, but otherwise it's strangely quiet. Neither of them says anything, and Malin has a sense that part of the universe has ceased to exist, a part she can't see but which is still real, important. She feels it inside her like a fluid vacuum, a hollowness, a chasm that is in constant motion.

At the next junction Elin turns left, at speed, and they head across the plain on an unpaved road, then turn right and carry on towards its yellow heart. In the distance Malin can see Vreta Kloster. The white tower.

And beyond it, the place where the body was found.

Not far from here.

'It should be that house,' Elin Sand says.

Stranded among fields of flowering rape and others left fallow is a large yellow house flanked by two red barns. The house and barns are half hidden by birch trees that form a huge hedge, but it's still obvious that they're badly neglected. A rusty red Ford is parked on the road.

This is a place that's seriously short of money.

What job does she do? Malin wonders.

'Let's stop here,' she says.

They get out.

The field to the left of the car is rust-coloured and dry, clouds of dust lifting in the gusts of wind from the lake. It's still light, but Malin still has to squint to see properly, as well as shield her eyes from the dust.

What are we going to find? she asks herself.

Julianna Raad assaulted a fellow police officer so badly that he lost the sight in one eye, so they need to be careful. Malin touches the pistol inside her shoulder holster, and can see the bulge beneath Elin's denim jacket.

Have we already got so far with this investigation that our murderer is inside that house over there?

Malin feels her stomach clench. Not from nerves, fear, or anger, but something else. An indefinable new feeling that can only be met with action. She knows that: her body's alarms can only be silenced by action or drink, and drink is out of the question for her, it would kill her.

Why did Julianna write those letters?

Why in Arabic?

To direct attention towards Muslims? To frighten Peder Åkerlund, and make him think he had a group of Muslims after him?

The letters weren't dated. Did she write them before or after he changed his views?

Or perhaps Julianna Raad isn't a left-wing extremist after all, but something else? A Muslim extremist? Are we blundering into some sort of jihad now? Malin wonders. She realises that she's turned Julianna into a monster without actually having met her.

They start to walk towards the house, and Malin can sense Elin Sand's fear.

'We'll take it nice and gently,' Malin says, as a sparrow flits past them, looking at them to see if they're edible.

Malin can feel the approach of night in the air.

She looks towards the dense yet fractured cluster of trees surrounding the buildings that are supposed to be Julianna Raad's home.

But she can't hear anyone. The voices of the investigation aren't whispering to her.

The fourth letter.

*We'll cut out your tongue. We'll leave you mute.*

## 18

The paper's newsroom can feel like the realm of the dead. Cramped and hot and abandoned, full of people who know that their days are numbered, that soon some number-cruncher will show up and draw a line through their names in the personnel files.

Daniel Högfeldt adds a full stop at the end of the last sentence of the third article he has written this shift.

His eyes feel gritty. The light at his desk is far too gloomy, his screen too old and decrepit.

Around him the others work on in silence.

The atmosphere in the newsroom is subdued.

No one seems to believe in a future for the printed edition of the paper.

For the free word in print. For the scrupulous examination of power.

The advertisers have more and more influence, Daniel thinks. A week or so ago he was told to go and cover the local ice hockey team, the LHC's annual sponsors' dinner at the Cloetta Center. Sheer sycophancy on the part of the paper, giving the city's big shots a chance to show off in the press.

He refused.

His boss issued a barely-concealed threat, but he stood his ground.

Refused.

They sent a trainee instead, and ended up with a double-page spread of local celebrities eating steak.

*LHC investing in the future*, the headline said.

No trace of critical analysis.

Who needs the free word now, when the bearers of the free word themselves demonstrate exactly how much it is worth?

Nothing. Not a thing.

If he gets fired he'll just have to find something else to do. There are PR jobs in the city. Soul-destroying, but better paid.

He sends the article off. Feels pleased with himself.

A strong, in-depth portrait of the murder victim, Peder Åkerlund, combined with speculation about his murder based on his background.

He tried to get a comment from someone in the police. But his source clammed up, and he never calls Malin about work. It would drive her mad, and would put him in an extremely difficult position.

But sometimes it would be so easy just to ask her for information.

Has a boil of racist pus burst in the city? Has someone had enough of the Sweden Democrats and murdered one of them? Or have the racists got rid of a former supporter who has been making a nuisance of himself?

Or is it a sexually-motivated murder? He was found naked, and the police have been tight-lipped about his injuries. No press conference until tomorrow.

He has a bad feeling about this story. Something really awful is going on.

Malin.

I'm forty-one now, Daniel thinks, looking at the faint reflection on his screen, the lines on his forehead that are getting deeper and deeper.

Malin can't have any more children. And I don't have any.

What's going to happen to us? Are we going to end up

a childless couple in Linköping? There aren't many of those, but do I even want children? If I do feel any kind of emptiness in my life, it isn't that sort of emptiness.

But I'm ready to take the next step. Ready to take it with Malin. End this limbo-life of ours and at least move in together.

He takes out his mobile.

Feels like calling her, hear how she is, what she's doing, tell her to be careful.

Tell her I love her.

Because he does. Has done for a long time now.

My hand against your cheek, then down, down over the steep curve of your collarbone, your hair tickling my fingers, and your voice saying something, anything at all.

He clicks to open a picture of Malin in the newspaper's archive. By mistake he opens one where she's being carried across a driveway on a stretcher.

Shot.

The shotgun pellets that hit her womb, and are still there. Tiny pellets of evil. They don't cause her any pain, and the little round scars have grown pale, aren't the angry red they were a year ago. He usually lets his fingers linger on them before moving further down, to where he knows she wants them, further down, and then in, and he can make her tremble with lust and desire, with longing for her lost self.

Because that's what sexuality is to her, she needs it to find something inside her that's been lost, something she has to find if she's to become whole again.

She makes love as if it's a matter of life or death.

And it is. His body is merely a tool for her dreams, her survival.

Where are you now, Malin?

Take care.

I couldn't bear to lose you.

# 19

Malin and Elin are approaching the farm, step by step. The gravel crunches beneath their feet and the sky is an endless evening blue.

No birds, Malin thinks. As if they've flown away from the world.

Elin seems nervous beside her, but focused, almost as if she's preparing for an attack and Malin is a lieutenant who's about to blow her whistle to send them out of their trench.

It's far from certain that Julianna Raad has anything to do with the murder, but anything could happen here.

There could be a trap lurking anywhere.

Is death here? Malin wonders.

The peculiar hedge of trees around the house. A wall of leaves.

They walk up to the white-painted gate. Elin pushes it open, and they're in the yard. The two barns flank either side of a weed-strewn farmyard, their roofs look ready to collapse at any moment. In front of them is the yellow-plastered farmhouse.

An empty porch.

Someone has taped brown cellophane over the windows, giving the house dark eyes and making the dark-grey door an open mouth. There's a vegetable garden on one side of the house, black soil, an abandoned cultivator whose blades glint in the last rays of sunlight.

Being watched.

She can sense that she's being watched, she's felt it before. Not just by eyes, but something else, something potentially lethal, and she yells: 'Get down, Elin, down on the ground, now!' And as she says the last word the first shot rings out.

Bang.

And stones fly up beside Malin's foot.

A rifle? A pistol, and out of the corner of her eye she sees Elin throw herself to the ground and crawl towards an upturned garden table for cover.

Malin is on her own in the open.

Bang.

Keep down, for God's sake.

The second bullet whistles past her head.

She can feel adrenaline pumping now, and she throws herself sideways and snakes towards the house, but she's completely unprotected out in the open yard.

Which window? she wonders, and yells: 'Fire, Elin, fire!' And Elin fires, a shot towards the façade of the building.

The next bullet lands in front of Malin's face. Broken glass rains down onto the gravel, and she gathers her strength, heaves herself up onto her knees, and sets off, running in a zigzag towards the porch, towards shelter, and she expects to feel a bullet hit her, knows how it feels to get shot, knows how much it hurts, yet she's still not frightened. Fear can come later.

More shots from the house.

They hit a few metres behind Malin, and she must be in the shooter's blind spot, and she runs faster, up the steps, turns sideways on, and hits the door with her shoulder.

Inside.

A smell of boiled vegetables and dirt. There are shabby rag-rugs on the floor, and the furniture seems to belong to another era.

Malin presses against one wall. The shots came from

the upper floor, but there could be other people in the house. She's not safe anywhere.

Sweat is trickling from her hairline, down into her eyes, and it stings.

'Stay there!' she yells to Elin.

Malin is breathing hard. She tries to take deep breaths, then realises that she's holding her pistol in front of her with both hands.

I need to get upstairs, she thinks.

I ought to check the rooms down here.

She hears another shot, glass breaking.

She crouches down.

If there's anyone down here I would have seen them by now.

The stairs. Just a few metres from her, the treads painted red.

I need to get up there.

She heads in that direction. Up onto the first step, the second, her pistol aimed upwards, and she's ready to fire, afraid now. Knows she doesn't stand a chance if there's anyone waiting for her up there.

She could get her head blown off.

'Julianna!' she calls out. 'We only want to talk to you.'

No answer.

Just a gun, a shot from inside one of the rooms upstairs, and Malin hears a noise behind her, there's someone there, and she spins around, movement, and as she takes aim, a black cat runs out through the front door.

Shit.

She turns around again, and heads up the stairs with her pistol raised, and she's angry now, what an idiot.

'Julianna!'

We're coming, I'm going to get you, and as Malin calls out she makes an effort to sound calm and authoritative.

Halfway up the stairs.

Her head almost level with the upper floor.

Above the floor.

A shot could ring out at any moment.

The landing. Two closed doors.

And Malin turns her body, lowers her pistol, no one inside on either side, and she runs up the last few steps and takes cover against a freshly-painted wall beside one of the doors.

Everything is neat and tidy upstairs. A chest of drawers with newspapers and books piled on top of it. A new rug.

The shots must be coming from the room at the far end, behind the red door.

She raises her pistol again. Walks along the passageway holding it in front of her.

No more shots.

She hears steps on the gravel, then Elin enters the house. But Malin keeps quiet, doesn't call out to Julianna again. Doesn't want to give her position away.

'I'm in!' Elin shouts. 'I'll make sure the downstairs is clear.'

Malin waits, hears Elin go from room to room, calling out: 'Clear, clear, clear!'

Then silence.

Just the sound of the wind in the trees.

Did one of the bullets go through the wall? Did they hit Julianna Raad? If it was actually her hiding on the other side of the red door.

It could be someone else.

Malin moves forward.

Towards the red door.

Tries to listen, but can't hear any sound from inside the room.

She stops beside the doorframe. Takes three quick steps back, then kicks hard. The door flies open more easily than she expected, and she stumbles in.

Fuck.

When she regains her balance and is about to raise her gun, she sees Julianna Raad standing at the far end of the room, aiming a pistol at her. Wearing a flowery pink dress, she seems almost to blur into the flowery red wallpaper.

A bewildered, hunted look in her eyes.

'Don't shoot,' Malin says. Keeps her pistol pointing at the floor.

Julianna Raad's hands are shaking.

'We just want to talk to you,' Malin says, thinking: Put the bloody gun down, don't shoot me.

The next moment she hears noises behind her back, then Elin Sand's voice: 'I'll shoot. Put the pistol down.'

And Malin looks at Julianna Raad. Loneliness, a realisation of what she's spent the past few minutes doing, but also fear and desperation.

'What the hell do you want?' she roars. 'Who the hell are you?'

'We're from the police,' Elin says. 'We're investigating the murder of Peder Åkerlund, and we need to speak to you.'

Julianna Raad looks even more bewildered, and then her expression changes again, anxiety, worry, and she says: 'I don't know anything about any murder.'

'We don't mean you any harm,' Malin says.

'No, you bastard cops never do.'

You're going to put your gun down now, Malin thinks.

But Julianna Raad goes on aiming at her, and Malin knows that Elin Sand has her in her sights, so she darts quickly to one side. Julianna loses her concentration, gets confused, and Malin throws herself at her. She kicks the gun from her hand with a high kick that could have come from a bad Hong Kong action movie.

Disarmed.

And Malin hits her on the temple. Julianna slumps to

the floor, her skinny body falls slowly, as if she somehow has the ability to float.

Elin is there in a flash. Sits on top of Julianna Raad, who appears to realise that there's no point resisting.

Malin takes out her handcuffs. Fastens Julianna's arms behind her back, and Julianna shrieks: 'Fascists! You're fucking fascists, that's what you are!'

# 20

I can hear the badgers' claws scratching against my coffin. There's a scraping sound.

Claws. I can hear them now, but no one can hear me. I know that.

Yet still I scream and scream and scream.

My joints are sore and my back aches. I try to roll over, but the coffin is too cramped.

I raise my head and let it fall back onto the wood. Hard, hard, hard, and I do it over and over again.

Pain is real. I'm alive.

Who buried me like this? And I scream again: WHO BURIED ME LIKE THIS?

What have I done? I don't deserve this.

Am I lying in a coffin?

Am I out on the plain, in the forest, or in a garden, or inside a house, under the cement floor of a cellar?

And what's that ticking?

A clock is ticking, and I take a sip from the tube. The water is fresher now, has someone refilled it? And I can feel that the air, my air, is running out.

Breathing, breathing, breathing.

Be still. I can't do anything, so I may as well save my strength.

The clock is ticking. Could it be attached to some sort of explosive device? That sounds mad, but this whole situation is mad.

Mum, Dad, I don't want to die. Not now. Not yet. I'm going to change the whole damn world.

Mum.

Dad.

You have to find me.

Even if I've treated you like shit, I need you now. My words bounce off the wooden walls and I barely understand them myself.

You have to hear me.

Why haven't you come?

Mum, Dad.

Sorry, sorry, sorry.

# 21

The taxi drops them off outside the *fin de siècle* building on Drottninggatan, up near the corner of Trädgårds-föreningen gardens. Bror Lundin looks over towards it. In the gloom, the trees are immoveable giants, and the bushes and flowers their cowering servants.

The building contains rented apartments, but only for the city's most affluent citizens. They're paying ninety thousand kronor per month for their five rooms.

Bror Lundin and his wife Beata have been lucky in life. He set up a business developing platforms for computer games together with some friends at university, and they've had a number of international successes. Beata is director of finance at another successful IT company.

They're wealthy, but not rich. He was forced to dilute his share of the business during the early years, when the company needed capital.

Bror helps the taxi driver unload their luggage onto the pavement. The golf bags are heavy, the clubs high quality.

Marbella.

A week of sun, golf, and rosé wine.

Beata taps in the code to the door.

He knows they're both hoping the same thing, that their daughter Nadja will be up in the apartment. Not waiting for them, that would be too much to ask, but he wants her to be there. Today was a school day. So she might be there.

She's only sixteen. But oddly opinionated.

Vegetarian, no, vegan, and an environmental activist.

She objects to more or less everything about the way they live their lives. She has a blog where she writes about the environmental damage caused by the city's industrial estates, and exposes companies and individuals, mostly celebrities, whom she considers to be living environmentally unsustainable lives.

There used to be a lot of conflict in the home, until eventually he and Beata realised there was no point arguing with her.

Nadja is who she is.

And he, they, love her more than anything. Their only daughter.

They haven't heard from her in two days. They've called, but she hasn't answered the phone, and she hasn't called or texted or emailed them either. There are no new pictures on her Instagram, and she doesn't use Facebook, that's 'for old people'.

But that isn't really so odd. She's probably at their summer house in Svartmåla now. She often goes out there after school or at weekends. She does her yoga there, and grows things in the large patch of garden she's cleared behind the house. The first harvest of vegetables she grew there did taste incredibly good.

They've bundled their luggage into the lift now. They're both tired. They missed their connection in Frankfurt, and had to wait another two hours for a flight to Stockholm instead of Gothenburg, so they're home much later than expected.

The lift rattles its way upward.

There's only just room for the two of them with all their bags and cases, and Bror Lundin looks at Beata. She's still beautiful. After thirty years together he can still see the beauty in her face, in her soft features and little button nose, and the blonde hair that time hasn't yet turned grey.

But she's worried now. He can tell from the tight little wrinkles around her lips.

'Don't worry,' he says. 'She's probably at home. After all, her school hasn't called to say she hasn't been there.'

'They don't ring about things like that, you know that,' she says tetchily. 'We should have called them.'

He feels irritation spread through his body.

Miserable cow.

But he holds back, like so many times before.

The lift stops on the third floor, and Beata pushes her way out and puts the key in the lock.

She disappears into the apartment.

Bror Lundin gets their luggage out. Carries it into the circular entrance hall, and his wife comes back.

'She's not here,' she says.

'Then she's gone to the country,' he says.

Beata looks sceptical, but says nothing.

They've tried calling the summer house as well, but got no answer there either. Mobile reception can be unreliable out there, though, and the Internet connection is fairly erratic. That means she could be there, and would explain why she hasn't posted anything on Instagram.

She usually posts at least three or four times a day. Pictures of environmental problems, or of herself and her limited number of friends. But perhaps she's got her hands full with the garden now that spring has arrived.

Beata turns and walks back into the apartment. To the sitting room looking out across the park.

Bror Lundin closes the front door and goes after his wife.

The clay-coloured Josef Frank sofas dominate the room, and there are two large oil paintings by Bengt Lindström on the walls. Grotesque faces, garish colours.

Beata has gone over to the window. She's gazing down at the trees.

Dusk over Linköping now.

And no Nadja.

But he needs to keep a cool head.

Should they call the police?

No.

He needs to check Svartmåla first.

He goes over to Beata, puts his hands on her shoulders and whispers in her ear: 'Don't worry, she'll be in Svartmåla. I'll head out there now.'

'Aren't you tired?' she asks. And he can hear from her voice that she's not asking out of concern, but more as a challenge: You're man enough to deal with this now, aren't you? Anything else is out of the question.

He lets go of her, and ten minutes later he's sitting in their BMW 4x4, heading out into the forests of Östergötland.

He's always struck by how beautiful Svartmåla is. The lake water is almost black at this time of day. But the fir trees are still reflected on the shimmering surface.

They bought the house when he sold some shares in the company five years ago. It was expensive, but the business has continued to attract investment, and Bror Lundin likes the fact that the house is so close to the city. In just half an hour you can be in another world.

Most of the houses are empty and shut up, but the Anderssons are home. They live out here all year round.

He takes two left turns and catches sight of the house, and the lake a little further on.

He painted it moss green last summer. Sanded and patched it up, then painted it. White wooden detailing. He's pleased with the way it turned out.

Bror Lundin parks. Then he walks firmly towards the front door, consciously choosing not to see any signs that Nadja isn't there.

That would be unthinkable.

She must be here.

Where else would she be?

He wants to see her beautiful face. Put his hands on her cheeks and kiss her head, tell her how nice she looks with her nose-ring, and that those fake leather shoes look good.

He wants to be nice. He wants her to listen. Not just see him as an old idiot who means well.

I'm forty-five. I can be part of her life.

The front door is locked.

But she could still be here.

Through the glass in the door Bror Lundin can see that the house is dark. He takes out his key and goes inside.

Something's not right. He feels it at once. The house smells aired, not shut-up and stale the way it usually does. He hurries into the living room.

The lake is pitch-black now, and the outside furniture, the barbeque and folded parasol on the terrace look like scorched bronze statues.

He sees what he doesn't want to see.

The glass in the terrace door has been smashed.

His shoes crunch as he moves around the room. The furniture is in disarray, the two Bruno Mathsson armchairs overturned, and the mat under the dining table is crumpled.

Broken vases.

The glass-fronted cabinet has been pushed over.

Glass everywhere.

Disorder.

Like after a fight. As if people had been fighting there.

Nadja's laptop is on the table, open, its screen black. Her brown cardigan is tossed on one of the sofas.

Bror Lundin stops. Breathes. Feels a cold wind blow through the broken terrace door.

He can't hear or feel his breathing.

Nadja.

NADJA!

He wants to call to her, loud and long. Drive her out of the forest with his cries.

Nadja.

You were here.

Someone came.

You fought.

You're missing.

Bror Lundin has never felt more scared in all his life. He feels the jaws of potential tragedy open up, can feel the beast's breath on his neck, knows it could swallow him whole.

He walks out onto the terrace. Looks out at the untouched vegetable garden.

Screams his daughter's name.

Over and over again, he screams her name.

But no sound comes out.

# 22

Dad.

Dad.

Are you calling to me?

Or is that you calling, Mum? Am I that close to you?
I dreamed your cries. When I was sleeping.

It's hot now, I'm sweating, I want to drink, but there's
no more water in the tube, it's run out.

I try to throw my hands out sideways.

I strike as hard as I can, but it's too cramped, and my
knuckles won't bleed.

I'm so alone that I can't even make myself bleed.

My sores sting and burn.

Please, Dad, find me soon.

## 23

Julianna Raad leans forward and spits in Malin's face.

'Cop bitch.'

Malin wishes she could reach over and grab her by the throat.

Julianna is twenty-two years old, and the most hate-filled person Malin has ever met. As if she were possessed by a demon.

She looks almost cute in her flowery dress and gentle features, but her eyes reveal a will of steel.

Elin Sand puts her hand on Malin's arm.

'Easy now, easy.'

Interview room number two is painted in various shades of brown. The chairs and table are metal, and the light from the halogen lamps in the ceiling reveal every detail of people's eyes and faces.

Göran Möller is watching behind the mirror.

'You won't provoke me,' Malin says, wiping the saliva from her face with the sleeve of her jacket.

'We'll see.'

'Why did you fire at us?' Elin Sand asks, in a friendly voice.

'I don't have to tell you a fucking thing.'

'No, you don't,' Malin says. 'But you're welcome to do so, if you like.'

You're looking at a lengthy prison sentence now, she thinks. The prosecutor will get attempted murder out of this, at the very least.

'You're in the shit.'

They've explained to her why they went out to the farm, and why she's now sitting in this interview room.

'Did you send Peder Åkerlund those threatening letters?'

Julianna Raad appears to consider the situation, then a light goes on in her dark eyes.

'It was me,' she says, and smiles. 'I wanted to scare the racist bastard. The way he scares other people.'

'He'd renounced racism,' Elin Sand says.

'How can you be so sure about that?'

'What do you mean?'

The pictures in his flat, Elin thinks. Adolf Hitler's artless landscapes. Why hadn't he taken them down?

'There are anonymous websites with posts from him. Updated long after he's supposed to have become a saint.'

'Which websites?' Malin asks.

Julianna Raad gives them some web addresses.

'So you believe he was still racist?'

'You can never be sure. But once a racist, always a racist.'

'When did you send the letters?' Elin asks.

'The first one last autumn, the last one two months ago.'

'But why in Arabic?'

'I knew that's what would scare him most.'

'How do you mean?' Malin asks.

'He wouldn't feel scared of me, a girl. But Muslims . . . they make people like him shit their pants.'

'And then you made good on the threats. Got hold of him somehow and killed him.'

Julianna Raad leans back in her chair. Throws her head back and bursts out laughing.

'I know you've got a forensics team searching my house now. Seizing my computers. But you won't find anything, because there's nothing to find. It wasn't me, someone else did it.'

'You threatened to kill him,' Malin says. 'You must appreciate that means we have to consider you a suspect.'

'I was just imitating the rhetoric of the jihadists. You know, the way they talk on YouTube before cutting off a hostage's head.'

Malin takes a deep breath.

'Do you sympathise with their views?'

Julianna smiles but doesn't reply.

'Why did you open fire on us?' Elin Sand asks again. 'You were trying to kill us, weren't you?'

Julianna Raad laughs once more.

'If I'd wanted to kill you, I'd have hit you.'

'So why did you shoot?'

'Like I said, I don't have to explain anything to you.'

A police-hater, Malin thinks. An anarchist. At least a century too late.

'Have you got a licence for your rifle?' Elin asks.

'Ha!'

'Where did you get it?'

'You think I'd tell you?'

She's capable of anything, could have done anything, Malin thinks.

'Why do you live on your own out at the farm?'

'I rent it.'

'How can you afford that?'

Julianna Raad doesn't answer.

'A good hideout,' Elin says.

'A good place to live.'

'Why did you open fire?'

'I heard about the murder on the radio. I thought you were his girlfriends or something. Sent by the racists to take revenge. Maybe they'd figured out that I'd threatened him and thought I killed him. I panicked, OK?'

'That doesn't sound very believable,' Malin says. 'How could anyone have known the letters came from you?'

Julianna raises her eyebrows.

'Let's try this, then,' she says. 'I realised you were cops, and got scared. I knew you'd grab any opportunity you had to hurt me because I hurt one of your colleagues. That's what you're like. An eye for an eye. Better to shoot first.'

'So you didn't kill the racist bastard,' Elin says. 'But you're pleased he's dead?'

Julianna Raad nods.

'People who think like him shouldn't exist. Get rid of them, I say.'

'But he'd changed his views. He was working for the same cause as you.'

'Doesn't make any difference.'

'So what do you want?' Elin Sand asks. 'Broadly speaking?'

'I want change.'

'What sort of change?'

'Of the whole fucking global order. If I end up like everyone else, I might as well be dead.'

She's not mincing her words, Malin thinks. Maybe the saliva from that mouth is slowly eating away at my cheek? You knew we were police officers, saw your chance to change 'the global order'.

'Do you have access to chemicals?' she asks.

'No, why would I?'

'What were you doing the night before last?'

'I was in the city. With a friend. I spent the night at hers. You can check. Stina Persdotter.'

'What did you do?' Elin asks.

'We watched a film. *The Hobbit*. It was shit.'

'I haven't seen it,' Malin says.

'You need to understand something,' Julianna Raad whispers, leaning across the table. 'There's a war going on. And if their voices aren't silenced, they'll silence ours. And their voices would destroy the world.'

Mad, Malin thinks.

But on the other hand . . . If no one protests against racism and injustice, and is prepared to go out on a limb with their protests, what would happen then? Would the worst of the maniacs take over?

'I'm prepared to accept the consequences of my actions.'

Julianna Raad leans closer to the tape recorder. Puts her lips to the microphone.

'I want this on record: you shot first. I was just defending myself against the fascist state.'

They let the uniforms take Julianna Raad to a cell in the custody unit. A long walk through the underground tunnels, Malin thinks.

Göran Möller hadn't wanted her and Elin to conduct the interview at first, thought they were far too agitated after being shot at. But Malin made her objections very clear.

'I arrested her, I question her, OK?'

She wasn't about to discuss the matter.

Göran Möller relented, and now the three detectives are standing in the passageway outside the interview room. They're all tired, but this case can't wait.

'I'll call her friend,' Elin says.

'Yes, we need to do that,' Göran Möller says, then goes on: 'Karin called a little while ago. They haven't found anything interesting out there yet. No chemicals, no drugs, nothing much at all.'

'Maybe she did only send the letters,' Malin says. 'Her explanations are more or less plausible. If you put them all together. I don't think she was lying.'

Elin Sand shakes her shoulders into place. As if her neck were sore.

'Me neither. But we can't be certain.'

'Nice work, girls,' Göran Möller says.

Malin feels like exploding, and Göran evidently notes her anger. He smiles.

'Just kidding. Nice work, bastard cops.' He goes on: 'I don't know how you managed to keep your calm when she spat at you.'

Malin replies: 'You underestimate me. I'll ask Johan to take a look at those websites she mentioned.'

Then Göran Möller's phone rings. He pulls it out from his trouser pocket, takes the call. Raises his eyebrows ten seconds later.

'I'll send Malin and Elin out at once.'

He ends the call. Looks at the two detectives.

'We won't be getting any sleep for a while.'

The clock on the wall in the interview room says 23.55.

The first day of the investigation into Peder Åkerlund's murder has gone at breakneck speed, and now something else has happened.

'You're heading out to Svartmåla. A man thinks his daughter has been abducted.'

# 24

I'd like to talk about Dad.

He was a bigwig. A man who made the decisions in the place where we lived. The socialist apostle of goodness. Used to preach justice and equality. A citizen beyond reproach.

Then he would come home to us. To me and Mum. He would put the bottle to his lips and preach with his fists about the place of women and children on earth and in the home.

And he went on hitting and hitting.

Me and Mum. Mostly Mum.

He threw a saucepan of boiling water at her. At the hospital they believed him when he said she tripped on the way to the sink.

Mum said nothing.

Because if she had, he would have taken it out on me. He would have killed me.

In the name of goodness.

Soon I'll talk about Mum. I'm just going to play for a while, even though it's late.

# 25

Night closes around the car like a flower. The headlamps light up the forest, and between the trunks of the pines Malin imagines she can see faces with rags stuffed in their open mouths.

Elin is firmly settled in the driver's seat.

As if nothing could shake her.

But Malin knows better. Everyone can be shaken, by life and what it can do to a person.

What's waiting for us out at the house?

A desperate father? A confused man who can't accept that his daughter has grown up and made her way out into the world without saying anything?

Is the girl really missing?

Göran Möller seemed certain: a girl has actually gone missing. This isn't a false alarm.

Svartmåla.

The psychologist, Viveca Crafoord, has a rather lovely summer house here. Has she still got it? Malin hasn't had any contact with her for several years.

Malin closes her eyes.

Thinks about Tove. Congo is in the same time zone as Sweden, there's no difference. She should have reached those mountain villages, perhaps she's sleeping in a tent. Malin would like to phone, but knows it's too late, and there's probably something like a one in ten thousand chance that Tove is actually within range.

It must have gone OK. None of the jungle's demons has got hold of her, no accident will have happened.

She has no idea what Tove is having to witness.

Doesn't want to know.

Thinks: What I see here is enough.

She tries to put Tove out of her mind. Thinks about Daniel instead.

His deep voice, how much she likes listening to the sound it makes, how much she would miss it. The love, comfort, and calm it provides.

She feels the car turn a couple of times before coming to a halt on what feels like gravel. When she opens her eyes she sees a smart man in a pink tennis shirt walking towards them, eyes wide open.

The fear in his face.

It's genuine. That's beyond any doubt.

Elin switches the car's headlights off, and the night turns dark.

They get out of the car and walk over to the man, who holds out his hand as he introduces himself.

'Bror Lundin.'

Malin shakes his hand. Hears him say: 'It didn't occur to me to switch the lights on. Follow me.'

He leads them around the house, and when they reach the terrace he says quietly: 'There's glass here,' and Elin asks him to turn some lights on. Bror Lundin clicks some switches on the wall of the house, and Malin finds herself looking at a neat garden sloping down towards Järnlunden. The lake spreads out into the night like a black lung.

Broken glass on the terrace, and in the living room.

A chaotic mess of furniture and papers.

There's been a fight in here, Malin thinks, that much is

obvious. Someone broke in, and a struggle ensued, and she glances at Elin. The look in her eyes says: This is serious.

Malin takes in the scene. The glass, the mess, looks for signs of a body being dragged off, a path through the chaos.

Bror Lundin stands in the middle of the room. Looks beseechingly at them.

'What do you think?' he says.

Nadja.

His daughter's name is Nadja.

Malin remembers the name now. It vanished from her head the moment Göran Möller said it, but she remembers it now.

Sixteen years old.

'Someone's taken Nadja,' Bror Lundin says.

Elin Sand goes over to him, puts her arm around his shoulders, and leads him off towards the kitchen, where she gently encourages him to sit down on one of the stools. Malin follows them, noting that Elin has a calming effect on the man who is Nadja's father.

'Yes,' Malin says. 'Nadja could have been abducted. But right now we don't know any more than you do.'

Bror Lundin shakes his head.

'I knew it would lead to trouble. I begged her to stop, but she wouldn't listen to me.'

Stop what? Malin thinks.

Then she flinches and pulls back. The realisation hits her, and creeps coldly down the lower half of her spine: Did you set this all up, Bror? Have you done something to your own daughter?

She asks: 'Is this how it looked when you arrived?'

'Nadja wasn't home when we got back from our holiday,' Bror Lundin says. 'We hadn't managed to get hold of her for a few days, and when she wasn't in the flat I came out here. She often comes out here to write and look after the garden. She does her yoga out here too, she likes doing it close to nature.'

'The front door wasn't open?' Elin Sand asks.

'No, but there was a mess in here, and the terrace door was smashed.'

'Why did you think she'd get into trouble?' Malin asks, and Bror Lundin seems to slump, even as his eyes reflect a sort of pride.

'She was very involved in environmental and social campaigning. She has her own blog, she's even written articles condemning the Sweden Democrats and Swedish immigration policy. She's precocious, she knows more than me about social issues, and she had an article about refugee children travelling alone published in *Dagens Nyheter*. She won some sort of essay competition. The winner had their piece published in the paper, and they ran it on the op-ed pages. But she makes too much noise, she doesn't understand the forces she's challenging.'

Malin's stomach clenches.

Peder Åkerlund.

Racist.

Murdered.

Nadja Lundin.

Anti-racist.

Missing.

Murdered?

Julianna Raad.

Anti most things, had sent threatening letters to Åkerlund.

All this at the same time.

'Did she have any enemies?' Elin asks. 'Had anyone threatened her?'

Bror Lundin throws his arms out.

'Do you think she'd tell me something like that? She doesn't listen to me at all. To anyone.'

'Have you got her laptop, her mobile?'

'Yes, they're here, you can have them.'

Malin nods, and studies the kitchen behind Bror Lundin. Shiny appliances in brushed steel, gleaming white cupboards. The antithesis of her kitchen at home on Ågatan.

She goes out onto the terrace. Looks over towards the vegetable garden, Nadja's, presumably. Thinks about what her father has just said about his daughter. Sixteen years old. She sounds very similar to Tove. Tove was stubborn, read a lot of books, and had very definite ideas about everything. And she could be dogmatic and foolhardy too.

Thank God it isn't Tove who's missing. But Tove could easily have been Nadja.

Malin stands still. Almost imagines she can see the shadow of someone sitting in the lotus position.

'We're going to find you,' Malin says quietly to herself.

Find me. I'm not dead yet.

Mum, Dad.

I'm alive, and you have to find me.

Nadja Lundin's internal whispers move through the ground, make their way through the vegetation and out into the night, up into the darkest corners of the Milky Way before returning to earth, to Malin Fors, as weary, swirling thoughts in a summer house in Svartmåla, not far from Linköping.

Find me.

Before the clock stops ticking.

She could still be alive, Malin thinks. She's found the path through the mess now, can see that someone has dragged a body through the house and out through a side door.

Where the forest begins.

Then nothing.

If Nadja Lundin is still alive, then they need to hurry.

Malin feels that now.

Feels Nadja Lundin breathing, feels her heart beat.

It's a new feeling, a feeling that's simultaneously hot and cold, a feeling that *is* her: incredibly brittle, yet strong at the same time.

'Don't give up,' Malin whispers. 'Don't give up.'

Malin looks at the photograph of Nadja Lundin.

Bror Lundin has just given it to her.

An aluminium frame containing a photograph of a beautiful girl with a nose-ring and dark, intelligent eyes. Long brown hair. A badge of Prime Minister Fredrik Reinfeldt depicted as a death's head.

It used to be Olof Palme, Malin thinks. Now Reinfeldt, or the Sweden Democrats' Jimmie Åkesson.

Everything must be silenced, nothing must be said.

Everything must be said.

Nothing is worth any reflection.

A car stops out in the driveway.

Karin, perhaps. God, she must be exhausted by now.

Or the dogs.

It's the dogs, and within minutes four Alsatians push past her, she can feel the musty smell of their fur, can hear their nostrils sniffing.

She doesn't wish their handler good luck. Because what could such a wish conjure forth from the dark face of the forest?

A dead girl?

# PART 2
# Waking death

[In silence]

Daniel. Your back, your skin, you.

I'm sweating, you're sweating, what we are together is sweating. Are we something more than people now, in this moment when we're both lost in each other?

You want to whisper, talk, but I hush you.

There must be only silence here.

The dogs bark in the darkness.

Divers search the blackness of the lake.

Where's Nadja?

The young, courageous girl, and Malin wishes she could remove Nadja from this moment with Daniel, but she won't go. This night belongs to her, too, and Daniel notices, notices that Malin is somewhere else.

Where are you, Nadja?

Tove is sleeping in a tent, in a mouldy sleeping bag.

That's what she's doing.

How dark is it where you are, Nadja?

I know you're alive.

Malin moves against Daniel, faster now, yes, like that, it will soon be over, but her body wins, thank God her body wins.

Fuck the crap out of me, Daniel.

Fuck the crap out of me the way the world fucks the crap out of all of us. Let me become one and the same person. What do I find in you?

Do it now.

Now.

And they surrender at the same time, and Malin rolls off him, trying to breathe.

Daniel.

His warm body, moist skin.

Close to mine.

This doesn't need words, she thinks, and slumps onto the bed, onto the white sheet, falls asleep and wakes up and falls asleep again inside what is actually a dream.

# 26

When Malin opens her eyes in the morning she doesn't know where she is at first.

At home in Ågatan, or in Daniel's flat on Sturegatan?

She stares up at the ceiling.

It's low, close to her eyes, depressing, not high and full of plaster detailing, and she breathes out. She wanted to wake up at home today.

Home, nowhere else.

She reaches out her hand. Daniel isn't there.

He was here during the night, wasn't he? He must have gone to the newsroom. She calls out to him, but gets no response.

A short while later she's standing in the kitchen. Her new laptop is switched on, and she's reading Nadja Lundin's article about refugee children travelling alone on the *Dagens Nyheter* website. She argues strongly in favour of their rights, and excoriates the local councils that have refused to accept them. And condemns people living in fancy houses who don't want the children living near them because they think the value of their homes will decrease.

One paragraph reads:

'If we should feel one thing for these children, it is sympathy, and if we can't feel sympathy, we should consider that we have to take care of the children as a matter of national pride. That is how we should be, as Swedes. The Swedes we know we can be: full of love, not hate like the Sweden Democrats.'

*

Sixteen years old.

What sort of thoughts did I have when I was sixteen? How did I express myself? I was interested in boys and clothes and getting hold of something to drink at the weekend.

Not even Tove was as precocious, as wise as Nadja Lundin. Unless Tove was even wiser. She had a different sense of proportion, she wasn't so obviously combative.

But they're clearly cut from the same cloth.

Malin clicks to open Nadja's blog. Finds pictures of Peder Åkerlund. Of other Sweden Democrat councillors.

Pictures from a demonstration against racism that took place in the main square last autumn. Julianna Raad among the sea of people. Do you know each other?

Beneath the picture of Peder Åkerlund it says: 'The biggest idiot in Linköping?'

High and low, considered and impulsive, all at the same time.

Your disappearance and Peder Åkerlund's murder are connected, Nadja, I'm almost certain of that. Unless I'm just imagining things, seeing a link that isn't there? But your paths have been too close to crossing for these cases to be entirely separate.

What does Julianna know?

Peder Åkerlund on Nadja's blog, the two of you, each other's opposites in every way, yet you could still almost be replicas of one another.

She sees an entry on the blog about the Democratic Republic of Congo. About the systematic rape of young children and women in the eastern part of the country. Pictures from mountain villages. Another post about two missing aid workers from Chile who were apparently trying to identify and prosecute a group of rapists.

Tove.

You're a long way from that part of the country, but

there's violence even where you are. Stay alert, Malin thinks, don't get involved, because if you get involved, someone will break into your tent or cabin at night and abduct you.

You might never come home again.

Malin switches the laptop off and takes out her mobile. Rings Tove's number.

The call fails.

She tries again, closes her eyes, and in her mind's eye she sees Tove walking through a jungle, carrying a naked baby. The child's skin is as black as crude oil, its head hanging limply to one side, and Malin knows that the child is dead. Tove is resolute rather than sad, and she walks right through Malin as the ringtone echoes down the line, ten rings before the connection fails.

Tove.

You don't usually answer; do you even know that I'm calling? I'd really like to talk to you now.

Have you been in touch with your dad? Should I call him?

No.

And she makes her way out of the flat. Heavy movements, bearing no trace of the vitality of spring.

## 27

Karin Johannison looks tired; the bags under her eyes seem to be making their way down towards her cheeks. But her eyes are full of fire.

She must have worked into the small hours out in Svartmåla.

She's standing next to the whiteboard in the meeting room, giving an account of her findings at the two scenes, and what she's discovered about the murder victim, Peder Åkerlund.

It's just past eight o'clock, and they're all there.

Göran Möller, Johan Jakobsson, Waldemar Ekenberg, Elin Sand, Börje Svärd, and Zeke Martinsson.

Twenty metres away, outside the window, the children at the nursery are playing in the spring sunshine. Some of them are wearing shorts, and look liberated, as if they've been released from the grip of a harsher season and are celebrating the fact that they can now do what they like.

Malin is vaguely aware of the children's excited cries. Their whoops of joy. The carefree way they're milling about. And she feels envious. The fact that they seem completely free in their games, completely unfettered, down to their very souls.

She hears Karin say that Peder Åkerlund had a high percentage of alcohol in his blood, about 1.1 parts per thousand, and that she's found traces of ether around his mouth.

Hydrochloric acid in his speech centre.

The quickest way to kill him would have been to inject the acid directly into his cerebral cortex, that would have paralysed the muscles around his lungs and he would have died instantly. But when the acid was injected into the language centre of his brain via his pupils, it isn't even certain that he would have lost consciousness at once. He could, according to Karin, have remained alive for a relatively long while after that sort of damage, fifteen minutes or more, while the acid spread through his brain tissue. He wouldn't have felt any pain during the process, because the brain has no feeling. But the injection must have hurt. Presumably the eye was chosen as the easiest way to reach that part of the brain. The skull and frontal bone are impossible to penetrate with an ordinary syringe.

Karin remains calm as she accounts for his injuries, factual, as if the brutality weren't real, and Malin is grateful for that, because otherwise this would be unbearable.

Karin takes a deep breath.

'Judging by his injuries, I estimate that he was murdered at approximately three o'clock in the morning.'

Karin remains standing beside the whiteboard. Awaiting the others' reaction.

But there isn't time for that. Waldemar asks instead: 'Hydrochloric acid. And ether. Where can you get hold of those?'

'I've checked,' Johan Jakobsson says. 'You can buy them from hundreds of sites online. Both of them. It's going to be hard to find out anything that way.'

'Is it even worth trying?' Göran Möller asks.

Johan nods.

'Once we've got a suspect. Otherwise it's practically impossible to find out who in Linköping might have got hold of the two substances. I can check to see if Julianna Raad has bought anything like that. If she used her own name, of course.'

Silence settles on the room. They all seem to be gathering their thoughts.

'Åkerlund is supposed to have left his friend's flat at half past one,' Göran Möller says, and Malin thinks he looks alert today, that meetings like this must be like oxygen to him.

But I really don't know anything about him, she thinks.

'So, an hour and a half from the time he left the flat until he was murdered,' Göran Möller goes on. 'He would have had time to get home.'

'He could have fallen asleep somewhere. On a bench. He was seriously drunk,' Elin Sand says.

'Or else someone abducted him. Took him off somewhere.'

Malin hears her own words. The way she pronounces them as if to test a potential explanation.

'Are there any security cameras in the surrounding area? Along his probable route?' Göran asks. 'Could he have been filmed somewhere?'

'We can check with the local council.' Johan Jakobsson wrinkles his nose, then goes on: 'There's bound to be at least one camera.'

'We ought to go door-to-door along any route he may have taken,' Malin says.

'Which leads us to the door-to-door enquiries in the area where his body was found,' Göran Möller says. 'Nothing, I'm afraid. Not a thing.'

'No one noticed a vehicle?' Börje asks.

Göran shakes his head.

A long silence spreads around the room.

The detectives of the Linköping Violent Crime Unit know that these first few days are vital, they can't have silence now. Because they also know that silence and undiscovered truths belong together.

'Shall I tell you about Nadja Lundin?' Karin eventually

says, brushing her blonde hair back. 'What I found out in Svartmåla?'

Göran Möller nods.

Malin is thinking what everyone in the room is thinking, the thought that struck her earlier: that these crimes are linked. The combined intuition of the officers in the room tells them that. Events like this don't happen so close together in a city like Linköping without there being some sort of connection.

One idea, one individual. Or both. The similarities between the victims. Politics, activism. The differences between them, even if they are supposed to have ended up on the same side.

What if Nadja has been kidnapped for money? The Lundin family is very well off. But if that were the case, they ought to have received a ransom note or something of that sort.

'Someone broke in at the back of the house. Tried to overpower her, and there was a struggle. I've found two types of blood, we can assume that one is Nadja's. I've also found hairs from a number of different individuals. They're being run through the DNA database as we speak.'

A match would be like hitting the jackpot, Malin thinks. But she knows that's unlikely. There aren't that many people on the register, and this wasn't an ordinary break-in. She can feel it.

'And I found something else,' Karin says. 'Tyre tracks. Identical to the ones I found by the locks. I think they were made by a relatively large vehicle. A van, probably.'

'So the cases are linked,' Waldemar says.

'It looks that way,' Göran Möller says.

'There's a ninety-nine per cent chance that it's the same vehicle. The pattern is an ordinary Michelin tyre, but the two tracks show the same signs of wear. Mind you, the vehicle doesn't necessarily have to be involved in the murder and abduction.'

'Good work, Karin. And I think we can assume that this vehicle is involved somehow.'

'Do we have anything else to connect the cases?' Börje wonders, and Johan clears his throat and says: 'It looks like Peder Åkerlund was a frequent commentator on Nadja Lundin's blog. Before his conversion.'

I missed the comments this morning, Malin thinks. Probably didn't know where to click.

'And she had a picture of him on her blog,' she adds.

'There must be other points of connection that we're not seeing,' Elin Sand says.

'We ought to interview more people from Sweden Democrat circles,' Göran Möller says. 'Spread the net more widely.'

'I got a list of people Nadja Lundin knows from her dad,' Malin says. 'He made it clear that it wasn't comprehensive, but it includes her teachers, a small number of good friends, and other people she was in touch with.'

'Have we got her phone and computer?' Waldemar asks.

Malin nods.

'Forensics are about to start work on them,' Johan says. 'They're also checking Peder Åkerlund's call log, and his computer. Julianna's too. They've cracked the password to Åkerlund's laptop, but haven't found anything special so far. But there are a number of locked folders, and the Internet history has been erased.'

'How does Julianna Raad fit into this?' Waldemar asks.

Malin went down to the custody unit before the meeting. Spoke to Julianna, who was calmer this time, almost like a different person. Her anger had been replaced by resignation. She was still refusing to answer questions, but did clarify one point: she was aware of Nadja Lundin, but didn't know her. Julianna asked if the exchange of gunfire had been reported on the *Correspondent*'s website, and seemed pleased when Malin said that it had been. And Malin found herself thinking that this could be one of the voices of the investigation.

'Her friend has given her an alibi,' Elin says.

'She wrote those threatening letters,' Malin says. 'And she opened fire on us. But I don't think she killed Peder Åkerlund.'

'Well, we're going to have to put in a lot of hard graft on every line of inquiry,' Göran Möller says. 'We can't rule anything out. Assume that these cases are linked, but bear in mind the possibility that they might not be. We don't know anything for certain yet. We need to question more people, talk to everyone on that list Nadja's father has given us. The dog patrol haven't found anything in the forest around Svartmåla so far, but they're going to carry on looking. The divers, however, have finished their search of the lake close to the house.'

'It's more likely that she was taken away from the house by road,' Malin says.

Karin nods.

'But the tracks from the house led into the forest, and I didn't see any footprints or signs of a body being dragged close to the tyre tracks.'

'So, someone who can fly,' Waldemar says. 'A ghost.'

Elin smiles dutifully, but none of the others laughs at Waldemar's strained attempt at humour.

'Loudmouths,' Zeke says. 'The one thing that Nadja and Peder have in common is that they both appear to have been really noisy. In terms of their opinions.'

Appear to have been, Malin thinks.

We don't yet know if Nadja is dead.

She isn't.

'I checked those websites Julianna told you about, Malin,' Johan says. 'Very briefly, anyway. They're openly racist.

And the choice of words does bear a definite resemblance to the worst of Åkerlund's pronouncements. For instance, that "the niggers ought to be cleared out of Berga".'

'Who's responsible for those sites?'

'Very hard to tell. But Forensics are working on that as well.'

'Åkerlund needn't necessarily be responsible. Other people could have imitated his choice of words.'

'That's highly likely,' Zeke says. 'Politics. That's what I mean, that you can never know for sure, if people are trying to get their opinions to become the norm. What they might be capable of.'

'I spoke to Peder's ex-girlfriend and her new partner yesterday,' Börje says. 'I got the feeling they were lying to me about Peder.'

'In what way?' Malin asks.

'Just a feeling, I'm afraid. They've got solid alibis. But Javier didn't seem altogether convinced by Peder's conversion. Maybe he didn't leave them alone like they said he did.'

A snake.

That's what the discussion resembles.

Back and forth, confused, squirming yet oddly heavy, and Malin misses Sven's focus, his ability to pull disparate thoughts into a definite direction. So far, Göran Möller hasn't really demonstrated that ability.

And he says: 'We've also received an anonymous tip-off. Peder Åkerlund is supposed to have been threatened by Muslims. Verbal threats. From a Suliman Hajif.'

Shit, Malin thinks.

Now things are getting really sensitive.

A few years ago Suliman Hajif was identified by *Expressen* as someone who was trying to recruit young men to the most extreme Islamist groups fighting in the civil war in Syria, and sorting out travel arrangements for them. He sued the paper, and referred to his record in community integration in his defence. And the fact that he did voluntary work in the mosque with teenagers who were starting to go off the rails.

The newspaper retracted its claims rather than pay considerable damages. Malin knows they came to an out-of-court settlement because the paper and journalist had no concrete, reliable evidence.

The whole thing looked like a massive journalistic error.

'It could be a scam,' Johan Jakobsson said. 'How did we get the tip-off?'

'An anonymous woman called early this morning.'

'Do we have a number for her?'

'No, just a pay-as-you-go mobile. We'll never be able to find her.'

Muslim extremists.

Activists on both the extreme right and left loathe them. Are frightened of them, and hate themselves for that. Hate their own fear.

'We should probably talk to Hajif,' Malin says.

Göran Möller nods.

Sensitive, sensitive, sensitive. He nods again.

'You take it,' Göran Möller says, pointing first at Malin, then Zeke. 'I've got to deal with the wretched press conference.'

Göran Möller feels the sweat start to break out at the base of his spine. They've requisitioned one of the rooms in the district courthouse, which is based in a former barracks just a hundred metres or so away from the police station. The reporters are lined up on polished pine benches. The photographers have their cameras ready, angry red lights flash from the television cameras. As he stands there at the podium he feels exposed, as if he were facing a firing squad.

Stick to the script, Göran, he tells himself.

Give short, concise answers.

Don't walk into any traps posed by the case's links to immigration and racism.

These wolves are going to try to bring me down.

They want to eat me alive. And if I make a mess of things again, I'm finished.

'Let's get started,' he says, in as brusque a voice as he can summon up.

'Is this a political murder? What can you say about the links to the Sweden Democrats?' are the first questions from the pack.

## 28

Börje Svärd is pacing up and down outside the head teacher's office in Folkunga School, waiting for the red light on the door to turn green. He walks over to one of the large windows that have been inserted into the almost metre-thick stone façade. Down in the playground he can see Waldemar and Elin talking to the pupils, asking about Nadja Lundin, questions they hope will bring her back from where she is right now, on the boundary between the living and the dead.

He hears a whirring sound, and the light on the door turns green.

Börje goes in, and behind a very tidy desk sits a woman his own age, attractive, he notes at once, with sharp features and a blonde bob. Her ring-finger is bare, and he holds out his hand and introduces himself.

'Börje Svärd, Crime Unit, Linköping Police.'

'Kristina Nederdahl.'

Her handshake is firm and gentle at the same time, and he tries to interpret the look on her face: open or closed?

She smiles at him as he sits down.

Open, definitely.

She knows why they are there, has read on the *Correspondent*'s website about the disappearance, the dog patrols, the divers.

She gave them permission over the phone to talk to Nadja's teachers and friends.

'Do you have any idea where Nadja might be?' Kristina

Nederdahl asks, leaning forward across the desk, her large bust resting on it.

Concentrate now, Börje.

'No. But we're almost certain that she's been abducted.'

'She wasn't at school yesterday. And that's unusual. She's never absent.'

'Not ill much?'

'Never. So, what can I do for you?'

Kristina Nederdahl smiles again. Playing the game.

'Tell me about her. Anything you think could be important.'

'How should I know what might be important to you?' Kristina Nederdahl says, smiling even more warmly. 'But I'll do my best.'

Börje nods.

'She loves spending time in the central library. She reads all sorts of things. A lot of history. She always keeps her history and social studies teachers on their toes. And it was a very big deal when she won that competition in *Dagens Nyheter*. Nothing like that had ever happened in Folkunga School before.'

'You've never noticed any threats against her? Anything odd?'

Kristina Nederdahl shakes her head.

'No.'

'Was she popular with the other pupils?'

'She's actually a fairly ordinary girl. She has friends, she's popular enough. She does her own thing. Most pupils here are only bothered about Instagram and what they're wearing. That commands a degree of respect.'

Kristina Nederdahl seems to pause for thought, and Börje notes how attractive she is when she's thinking.

Then she exclaims: 'Christ, how could I forget that?'

'Forget what?'

'Sorry for swearing.'

'Don't worry.'

Kristina Nederdahl takes a deep breath.

'Just after her article was published in *Dagens Nyheter*, something did actually happen.'

Elin Sand has withdrawn into the shade of an old oak tree. In front of her stands a thin, sixteen-year-old girl, with streaked blonde hair and a small star tattooed at the base of her neck.

Sirje Rapp.

A slight but by no means mild person.

Nadja Lundin's best friend.

She's just explained that Nadja went to the house in Svartmåla at the weekend. That she had seemed normal beforehand, that she hadn't received any specific threats, apart from 'the idiots from the Sweden Democrats' who had visited her blog.

'Nadja's not scared of anything.'

Just like you, Elin thinks.

'This evening we're supposed to be handing out leaflets in the city centre. We want them to set up a refugee centre at the old air base in Malmslätt.'

'Is that likely?'

'It's been planned for a long time, but the people living nearby are protesting.'

A breeze passes through the crown of the oak, and the shadows move anxiously across Sirje Rapp's face.

'Is there anything you can tell me about Nadja? Anything at all?'

'She's kind. And far more engaged than me. I'm pretty quiet, really, but she wants much more.'

'Is she always kind?'

'Almost. Sometimes she can get impatient. Make fun of people. She's so smart that she almost can't help it.'

'What sort of thing does she do?'

'Like, if we're at a café – she'll order a latte, then make them give her a fresh one because the milk wasn't organic. If they object, she gives them a long speech about consumers' rights. Or in H&M. She can make the staff feel stupid by talking about their factories in China.'

'OK,' Elin says. 'It sounds like she is just trying to show how smart she is.'

'Kind of, but she doesn't mean any harm by it.'

'Do you know if anything special had happened to her recently? Has she mentioned anything?'

'When her article was published in *Dagens Nyheter*, some time after that, there was a man in a hoodie standing outside the school yard for a few days.'

'What?'

Elin Sand takes a step back, and turns to look in the direction Sirje Rapp is pointing. Part of the wall surrounding the playground is lower, and beyond it she can make out a red-brick admin block.

'Yes, there was a man. He stood there watching us. Mostly Nadja, it looked like. He was pretty creepy. And it was cold, but he wasn't wearing much. Some sort of black hoodie. You couldn't see his face. I think we saw him three days in a row. Then the head phoned the police, but he was gone by the time you arrived.'

Kristina Nederdahl is on her feet now.

She is pouring coffee for the two of them from the machine on a small sideboard.

'I saw him standing there,' she says, 'looking into the school yard. He didn't seem dangerous, so I ignored him. Our pupils are relatively mature, and there's nothing illegal about looking into the school grounds.'

Börje nods.

'But on the third day I decided to call the police anyway.'

'Did you try to talk to him?'

'That was why I called.'

'How do you mean?'

Kristina Nederdahl passes Börje his cup before sitting down again.

More beautiful than most women my age, he thinks. I wonder if she ever goes to the gym? No, she's not the type.

'I went outside to talk to him, and he ran off. I thought that was a bit odd.'

'Did you see his face?'

Kristina Nederdahl shakes her head.

'Do you know the names of the police officers who came?'

'No, I don't remember what they were called. They were in uniform.'

'There'll be a report about it.'

Kristina Nederdahl nods.

'And you're sure it was a man?'

'I can't be absolutely certain. But that's the impression I got from his build.'

'No car?'

'No.'

Börje drinks a sip of coffee.

'Was he looking at Nadja in particular?'

'Impossible to say. Her friend Sirje thought he was. And of course he could have been, seeing as it came right after the publication of her article. I seem to recall that the *Correspondent* made a big deal of her winning the competition.'

Börje sits in silence.

Doesn't know what else to ask. Well, he does know, but he wants this moment to last, doesn't want to leave the room.

'We never saw him again,' Kristina Nederdahl says, answering the question he was on the point of asking.

Börje puts his hand in the inside pocket of his jacket. Takes out a card and hands it across the desk to Kristina.

She takes it.

And her face changes. From determination to an anxiety that seems to verge on hatred.

'You have to find her,' she says. 'Young girls have to be able to make their voices heard without suffering any repercussions.'

'We'll find her,' Börje says. 'Get in touch if you think of anything else.'

'I'll give you a call,' Kristina Nederdahl says, flashing him a smile full of anticipation.

Sirje Rapp is still standing beneath the oak with Elin Sand, who has put her hand on her shoulder.

'Is he coming for me next?'

She's repeated the same phrase ten times now, and Elin Sand says: 'We don't even know if there is a *he*.'

'What should I do?'

'Don't go out alone. Never, not even during the day. Don't be alone.'

'So there is a threat?'

How can I answer that? Elin Sand thinks. Do I say that a sixteen-year-old in Linköping ought to be afraid, that fear might be the smart choice?

'Just be careful,' she says. 'Until we know what's happened to Nadja.'

# 29

Elin Sand watches Sirje Rapp walk off towards the main school building, and its heavy, curved stone frontage seems to want to make her feel small.

Sirje had an alibi for every evening for the past week. She's been at home; they've got relatives visiting.

Could the man in the hoodie have been Peder Åkerlund?

Or was it someone else?

The murderer, the kidnapper? Or one of them, if they're different people?

There'll be a report of the incident in their records. In all likelihood nothing will have been done about it.

Sirje Rapp skips up the wide stone steps.

Opens the wooden door.

Swallowed up by the darkness of the building.

Linköping's mosque is tucked up against the maples and lime trees on a hill in Berga.

The imam is known for being a moderate. A man who understands both the weight of tradition and the ostensible lightness of the modern world.

They've left the car in the centre of Berga, and as Malin and Zeke walk towards the mosque past blocks of flats, their balconies bristling with satellite dishes, she tries to recall what they know about Suliman Hajif.

Johan has checked his website. It contains guidance for how Muslims should fit in to society. A benevolent tone. Completely at odds with the supposed threats.

Then there was the newspaper article about his supposed attempts at recruitment. None of it makes sense, and the contradictions can't help but remind Malin of Peder Åkerlund, and the doubts surrounding his conversion.

But perhaps genuine Islamists are involved in the murder?

Too obvious. And if the murder and Nadja Lundin's disappearance are connected, why would Hajif attack her?

Suliman Hajif is twenty-seven years old, but in the pictures in the paper he looks more like fifty, with his dark, unkempt beard and thin face. Dressed in a white kaftan.

Some pigeons are pecking at the arched tin roof of the mosque. There's no one in sight, and Malin feels an urge to draw her pistol from its holster under her jacket, but knows she's just being paranoid. Fear driven by prejudice is playing tricks on her. She's had dealings with the imam before, he's a sensible man, and she knows that he's asked Suliman Hajif to be there, that he's waiting inside ready to talk to them.

The small room is covered with Persian rugs, and Suliman Hajif is sitting on the floor next to the imam, Samid Samudra. His brown eyes are tranquil, but Malin imagines she can see hatred in his expression.

A woman!

A police officer!

Threat. Fear.

That's exactly what Jimmie Åkesson and his followers in the Sweden Democrats want me to feel in the face of a man like Suliman Hajif. In the face of the imam.

They've introduced themselves, he shook her hand and poured them some tea, and now they're sitting opposite each other in the overheated, windowless room, drinking tea that's too hot.

But that's all fine.

There's no time for pleasantries.

Just as well to get straight to the point.

So Malin says: 'Peder Åkerlund. Did you know him?'

'I didn't know him, but I knew who he was.'

'What was your opinion of him?'

'I'm opposed to all forms of racism. But he had changed his views, and was therefore forgiven.'

'We've received an anonymous tip-off claiming that you threatened Peder Åkerlund,' Zeke says.

'Why would I do that?'

'You had very different opinions.'

Suliman Hajif smiles.

'If you're working to promote integration, that's not a problem.'

'What were you doing on the night between Sunday and Monday?' Zeke asks.

The imam holds up his hands.

'Do you really believe that Suliman had anything to do with this?'

'Let him answer,' Malin says.

'I was at home with my brothers. I'll give you their numbers so you can check.'

Malin adds the numbers to her mobile.

'Do you know anyone who might have wanted to kill Åkerlund, anyone who might be involved? For religious reasons?'

'No. That would be too easy, wouldn't it? Too obvious? I don't believe in violence, and I don't know anyone here who would be capable of doing something like that.'

So you don't believe in violence? Malin thinks. Why don't I trust you?

My own prejudices.

But, on the other hand, she remembers the article in *Expressen*. And how he sued the newspaper.

'Nadja Lundin,' she says. 'Do you know her?'

Suliman Hajif looks at Malin, clearly surprised.

'I don't know anyone called Nadja,' he says. 'Who is she?'

'It doesn't matter,' Zeke says.

Suliman Hajif suddenly gets to his feet, and the imam tries to stop him, tugging cautiously at the white fabric of his kaftan, but Suliman stands up and stares down at Malin and Zeke, and says: 'Is this all you've got? You call me here and insinuate that I'm involved in a murder? What right do you have to bother me?'

And Malin feels like snapping back: Murder. Of a man you're said to have threatened.

What the hell do you think?

She feels Zeke's hand on her knee. He squeezes it gently.

Easy. Don't lose your cool now, Malin.

Suliman Hajif storms out of the room, leaving Malin, Zeke, and Samudra sitting on the floor.

'Forgive him his youth,' the imam says.

Malin nods.

'We might need to speak to him again,' Zeke says. 'Or with some of his friends.'

Outside the mosque Malin feels that the world is spinning far too fast. She can't make sense of anything.

She forgot to ask Suliman if he was the man in the hoodie outside Folkunga School, the man Elin called to tell her about. She'd meant to ask, just to see his reaction. But why would he be that man?

She turns her face to the sky. Low, dark clouds are skimming the rooftops now. Rain soon, no question.

Nadja.

Peder Åkerlund.

Connections.

Visible and invisible.

How does this fit together?

It does fit together. All the particles of the earth are linked to each other.

We all come from the same earth, and shall all be laid to rest in the same.

Until then, we have to cope with living alongside one another.

And she sees Nadja Lundin in her mind's eye.

A lonely face surrounded by even lonelier darkness.

# 30

I'm so hungry. And the tube is still empty.

My muscles are cramping, I need water.

I'm whispering now. Hoarse. I don't think I can last much longer.

I whisper, but nothing can be heard.

My room has walls of silence and a ceiling of stillborn words.

How did I come up with that?

I breathe in my own sentences.

Everything ends, I can feel it.

The clock is ticking. There's a rushing sound in my ears, and it hurts so much when my calves tighten.

So hurry up. Hurry up.

# 31

The rain lashes the metal frame of the car. The noise drowns out the radio, the newsreader talking about their case.

Malin turns up the volume.

'*The police suspect that the disappearance of sixteen-year-old Nadja Lundin is connected to the murder of former local councillor for the Sweden Democrats, Peder Åkerlund. At a press conference this morning Göran Möller, who is leading the preliminary investigation, has confirmed that there is evidence to suggest that the two cases are linked . . .*'

Göran evidently handled the press conference well.

She lowers the volume again, and soon there's nothing but her and the roar of the rain, the sound of the engine a distant hum.

It's lunchtime, but she isn't hungry. She's on her way to the forests of Svartmåla.

The dog units.

She was blunt with Zeke: she needed to go out there on her own. Try to make sense of her thoughts.

Malin drives along the main road for twenty minutes before turning off onto a forest road. She knows the patrols set out from there that morning.

They're searching deeper and deeper into the forest.

She pulls in behind the three police cars that are parked in a clearing. Puts on her yellow raincoat, remembers coming to these woods after Peter betrayed her, how she burned all the crap he'd given her, including that ridiculous oilskin coat.

She gets out of the car. Walks off into the forest, calling: 'Nadja, Nadja, Nadja.'

But she knows there's no point. There's no Nadja to hear her cries, and that's not why she's calling. She's calling out because she's missing something, because the forest and people and earth are silent.

The raindrops are cold and refreshing on her face. Like the beads of condensation on a glass of beer.

'Nadja, Nadja.'

Why would someone want to hurt you?

You and Peder Åkerlund. Was Karin wrong about the tyre tracks? What if it's just a coincidence?

She can hear the dogs now. Barking. Getting closer to her.

Then she sees the first one, an Alsatian, and its waterproof-clad handler.

Then a second animal.

A third.

And their handlers.

Malin looks down at her feet. Beneath her the ground is starting to turn to mud.

One of the dogs pulls free and rushes towards her, as its handler cries: 'Stop! Stop!'

Malin flinches, but the dog suddenly stops, recognises her, wants to say hello. And in the rain Malin reaches down with her hand, feels the tongue against her skin.

'Have you found anything?' she asks the first dog's handler.

'Nothing. I don't think she's anywhere around here. We'd have found her by now.'

'She's alive,' Malin says.

The three men in front of her hold their dogs close to them, the looks on their faces indicating that they don't agree with her.

Nadja Lundin is dead.

Dead in the way that only young girls can be dead, with a feeling that this is wrong, yet still predictable. As if this tragedy were written into the passage of her life right from the start, and that all they are really doing in this godforsaken forest is locating and confirming that.

'Nothing at all?'

'Not even an elk,' the third handler says, pulling the hood of his raincoat tighter over his head.

A man or woman in a hoodie.

Elin Sand is sitting on the toilet at the police station. She has to fold her legs uncomfortably to have room in the cramped space.

Life often makes her feel clumsy that way. As if her presence were troubling the world. And in that feeling is a sad loneliness.

Am I going to have to leave Linköping to stop feeling alone?

Is there any future for me and my desires here?

She leans forward.

Hydrochloric acid, injected directly into the brain.

What sort of sick individual would come up with an idea like that? What sort of sick soul could commit such an act?

A man in a hoodie.

Waiting for a girl whom the world had equipped with a conscience and the willpower to match it.

Malin, Elin thinks. I see you work, I want to be more like you, and I think I can do it. I want to listen to the voices of the investigation, the way you do.

I want to open myself up, she thinks, as one of her knees hits the pedestal beneath the basin. The porcelain hits a nerve and almost makes her cry out in pain.

She shuts her eyes.

Black on black.

Linköping has long been a playground for violence. The city's memory is full of unsolved murders, murdered girls and boys.

There's everything here, but is there anything here for me?

Elin Sand can't help herself. She leaves the station, alone, and heads down to the building on Drottninggatan where Nadja Lundin's parents live. Using the post office's entry code, she goes inside and is soon standing outside their door, dripping with rain. She rings twice, and hears footsteps. The door opens, and Nadja's mother is standing before her. She was questioned by a couple of uniforms this morning. Nothing of interest emerged.

Elin holds out her ID.

'Can I come in? I'd like to ask a few questions.'

A thin, once beautiful face.

They shake hands.

'Beata.'

Now that face is edged with anxiety. The past twenty-four hours must have aged her at least ten years, Elin thinks.

She follows Beata Lundin into the sprawling apartment, past the golf bags in the hall.

The rooms smell of money. Designer furniture, genuine oil paintings on the walls, thick rugs on the floor.

'My husband's at work,' Beata Lundin says. 'He's a game designer. He runs a business with thirty employees that supplies game platforms to the big companies.'

'It looks like it's going well.'

Beata Lundin nods as she sits down on a well-upholstered white sofa. In her white dress she almost drowns in a sea of fabric.

No question of coffee or anything else to drink.

Elin sits down in an armchair opposite her.

'How can I help you?' Beata asks.

And it strikes Elin that she doesn't know what to ask. She came here because of her suspicions.

'We're going to find her,' Elin says.

'You came here just to say that?'

'No. I'm wondering if you or your husband have ever seen anyone behaving in a suspicious manner in your vicinity when Nadja has been with you. A man in a black hoodie, for instance.'

Beata shakes her head.

'No, never. So who might this man be?'

'We don't know.'

Beata takes a deep breath.

'I know what she writes makes people angry. But I'm proud of it, of her. If everyone was like Nadja, the world would be a better place. She loves nature, everything that grows in the earth. When she explained yoga to me, and how it takes her closer to some sort of original state, I didn't understand a thing. I'm more grounded. But we often make vegetarian dishes using the vegetables she's grown. I know how to cook, and she wants to learn. Most of the time she thinks I'm an idiot, but when it comes to food she respects me.'

'Her friend Sirje said Nadja could be a bit arrogant towards people at times.'

'She's a smart girl, and smart people are sometimes arrogant. Sure.'

'Could she have made someone angry?'

'When it comes down to it, she's extremely kind. But the staff at the ICA supermarket near here probably think she's a real nuisance. She keeps arguing with them about the fact that they should only sell organic vegetables.'

Elin smiles.

'She wasn't home when you got back?'

'No. What an odd question.'

'And your husband went off to the cottage at once to look for her?'

'Yes.'

'Did he call there first?'

'I don't know. Why?'

'No particular reason,' Elin Sand says.

Beata nods.

'I admire him for being able to go to work at a time like this. I couldn't do that.' She goes on: 'He goes mad if he can't work. He loves those little pretend worlds where he can kill everything that moves and you're allowed to be a hero.'

## 32

Malin makes her way along the rows of books in Linköping Central Library. Takes deep breaths, tries to draw air from up near the rafters of the twelve-metre-high ceiling.

Stories.

About life and death and everything in between.

Nadja Lundin is said to have enjoyed studying here. According to the head teacher Börje talked to.

And Malin inhales the smell of books, the pleasant, gently mildewed smell of learning.

The library is one of Tove's favourite places in the city. She's spent hours sitting here reading, dreaming herself away, perhaps. Malin has tried to call her again, but couldn't get through. The line was completely dead, and Malin couldn't help seeing her in front of her, raped, speechless, shaking with fear in the rain.

A fiction. Like almost all the novels in here.

Pointless fiction.

She goes downstairs. Catches sight of someone, a man in his mid-thirties with weakly defined features, short, bleached blond hair, and grey skin. A bandage around his arm.

A real bookworm.

He's pushing a trolley laden with bound volumes, and stops every few metres to put books back on their shelves.

Malin watches him for a while before going up to him.

She holds out her hand. Introduces herself, and he says his name so quickly that she doesn't catch it.

'Curator,' he says. 'I'm a curator and restorer here, but have time for a bit of librarian work as well.'

Malin holds out a photograph of Nadja Lundin.

'Have you ever seen this girl here?'

The man nods.

'Nadja,' he says. 'She comes here a lot. I often have to find books on different subjects for her. Most recently on the history of the Ottoman Empire. I think she was working on some sort of essay.'

'Do you talk to her much?'

The man looks surprised.

'Obviously I talk to her occasionally. She's very friendly and cheerful. Most of the people who sit down here reading aren't exactly extroverts.'

He doesn't appear to have any idea of what has happened to Nadja, that she's missing, possibly murdered. Presumably he doesn't read the papers or watch television.

'Would you say you know her well?' Malin asks.

'No, not at all.'

The man gestures vaguely towards the book trolley.

'If you'll excuse me?'

'Of course, I don't want to stop you,' Malin says, and presses up against a bookcase so he can get past.

I'm not going to tell you, she thinks, and starts to walk towards the stairs, pushing past another man, keen to get out of this book-lined crypt.


Elin Sand has driven down to the library. Beata Lundin said it was one of her daughter's favourite places. That's enough for Elin. She wanted to go there, walk in Nadja's footsteps, see what might crop up.

She called the station on the way. Asked Waldemar to check out Nadja's dad particularly carefully. Something's nagging at her. He could have driven out to the summer house and staged the whole thing, couldn't he?

And now Elin is heading towards the spiral staircase leading down to the catacombs full of old books, the ones that survived the fire of 1996.

Someone's coming up the stairs.

She sees who it is.

Malin.

And Malin looks at her, her jaw drops in surprise, then she says: 'Looks like we had the same idea.'

The next minute they're sitting in the library's cafeteria with two cups of bitter, watery coffee in front of them.

She's getting better and better, Malin thinks, looking at Elin Sand. Soon she'll be a fully-fledged detective who can hear the most muffled voices, see the slightest details, the most opaque connections. The ones you sense rather than see with your eyes.

'What do you make of all this?' Malin asks.

'I think there's going to be some sort of explosion soon,' Elin says. 'It's far too quiet considering how gruesome the murder was, and given that a sixteen-year-old girl has gone missing. The city ought to be simmering with fear, but everything's completely calm. A very odd sense of calm.'

I've been thinking the same thing, Malin thinks.

It's as if someone's lying in wait, watching to see what we do. As if there are invisible eyes watching our every move.

But Malin doesn't say any of this. Instead she says: 'I think you're right. Soon all hell is going to break loose. There's a serious chance that something else is going to happen.'

She leaves a dramatic pause.

'I'm convinced Nadja's still alive.'

Elin Sand takes a sip of the coffee.

Pulls a face.

'Rat poison,' she says. 'Are you coming down to the gym instead?'

Malin nods.

'Assuming nothing else happens.'

# 33

Johan Jakobsson can see Stella's fingers quiver with her juvenile rheumatism, and his daughter grimaces with pain, and he feels like shouting out loud: Why? Why her?

The chemical hospital smell catches in his nose, and the speckled brown floor glints. The doctor is sitting on a metal stool, and Stella is lying on a paper-covered bed. The room is completely anonymous, as if all attention should be focused on the illness. The corridor outside has been decorated to appeal to children, with drawings of famous Swedish cartoon characters, but in here everything is serious. So much so that an eleven-year-old would notice.

They were given the initial diagnosis in a room not far from this one.

'Your lives will never be the same again.'

Stella was pumped full of cortisone then, as well as anti-inflammatory tablets, and nothing seemed to help except the cortisone, which would slowly consume her from within.

Over the past six months he's had to watch as his daughter learned what real pain is.

And he hasn't been able to help her at all.

He knows that's why she wanted him to wait outside the treatment room today. Because the only thing he has to offer her is his own mental anguish, and what good is that to her?

Someone's toying with us, he thinks. God? But He doesn't intervene in our lives. He deposits us on earth and leaves us to our own devices. But perhaps He feels like playing from time to time. And so He gives a child a painful, lifelong illness. Or some unforeseen talent.

I have trouble imagining a God who doesn't want to control things, Johan thinks. Why else would He have the power?

Johan can't bear to see Stella suffer. Can't bear to see the tears welling up in her eyes.

Give me strength. But most of all, give me patience. The energy to find sympathy beyond my own pain.

'All done,' the doctor says. 'That wasn't so bad, was it?' he says, and Stella wipes her eyes on her sleeve.

Johan feels like punching the man. No more. No less.

Waldemar and Börje aren't in the station when Malin and Elin arrive back. They're probably out questioning people connected to Peder Åkerlund.

Zeke is sitting at his desk. When he sees them arrive he calls out: 'Got your thoughts clear, Malin?'

'Hardly. Unfortunately.'

Zeke lets the matter drop. Over the years he's got used to her going off on her own, to the fact that she sometimes does things entirely her own way.

Malin watches Elin go off towards Johan. They start to chat, and Johan seems agitated, probably talking about something new he's found. But then she remembers. Johan was taking his daughter to hospital today. He's probably feeling off balance, and who wouldn't be? He can't have been back long.

Elin told her about her suspicions regarding Nadja's father. The same thought had also occurred to her.

Could there be something in that?

Doubtful.

Why would he harm his own daughter? Or Peder Åkerlund? He has an alibi for the murder. No, Nadja's dad has nothing to do with this. Even if there's something a bit odd about a grown man making his living designing games.

Malin switches her computer on. Opens her email.

The usual internal memos.

A summary of the state of the investigation from Göran Möller. Concluding that although all the lines of inquiry seem to be pointing in different directions, the connections are there somewhere, the answers, the truth.

She scrolls down.

Spam that's found its way through the filter. Some new decree from the Public Prosecutors' Office.

Hang on, though.

Nadja little, ever so brittle.

The heading of an email some way down her inbox. Malin opens it.

Her hand is shaking as the computer brings up the unknown message, far too slowly.

This isn't an ordinary email, and she feels that something's about to explode, to use Elin's phrase. While her antiquated computer slowly does its thing, the realisation hits her.

The police aren't in control of this investigation.

Someone else is.

A childish rhyme.

A missing girl.

Hydrochloric acid.

Hajif.

Malin reads the email, sent from a Gmail address that consists of an apparently random combination of letters and numbers. Untraceable, in all likelihood. Created to look as neutral as possible. She reads the message over and over again, tries to understand what it says. Both in its words, and beyond them.

Go to Stenkullamotet, dig beneath the magical
tree. What will you find?

Then, after a gap of about ten blank lines:

Acid against sayings leads to slayings.

Malin feels her heart skip a couple of beats.
The fact that acid was injected into Peder Åkerlund's
brain hasn't appeared anywhere in the media.
No one but us and the murderer, and any potential
accomplice, knows about that.
So: the email was probably sent by the murderer.
Making contact.
Issuing a challenge.
Sending silly rhymes.
As if this is a game. Red against blue, words against
words, where nothing except silence necessarily means
anything.

Go to . . .

Malin calls the others over, and soon she can feel Zeke,
Johan, and Elin's breath on the back of her neck. Calm,
focused concentration.
'Bloody hell,' Zeke whispers.
'Are we going to find her now?' Elin says, and Malin feels
like saying 'There's no way of knowing,' but stays silent.
'I can try to find out what server the email was sent
from,' Johan says. 'What IP-address is behind that Gmail
account.'
He sighs.
'But it'll be bloody difficult. And it seems to have been
chosen specifically to prevent it giving us any clues.'
'Has something happened?'

Malin hears Göran Möller's voice, and the four of them turn towards their new boss, who is standing just behind them in his blue summer suit.

'Yes, something's happened,' Malin says.

Göran Möller reads the message.

'So we're dealing with a game-player.'

'Nadja's father is a game designer,' Elin says.

'That doesn't necessarily mean anything,' Malin says.

'Do you know Stenkullamotet?' Göran Möller asks.

Malin nods.

'It's out on the plain, a few kilometres from Klockrike. There's an ancient, misshapen oak tree with two trunks there that's supposed to possess magical powers. That sort of thing.'

'Then I think you and Zeke should head out there with Karin Johannison and see what you can find. Johan, see what you can find out about the email. Elin, get the reports written and take charge of our dealings with Folkunga School.'

'Already on it,' Johan says, and disappears off to his desk with Elin.

'"Acid against sayings leads to slayings",' Göran Möller reads. 'The bastard's certainly not a poet.'

## 34

An email from a lunatic.

But containing information that no one but the murderer could know. Assuming no one in the police station or in the forensics team has leaked it.

Malin tries to stay calm in the car, but is aware that she's never faced anything like this before.

Playful sadism.

The sort of rhyming riddles some Swedes put on the labels of Christmas presents. And these presents contain violence and death and grief.

Karin Johannison's car is in front of Malin and Zeke's.

Put your foot down, Malin thinks.

But Karin sticks to the speed limit.

They follow the rear lights of her Volvo estate as they cruise across the Östergötland Plain, through swaying yellow rape and ochre-coloured fields that have been left fallow. Blue sky again now, the rain has left the world looking greasy.

Zeke's hands on the wheel. There's no more reassuring sight, Malin thinks. I've seen it a thousand times, and it often keeps me calm.

How are you doing? Malin wonders.

I know you like Tess, Karin's adopted daughter from Vietnam. You're a good dad, and I know you're in a good place, the sort of place I want to be in with Daniel.

Are we OK, Daniel? Have we got something?

Does he want children? And Malin runs one hand over

her stomach, the scars from the gunshot under her blouse. A damaged womb, and she closes her eyes, forces back the sudden flare-up of longing and thirst, digs the nails of her forefingers into her thumbs the way she has taught herself.

Do I deserve to be in a good place?

Daniel doesn't really love me. That's just something he says, words among the thousands of other meaningless words we utter to get what we want at any given moment.

In the distance Malin can see the spires of different churches. Ljung, Klockrike, Fornåsa. They're approaching Stenkullamotet, where three roads converge, roads that seem to curl around each other in a wide circle, linking the most remote parts of the Östergötland Plain with larger roads that lead to Linköping, Motala, and Vadstena, that metropolis for nuns and fools.

At last, they arrive.

Karin's brake lights go on as her car pulls up beside the misshapen oak whose hat-shaped crown rests on two gnarled trunks, legs with no body, with a magician's hidden head. Long branches stick out of the crown like magic wands.

Malin and Zeke get out.

The oak stands on a small patch of farmland twenty metres away from the point where the roads meet.

Silence reigns.

Why isn't the wind in the tree audible?

This is the sort of place where anything could happen, Malin thinks, a place where life could go in any direction at all. She can see why it's regarded as magical.

They walk over to Karin.

'How do we proceed?' Malin says, feeling the spring sunlight on her face, trying to burn her skin, make her sweat. 'It said we have to dig.'

'We check the ground,' Karin says. 'Carefully, looking for signs that the soil might have been disturbed recently.'

Malin nods.

Zeke opens the boot of their car to take out the battered shovels they brought with them.

'We'll divide the area around the oak into three zones, and search one each,' Karin says.

'Sounds sensible,' Zeke says.

'Of course it's sensible,' Karin says irritably.

'Please . . .'

Karin stops. Smiles at Zeke, then Malin.

'Sorry.'

Malin is soon standing in the shadow of the oak with a spade in one hand. She inspects the ground impatiently, wondering if it could be hiding something that might lead them to Nadja. The earth is dry, sheltered by the dense crown, but her shoes are muddy from walking across the wet field.

A car drives past, the children in the back seat stare at them.

Who are you? What are you doing beside the magic tree with spades in your hands? Stop, Daddy! We want to dig too!

Should we be frightened? Malin wonders. More cautious than we're being now? Am I getting carried away? Who knows what someone who sends emails like that might be capable of?

But she doesn't say anything. Suppresses her anxieties. Why would there be a trap here? A bomb?

On the other hand, why not?

She goes on looking.

Centimetre by centimetre she scans the ground, looking for anything unusual, a sign that the earth has been disturbed. She has a feeling that someone is watching them. She looks out across the fields, but there's nowhere anyone could hide without being seen.

She looks up at the crown of the oak. A wind blows

through the leaves and she can hear them rustle now, and in the rustling are words she can't make out, the mute whispers of the dead, and she gets a sense that it's all too late. That Nadja Lundin is dead after all.

'Here!' Karin calls. 'Look at this!'

And Malin looks over at Karin, who is standing some thirty metres away in the field. In the fierce sunlight on the other side of the tree she is pointing at the ground with her spade.

'Be careful as you approach,' she says.

Malin and Zeke head towards Karin, treading in her footprints.

The patch she's pointing at is a different colour to the surrounding ground. A more porous, darker patch of mud, flecked with grass, and she says: 'Someone's been digging. Before we set to work, I want to secure the ground around here.'

Malin and Zeke wait in the shadow beneath the oak as Karin combs the ground for clues. She doesn't seem to be finding anything, the rain must have destroyed any evidence.

They're sitting on the ground, each leaning against a trunk, and it occurs to Malin that it would be impossible to bury anything close to the oak. The roots must be dense, ancient, much older than her, and then she asks Zeke: 'Are you OK?'

'What?'

'You heard.'

'We're fine. I've never felt happier.'

'Good,' Malin says, and Zeke asks: 'How about you? With Daniel?'

'We're trying.'

Then they sit in silence alongside each other, watching their colleague and Zeke's partner do her job, and before too long she calls to them: 'We can start digging now.'

★

Spades in the ground. They dig quickly but carefully.

All three of them are wondering what they're going to find.

Nadja's body? A violated, damaged girl's body? A different body? An unknown victim of this spring's evil? A victim they don't yet know about?

They keep digging down.

Spade by spade, at an even pace, and sweat breaks out under their clothes. The sun laughs at them, the earth too.

Malin feels the spade in her hands, and can feel the start of blisters. Her skin isn't used to this sort of work.

But there's something here. She's sure of it.

They're a metre down now, and another car, a dark blue Passat, drives past, slows down, and Malin tries to see the passengers, but it's impossible with the light against her, and then the car drives on.

A large heap of earth is growing beside them.

Dusty now, now that they've reached completely dry soil.

No roots. A few dry, dead worms.

Then her spade hits something solid.

Zeke and Karin notice. They stop what they're doing, look at each other.

They keep digging. Scrape with their hands.

Is it a coffin?

No, it's too small to be a coffin. A body? No, too hard to be a body.

They uncover the object. It is a coffin, a tiny wooden coffin, painted white, suitable for a doll or a baby, and they lift it out from the hole and carry it over to the dry ground beneath the oak. They know they should have left it in the hole, and a thought suddenly occurs to Karin.

'Dare we open it? Or should we call out the bomb squad? We have no idea what it is.'

Malin digs her fingernails into her thumbs.

Is there a small child in the coffin? Alive? No, it would have to be dead. Could the coffin contain part of Nadja's body?

'We open it,' Zeke says.

'You two stand back,' Malin whispers. 'If it does explode, there's no point in it taking all three of us with it.'

Zeke and Karin do as she says without protest. She waits for them to reach cover behind Karin's car. Then she bends down and carefully unfastens the catches on the side of the coffin.

Is it going to explode?

Malin listens out for sounds across the fields, but can no longer hear the wind. Just an all-pervading silence, as if all the unspoken words had the power to extinguish the sun if they wanted.

Then she opens the coffin.

# 35

Malin, Karin, and Zeke are looking down at the contents of the coffin, the piece of flesh, the oblong, greyish-red lump, the amputated tongue. And they look at each other with shared confusion.

What's this?

They pull back from the coffin, away from the stench of the rotting muscle.

'Is that a human tongue?' Malin says.

Karin looks down again.

'Not impossible, it could be.'

A vehicle pulls up behind them and Malin turns around. It's the *Correspondent*'s blue car, and Daniel gets out, together with a young, female photographer. He starts to walk towards them, and she feels like fending him off, yelling at him to get lost. But most of all she'd like to fall into his arms and let him take her away from this madness. But the madness is everywhere, impossible to escape.

Malin knows that.

The only momentary escape is in ecstasy.

'Stay up on the road,' Zeke calls. 'This is a crime scene.'

Daniel and the photographer stop. How come they're here? Nothing's been said on police radio. But the station leaks like a sieve. Malin turns her back on Daniel, looks down at the tongue again, is that Nadja's tongue, but could something that large really fit inside a human mouth? She realises how badly she's sweating, and says: 'We need to calm down.'

The frenetic digging.

An email. A coffin.

A murdered former Sweden Democrat of the most extreme, right-wing variety, a missing left-wing activist, a buried tongue.

'I am calm,' Karin says.

'I can't make any sense of this,' Zeke says, as if he could read Malin's mind. 'None of it makes sense.'

'The tongue is controlled from the Broca's area,' Karin says. 'Where the acid was injected. And now we have a tongue.'

'If the motive is political,' Malin says, 'then the perpetrator is someone who stands to gain from firing in both directions. Left and right.'

'Why would anyone do that? In Sweden? Today's Sweden?' Zeke says. 'This is the work of a madman.'

Malin doesn't reply. She realises the limitations of the political angle. But, on the other hand, perhaps there's someone who stands to gain from chaos? People with different goals, but whose interests might just coincide.

The two trunks of the oak seem to be clutching at each other now. And sucking strength from their muscles. Malin says: 'But, as Karin says, there's a very odd connection here. Between language and silence.'

'It's not a human tongue,' Karin says. 'I can see that now. It's too big. It could be from a calf.'

'Where would you get hold of a calf's tongue?' Zeke wonders.

Good question, Malin thinks. Replies: 'In any supermarket. It's the sort of thing poor pensioners boil up to eat.'

The click of a camera. Daniel's voice.

'What have you got in the coffin?'

'None of your business,' Malin shouts.

Why so unfriendly?

He's a journalist now, and I hate them.

Get lost.

It's possible to love and hate at the same time. And she wants to hug him, kiss him. Tell him she loves him.

A fucking calf's tongue. Karin prods at it with her tweezers.

'So we know it isn't Nadja's,' Malin says.

'She might still be alive,' Zeke says. 'Is that what you mean?'

Malin nods, wipes the sweat from her forehead. And she realises that Stenkullamotet has its own microclimate. It's much hotter here than in the city.

'Look at this,' Karin says.

She pulls a bloody piece of paper out of a hole in the tongue. She puts it down on the coffin lid, carefully unfolds it, and words in blue ink, neatly handwritten, stare mockingly up at them.

*We humans have freedom of speech. Most of us.*
*What do we do with this speech?*
*We abuse and neglect it.*
*Shriek and yell without reflection.*
*I know the price of words.*

*I shall burn these words to secure them.*
*I shall speak through murders.*
*Peder, Nadja, and others.*
*I shall create order in the mass of humanity.*

*I am the mask burner.*
*You can never silence me.*
*But you can play for a while.*

Malin reads the words on the note several times, as do Karin and Zeke.

'We're obviously dealing with a madman,' Karin says.

'Or a smart madman who wants us to think he's mad,' Malin says, thinking: Is he trying to say that Nadja is dead?

Zeke stands there silently.

Breathing in and out, then rubs his head with one hand.

'The bastard has a point, though,' he says. 'What do we do with our freedom of speech? Write a load of crap about celebrities, a lot of drivel, spewing out anything and everything.'

That's what scares me, Malin thinks, looking over towards Daniel and the photographer. That evil seems to have a point this time, that it loves something, has a passion that every thinking person must surely sympathise with.

The importance of words.

An evil that loves humanity. An evil that is so black that it becomes white, and then red? Beyond the white light where she found Maria Murvall's nemesis? That case took years for her to solve.

Malin walks away from the others, towards Daniel.

He's about to ask her something when she reaches him, but something in the look on her face stops him.

Instead he holds his arms out to her.

And she lets herself fall into his embrace.

## 36

*You can never silence me.*

Göran Möller has written those words on the whiteboard in the meeting room.

Outside, the sun is sinking in the sky, making it pulse in shades of pink, playing tricks on Malin's tired eyes.

What colour am I?

Now pink, red, yellow, then icy blue, and soon black.

Malin can see confusion in her colleagues' faces. Where is this going to end?

And the certainty: there is a desperate urgency.

Nadja Lundin might still be alive. Even if the message implied that she's been murdered.

*You can play for a while.*

Whoever it is they're hunting, whoever it is they're being hunted by, that person sees murder and kidnap as a game, a diversion.

A buried calf's tongue beside a magic oak. A cryptic but not so cryptic message.

'So what have we got?' Göran Möller asks. He's standing by the whiteboard, dressed in a thin white shirt. 'The floor's all yours. Because I have no idea where we should start.'

At first Malin feels irritated by Göran Möller's passivity, his admission of weakness, but then she has to admit that he's doing the right thing, he's showing them what they've got to work with, showing that we're in the eye of the storm and that there are rules here that we don't yet recognise, we need to react and act accordingly.

'We've checked out Nadja's father,' Waldemar says. 'Nothing remotely suspicious about him. His business looks very solid, and I can't find anything else odd about him.'

'He works in game design,' Börje says, 'and we've been contacted by someone who wants to play with us.'

'That's just a coincidence,' Göran Möller says.

'What about the political angle?' Börje goes on. 'Could this be a sick way of attracting attention? Getting rid of enemies? A confused young person in some political camp who's gone berserk?'

'This isn't the result of an outburst of anger,' Malin says. 'This has been carefully planned.'

Göran Möller adjusts the collar of his shirt.

Looks first at Elin Sand, then at the other detectives.

'We've interviewed a number of people in relation to that line of inquiry. And so far we haven't found anything that indicates any political connection to Peder's murder, or Nadja's disappearance. Everyone we've spoken to has been surprised and afraid.'

Except Suliman Hajif, Malin thinks.

'But the crimes are connected,' Göran Möller says. 'That much is clear.'

'Can we be one hundred per cent certain of that?' Malin says. 'Couldn't the tongue and that note be a way of focusing our attention in the wrong direction? Maybe we've been contacted by Peder Åkerlund's murderer, and Nadja is a completely separate case?'

Malin hears her own voice, the underlying tone. She doesn't actually believe her own doubts, just wants to toss them into the room, see where the uncertainty can take them.

'Maybe,' Göran Möller retorts. 'But that's not very likely.'
He pauses before going on: 'The search of Max Friman's
flat hasn't produced any results.'

Perhaps he wasn't hiding anything after all, Malin thinks.

Waldemar coughs.

Then he says: 'Let's just hope it's a darkie next time.'

And Malin feels like punching him in the head. The
others are sitting there open-mouthed, even though they're
used to Waldemar's idiotic remarks, and Göran Möller
says: 'For fuck's sake, Waldemar!'

Silence settles on the room. Because they're all starting
to realise that there will be a next time if they don't succeed
in their work.

'Our conversations with people who know Nadja haven't
come up with anything either,' Elin says. 'Her teachers are
just ordinary people, her friends, ordinary teenage girls.'

'And the man in the hoodie? The one outside the school?'
Göran asks.

Elin shakes her head.

'He feels like a ghost,' she says. 'I found our report, but
it didn't say much. We haven't had time to knock on doors
near the school to find out if anyone noticed anyone
matching that description.'

'Anything new from Forensics?' Malin asks.

'They haven't found anything special so far in any of
the computers or mobiles,' Johan says. 'Andersson called
me a little while ago. And we haven't managed to identify
any security cameras along Peder Åkerlund's route home.
I'm sorry, but everything's been moving so fucking quickly,
and the council are pretty bloody slow, to put it mildly.'

Johan swearing.

He never usually does that, Malin thinks, then says:
'Words. He or she seems to be obsessed with words. What
does that mean?'

'There are people who say that everything begins with

words,' Göran Möller says, and Malin sees Börje and Waldemar glance suspiciously at their new boss. 'Or with colour, nuances,' Göran goes on, and now they're looking at him as if he were mad.

What the hell does he mean? they seem to be wondering. Hippy nonsense? Now?

'What the hell does he mean?' Waldemar hisses.

'The tone,' Zeke says.

'Sorry.'

'I mean that for this individual, perhaps words are the most important thing. Taking care of them. That that's more important than what anyone thinks. And that's why he or she – or they, for that matter – attacks people who've expressed unambiguous views. The perpetrator may not care about the content of those opinions, but is somehow angry that they were expressed at all.'

'That's some serious anger,' Elin Sand says.

'There's a madness in that way of thinking,' Malin says. 'A madness that somehow seems to fit perfectly here. It's so odd that it could actually be true.'

For the first time she's been impressed with Göran Möller. The sensitive way he's dared to approach their case.

'Have we got anywhere tracing the email that led us to Stenkullamotet?' Göran Möller asks.

'Forensics are working on it,' Johan says. 'It's very complicated. I'm not up to it, but they've got someone new who might be able to do it.'

Malin notices how tired Johan sounds. The more digitised the world has become, the more work there is for him. But he's never seemed tired before.

Outside the windows, darkness is slowly falling.

As yet invisible stars have occupied the sky, making it their own, and silent voices whisper down across the Earth from their points.

But whatever those voices are whispering, the detectives in their meeting room don't hear it.

They just hear their own silence.

And a recently-appointed boss saying: 'Go home and get some sleep now. And we'll try to take another look at this with fresh eyes tomorrow.'

And Malin knows that they're nowhere close to the end yet. This is only the beginning.

I'd like to talk about my mum.

She had boiling water thrown over her, trying to protect me.

She went to the police in the end. Told them about the abuse, the water, the cruelty, about how the town's angel was a monster.

The police didn't believe her. Asked her to leave.

What evidence did she have?

Wasn't she simply being jealous? Everyone had heard the rumours about his mistress in Stockholm.

She left. Thought she could hear them laughing at her behind her back.

Thought they were toying with her.

Then he came home one day after the party conference. He hadn't managed to get the position on one of the committees that he'd wanted.

So he drank and turned violent, and Mum shouted at him to stop.

I was nine years old at the time.

I saw him hit her head against the radiator. Fill her mouth with plant soil.

Old women and kids should shut up, he yelled at me before walking out.

I sat there for days and nights.

Staring at Mum.

I never saw Dad again.

He hanged himself in his prison cell.

And I didn't say a word for the next four years.

Karin is bent over a microscope when Malin enters the laboratory. The fluorescent lights in the ceiling make her face look pale, make her look older than she is, and the heavy metallic smell in the air makes Malin feel sick.

She didn't want to come here. Would rather have gone to the gym with Elin, or gone out for a run, or home to Daniel, but she came anyway.

Karin looks up from the microscope. Her white coat lends her an air of authority, and Malin suddenly feels uncertain.

'Hi, Malin.'

Her voice is soft, and Malin's uncertainty vanishes.

'How are you getting on?'

'Not great. I've examined the coffin. Nothing on it but soil. No fingerprints on the note either. I'm trying to get something from the tongue, but that's probably pointless. And I've just had the results of the DNA comparison from the hair found out in Svartmåla. No match in the database.'

'Zeke went home,' Malin says.

Karin nods.

'He just called. He's sent Tess's babysitter home.'

Karin seems pleased that she's there, and Malin looks at her colleague, thinks about the secrets they share, the closeness that brings.

'Of all the crazy things,' Malin says.

'Seems to be a methodical individual, at any rate,' Karin says. 'Bearing in mind the acid in the brain. The note hidden inside the tongue.'

'What do you think about Nadja? Is she alive?'

Karin lowers her eyes towards the microscope and stares at it for a moment before looking up at Malin again.

'I hope she's alive, Malin. I hope so.'

In the basement of the police station, Elin Sand is doing push-ups.

Three times fifty, and she feels the weight of her breasts against the floor, how her stomach muscles have to work to keep her body straight, the way her arms tremble as she approaches her target.

Am I going to make it?

She pushes and pushes and pushes, and then she's there, and lets herself sink down onto the sweaty mat.

Should we all be frightened? she thinks. Anyone in Linköping who has ever expressed an opinion?

She rests her cheek on the mat. Enjoys its relative cool. And the sensation of living in a present where the past doesn't matter too much.

I can live here, she thinks. Right now, I'm OK here.

Waldemar Ekenberg and Börje Svärd are sitting in silence in Börje's kitchen, at either end of the table.

In front of them on the table is a bottle of whisky and two glasses filled to the brim with liquor and ice. A pan full of beef stroganoff is bubbling away on the stove.

They've got into the habit of doing this sometimes after work.

Preparing a simple meal together.

Getting drunk.

Then Waldemar stays over in what used to be Anna's room.

They never talk much. Don't need words, and what would they say to each other anyway? Talk about their feelings?

Work?

Gossip about their colleagues?

Neither of them is interested in any of that.

'How are the dogs?' Waldemar asks.

'Fine,' Börje says, 'but I've been thinking about getting rid of them.'

'Why?'

'I'm ready for something new,' Börje says. 'So the dogs will have to go.'

'Just like that?'

'Big changes have to happen suddenly. Like an explosion.'

He finds himself thinking of the head teacher at Folkunga School, Kristina Nederdahl, and the game they were playing with each other. He hopes she's going to call, believes she will.

'You'll miss those dogs,' Waldemar says. 'Just like I'd miss the old woman if I threw her out.'

'You'll never throw her out.'

'It's only a matter of time before those kennels are empty,' Waldemar says. 'Once you've said it, that's what happens, isn't it?'

Börje Svärd grins towards his friend, takes a deep gulp of the whisky, and says: 'Words. Everything starts with words.'

'What a load of fucking shite,' Waldemar says.

Karim Akbar strokes his seven-month-old son Abel on his cheek. He's sleeping softly and soundly in his cot in the little room in their villa in Lambohov. They haven't had any problems with him. Vivianne has turned out to be the perfect, reassuring mother, and his own paternal efforts have been better this time around.

Mummy, daddy, baby.

The game, the seriousness of that.

So serious that it's incomprehensible, and so he's playing

instead. As hard as he can now that he's on paternity leave. Making a fool of himself with Abel. Playing peekaboo.

If we can't deal with being grown up, Karim thinks, we play. And if we were never allowed to be children, we play.

He looks down at his son. Hears Vivianne preparing dinner out in the kitchen.

He remembers his own father, hanging from the noose in the bathroom. Remembers the way words were taken from him.

The way his own childhood was snatched away from him at that moment.

And he feels like waking Abel.

And playing and playing and playing with him. Play with him until the end of the Earth and back.

Johan Jakobsson has gone home. He's made dinner for his family, and now he's sitting in his study in the basement, searching on his computer for a crazed individual who might fit the contradictions of their case.

But he can't find anyone.

For people today, opinions themselves are the important thing, he thinks. Being able to self-identify, starting with 'I BELIEVE'.

Not 'I THINK'.

Sometimes he feels tired of police work. With his skills, he would easily be able to find another job that paid a good deal better. He could even move to Malta and earn three hundred thousand kronor a month, tax-free, as a hacker. The heat would doubtless be good for Stella, and their health insurance would work out there.

Occasionally he feels tempted. But usually not.

He hasn't mentioned anything to his wife about the opportunities that are actually out there. A freer, richer life. When they sat down to plan their holiday that summer, he realised they couldn't even afford a package deal.

Shit.

'That wasn't so bad, was it?'

Stella is asleep now, and he wishes he could comfort her in her dreams. Tell her the pain is gone now.

He's found his way onto a website belonging to an anonymous right-wing extremist.

Exterminate Sweden's Niggers.

Death to Judaism.

Dear God, Johan thinks. What am I doing?

We need to try to improve things.

A few of the folders on Peder Åkerlund's computer still haven't been cracked. From his bag he pulls out the copy of the hard drive that Forensics gave him, and delves into it.

He spends hours sitting there in the darkness, trying to find his way past the passwords.

And in the end the folders open up.

And there they are.

The text and images from the websites they were told about by Julianna Raad. All dated after Peder Åkerlund's supposed conversion. Johan clicks from file to file, and there's no doubt at all. Peder Åkerlund was behind those websites, no one else.

He remained a racist until his dying day.

Anything other than that was merely playing to the gallery.


Göran Möller is sitting alone in front of the television in his two-room flat beside the Stånga River. He bought the flat as soon as he moved to Linköping, thought it best to settle down quickly, prove to himself that he was here to stay.

The case they are working on now troubles him. Not so much because of the violence, but the ideological aspect. The calculation, the madness of it.

People can say things they don't really mean out of fear and anger.

But, on the other hand, those words reveal the structure of thought processes that are usually invisible to the speaker.

He channel hops from a film to a repeat of a talk show.

What are they on about?

Some non-issue.

He makes his way to the Knowledge Channel, which is showing a documentary about the artist Gerhard Richter. Göran has seen it before, but is happy to watch it again. He loses himself in the concentrated, constantly shifting brilliance of the German artist. Canvasses covered in running paint. The investigation feels very similar. As if it were constantly running away from them, stopping a clear image from appearing.

He switches the television off.

Sits quietly in his lonely darkness, and thinks about Malin Fors. He had heard about her long before he moved to Linköping. An edgy, broken, but brilliantly talented detective. Sven Sjöman gave her a lot of freedom, but simultaneously held onto her reins tightly: she was worth the risk and the worry, because of the results she achieved.

She seems much calmer than her reputation now.

Presumably because she's not drinking.

She seems absorbed by her own dullness, the way a lot of sober alcoholics can be. Then they start drinking again, simply as a way to put up with themselves.

Malin is lying in bed next to Daniel. He wanted to have sex, but she pushed him away, just wanted to feel his warm body against her skin. He's asleep now, with his arm around her. Breathing heavily, and he smells good, and she could lie like this for ever.

She's tried calling Tove again. The call didn't get through.

So she called the aid agency instead, but only got an answerphone message giving their office hours.

The darkness of the bedroom contains anxiety, monsters.

Longing.

And Tove's silence.

What if she's lying somewhere, her body cut to shreds, screaming, but no one can hear her?

Malin pulls free from Daniel. Goes out into the kitchen. Opens the cupboard under the sink and reaches in, right to the back. Pulls off the loose wooden panel, fishes out the bottle of tequila she hid there.

She's thinking about Tove.

Where are you?

An amputated tongue.

Screams, but no one to hear.

Malin opens the bottle. Puts it to her lips.

And she feels the warm liquid inside her. Wonderful at first, then it becomes nothing but blunt violence against everything that could be her.

# 39

Suliman Hajif turns off the lights in Linköping mosque before locking the door and heading out into the darkness of early night.

He's emailed his contacts in Syria. He does that via an encryption program he's installed on one of the mosque's computers. The old imam doesn't understand things like that, and for some reason he appears to trust me, Suliman thinks.

Two guys in Ryd. Eighteen years old. They're travelling to Turkey tomorrow. Then they'll carry on from there, and, if everything goes according to plan, before the summer comes to an end they'll have blown themselves to pieces along with dozens of Assad's supporters.

It's no more complicated than that.

There's so much confusion, so much weak-mindedness to exploit.

'Why waste your lives here, when you could die a martyr's death in a holy war?'

'Get to paradise.'

'Have all the women you want. Like the Prophet says.'

They swallow everything I say, Suliman Hajif thinks as he walks towards the forest behind the mosque. He's going to cut through the woods and then head home to Berga down the narrow path behind the blocks of flats in Ekholmen.

There's a madman on the loose in the city.

He looked at the *Correspondent*'s website just now, as well as the online editions of *Aftonbladet* and *Expressen*.

Their reporters have gone crazy over the story, and
there are pictures of the little whore on all the sites, right
at the top: *Where's Nadja?*

Hope the whore is dead. Then there'd be one less, at
least.

The forest is dark, and he switches on the little torch
on his mobile, and shines it down at the ground so he
doesn't trip over or step in a hole.

His kaftan isn't particularly practical, nor is his beard,
actually. It sometimes itches badly, just like the kaftan, but
he wants to dress like the person he is, knows how important that is in the young men's eyes.

He can see the path now.

The street lamp.

The black van parked just beyond the cone of light.

What's it doing here at this time of night?

I recognise it. Where have I seen it before?

His stomach clenches with fear, and then he hears a
rustling sound, feels something cold against his nose, a
sharp, acrid smell, and there's no time for him to put up
a fight before he collapses onto the twigs, moss, and damp
ground.

He drops his mobile.

But his eyes work in the dark.

And he sees the treetops etched against the starry sky
as he is dragged through the forest, then pulled upright,
his head lolling from side to side, the world is shades of
black and grey, and he hears the door of the van close.
Above him the sky is low and black now, and he tries to
scream, but his tongue won't obey him.

It's as if it's never been part of his mouth.

# PART 3

# At the end of longing and the start of everything

[In silence]

The Östergötland Plain is moving in the night.

The ploughed furrows twine around each other, becoming so deep that no starlight can reach the soil hidden at the bottom.

The ears of the plain are full of earth.

There's nothing to hear the knife slicing through flesh.

There's nothing to hear the screams from the coffin.

On a sofa in the city, a man and a woman are sobbing, their grief as endless as the movements of the ground. An anxious father walks up and down inside a flat, his wife driven into a dreamless sleep by alien substances.

The air will soon run out.

The water ran out a long time ago.

The girl feels it in her cramps.

She tries to fill her lungs, scrape the wood, but her fingernails are no longer there, just open, stinging wounds and a feeling of never being able to breathe again.

A breath.

Another breath.

She wants to escape from herself, become one with the earth beyond the wood.

But that's impossible. There's only one reality here.

So she plays a word game. Thinks of a colour that becomes a thing that becomes a feeling that becomes a nothing.

The nothing that existed before a tiptoeing death.

# 40

Brush teeth, brush teeth, brush teeth, and be happy.

Malin has switched on the light in the bathroom. She's looking at her teeth in the mirror, as they are covered by more and more froth from the toothpaste.

Not be sad.

She moves the hand holding the toothbrush manically, to and fro, trying to get rid of the taste of alcohol in her mouth, the stench, the shame at having given in. She swallowed two mouthfuls, then tipped the rest of the tequila down the sink and slipped quietly out into the stairwell to drop the bottle down the rubbish chute.

Doesn't want Daniel to know anything.

The drink was hot in her mouth, burned her tongue as if it were an open wound.

She felt the alcohol spreading out through her body, and had to hold on to the cold draining board to stop herself from falling over. Her legs turned to cotton wool, the clock of St Lars Church struck one o'clock, and it was as if her body disappeared for a few brief seconds, and she started to float, no longer tied to the earth.

And she wanted more of that feeling.

But resisted.

Because she knows that it could kill her, and that real-isation makes her brush with increased frenzy, and her gums are bleeding, the taste of iron making its way beneath her tongue.

Tove.

She has to find a way of suppressing her anxiety.

She spits. Holds her hand in front of her mouth, breathes out hard, then in through her nose. No smell.

She turns the tap off, rinses her mouth, and goes into the bedroom. Sits down on the side of the bed, shakes Daniel.

He wakes up slowly and opens his eyes. The whites are like small lights in the darkness, his breath heavy yet pleasantly sweet.

'Is it morning?' he asks, weary but not annoyed.

Malin shakes her head.

'Middle of the night.'

She breathes on him, and he grimaces. Can he smell the alcohol? What would he say if he could? She hasn't had a single drink since they got back together, so her problem has been a non-issue, it hasn't needed discussion, and so they haven't talked about it.

Better without words.

Words can uncork a bottle.

'Have you brushed your teeth?' Daniel asks.

'Yes, my mouth felt disgusting.'

'Shall we try to get back to sleep?'

'I want to talk,' she says.

And Daniel sits up, because she hardly ever wants to talk about anything, even though she knows that he finds her silence about most things difficult.

'I want to talk about the case,' she says. 'There are loads of things we haven't released to the media.'

'I don't want to know,' Daniel says.

'But I have to be able to tell you. I'll go mad otherwise.'

'Then I have to be able to write about it. You have your responsibilities, I have mine.'

'We have to be able to talk about things.'

Daniel leans over and takes her in his arms.

'Talk,' he says. 'Say what you need to say.'

And Malin knows he won't write about anything she tells him, knows she can trust him, can't she?

'Thanks,' she says.

She pushes him away gently.

'I feel a silence inside,' she says. 'As if something's disappeared, as if I'm missing something.'

Daniel says nothing, thereby encouraging her to go on.

'It feels like the silence is connected to the case, but I don't know how.'

She tells him about Peder Åkerlund.

The acid in the speech centre of the brain.

The tongue.

The message they found inside it.

Daniel remains silent, lets her tell him at her own pace.

When she's finished, he says: 'Sounds like you're dealing with a real lunatic.'

Malin nods.

'And he's not done yet.'

'Have you got any suspects?'

'We haven't got anything,' Malin says. 'We've spoken to people who knew Nadja Lundin and Peder Åkerlund, but we haven't found anything useful. And their relatives are all spotless.'

She doesn't mention the text Johan sent her a little while ago, telling her what he's found out about Åkerlund's duplicity. But does that actually change anything? OK, one of his opponents may have found out about it, or suspected it, like Julianna, and crossed the line in their fury. But there's no need for Peder's parents to know about that.

But it fits somehow with the idea of a game. How everything has more than one side, can change and end up as anything. If there's just the one perpetrator, he likes killing and displaying his victims, or kidnapping and killing them. Everything's possible in this game, so the same applies to the case. Even the fact that there doesn't seem to be a clear pattern could be relevant.

'What does the murderer want?' Daniel wonders. 'What could the motive be?'

'I think he's trying to say something,' Malin says.

'What, though?'

'I don't know yet.'

Then they sit in silence next to each other in the night.

'You won't write about this, will you?' Malin asks after a while.

'I promise.' Daniel strokes her cheek. 'This is more important.'

And then Malin talks about Tove, and how worried she is that she can't get hold of her.

'I've got a contact I can call tomorrow,' Daniel says, and sinks back on the bed, stretching his arm out, and she lies back on top of it. She falls asleep in a matter of minutes, while Daniel lies awake, feeling her weight against him, just as he sensed a faint trace of tequila on her breath a little while ago.

He didn't want to say anything.

He knows what she is.

And he loves her.

The thing about people, he thinks, is that you can never have one thing without the other.

Life and death always exist within the same body. And you have to dare to love them both.

# 41

'You're going to die now.'

Suliman Hajif hears the voice as if it were coming out of a tin can. Subdued, neither masculine nor feminine, without any real emotion, despite the fact that the words are repeated over and over again.

'You're going to die now.'

His brain, his thoughts are perfectly clear, just as clear as the burning pain coursing through his lower body and up to his head, overwhelming everything but fear.

Why am I here? Suliman Hajif thinks, and he jerks his head and tries to get up, but that's impossible because thick nails have been hammered through his shins and lower arms.

Suliman Hajif didn't hear the nail-gun.

The quick, muffled sound as his unconscious body was nailed to the textured metal plates on the floor. But he feels the pain, and wants to scream, but can't because his mouth is full of earth, and he feels thirsty, could drink a whole lake.

Within him he sees eyes.

Dead people's eyes.

People who see suicide bombers, the ones he sent, seconds before their bombs go off. People who realise they're going to die, but who don't have time to scream before they are torn to pieces, who never have the chance to say goodbye to their loved ones, who never get to feel soothing hands against their skin before they pass on.

They stare at him, challenging him.

But they don't want to kill him.

They want to see the man circling around him inside the van with a glinting knife in his hand do it. The man who is moving closer and closer, like a hunting beast about to attack its prey.

Suliman Hajif can feel how much the man is enjoying this moment, the power of this act. This isn't some cold, emotional murder for the sake of survival.

He comes closer to Suliman Hajif, sticks the knife into his bare legs again, slices across his stomach again, and twists the nails in his arms, watching his face contort.

'Scream, scream,' the man says. 'Get it all off your chest. Reveal who you really are,' and then Suliman Hajif feels fingers picking at his mouth, and the earth filling his mouth is pulled out in big, wet lumps, and he feels his tongue move again, but his screams are nothing but gurgles, and what can he say?

All conviction is gone.

The man is laughing at him now, and behind the black mask his eyes are ecstatic, and the man pulls the mask off, and Suliman sees a face, a smile, and there's love in that smile, isn't there?

Is this what death looks like? Suliman thinks.

Did you see a smile like that?

Then the man holds his head against the floor, and Suliman Hajif tries to resist, but he's too tired, too weak, not even the adrenaline of fear can help him now.

His mouth is opened.

He feels the knife push inside.

Sees the gleam in the smiling eyes.

The blade cuts into the root of his tongue. His head explodes, and he gurgles, roars, the sensation is impossible, he stares at his own tongue, and blood gushes down into his lungs and stomach.

# 42

Water, air.

No water, only a little air, as if I'm breathing through a straw.

A hissing sound when I breathe. I'm shaking. I'm so thirsty I could drink my own urine.

I'm not struggling any more. There's no reason to. That only makes me lose my mind.

Perhaps no one will ever find me.

A thought struck me. Was it the man in the hoodie outside the school who brought me here?

Why?

I don't know, but I have a feeling I'm lying in a coffin that's been buried out on the plain, or in a garden. I see a red house with white eaves, or a large tree, or a dense patch of woodland.

Perhaps they'll find me in ten years' time.

Decomposed, gone, apart from my skeleton, a skull with teeth that can be identified as mine: Nadja Lundin's.

I want water.

Air.

Otherwise I'll die.

I can hear something now.

Footsteps above me?

Silence.

Then more steps.

I put my mouth to the tube and suck moisture into my mouth, and I scream with happiness. Suck up the water.

And the air.
It's clearer again.
I breathe and drink.
How long?
An hour?
I drink it all.
I breathe. The air gets stuffier again.
TICK, TICK, TICK.
I'm still alive.
Do you hear?
I'm alive.

## 43

Malin moves slowly through Linköping. The time is a quarter to seven, and at this time of the morning the city is strangely deserted. She walks up St Larsgatan towards Trädgårdstorget, past H&M. She sees the sale posters in the windows, they're early this year, sales of summer clothing must have been slow.

As she walks past the tobacconist's she reads the previous day's flysheets.

*Expressen*: 'Sweden Democrat Found Murdered, Girl Missing.'

*Aftonbladet*: 'The Canal Murder in Depth. Where is Nadja?'

A small photograph of her beautiful face.

*Svenska Dagbladet*: 'Murder in Linköping.'

*Dagens Nyheter*: 'Hate-Murder in Linköping.'

A red bus pulls up at its stop. A few people get out. Three of them are wearing traditional folk costumes. They're holding Norwegian flags. Malin tries to read the looks on their faces. Is there terror in their expressions, anxiety?

No.

She sees only tiredness in the people in normal clothes, happiness is those who are dressed up. Here we are, showing off our culture!

A few cars drive past. Some bicycles.

She stops by the toy shop just beyond the tobacconist's. Vast amounts of coloured plastic. Games, cars, advanced technical gadgets.

*You can play for a while.*

OK, Malin thinks. With your permission, we'll dance to your tune.

This is a game. You can have it your way. What is a game? It's when you conjure up the world through imitation, in order to make it comprehensible, understand how it works, how its component parts fit together.

Is that what you're doing?

Making the world comprehensible to yourself, manageable? You're just trying to survive, aren't you?

She used to love playing on her own as a child. Going off with her things and conjuring up her own worlds, alone in her room in the house in Sturefors, alone with all her suspicions and ideas, all the betrayals.

Sometimes she felt like cutting the heads off her cut-out dolls. Swapping the boys' and girls' heads around. Changing the world.

Maybe you're trying to make everything better as well? Not just survive? In your own screwed-up way, you want to change your world into something more beautiful, more loving, a world that you can control completely.

Is that how I'm going to get closer to you? Malin wonders. By assuming that you want a more beautiful world? Because you think you've already created it?

She walks on.

Past McDonald's, where a few hungry customers are eating a revolting breakfast, then turns the corner into Drottninggatan, passing Karin Johannison's door. She can't help wondering if Karin and Zeke are making love up there right now, quietly so that Tess doesn't hear them. Probably not, they must have their hands full with the morning routine.

She walks through the Trädgårdsföreningen gardens, trying to enjoy the preened greenery and the smell of spring, but can't summon up anything close to a gentle feeling.

'Malin!'

The call comes from behind, and she turns around, and, over by the entrance to the park from Linnégatan, she sees Elin Sand.

She's wearing a blue dress and black leather jacket, and from a distance she looks unbelievably cool, like something from a Hollywood film, and Malin stops to wait for her colleague. She always manages to look so young.

When Elin catches up with her the illusion crumbles. She looks tired.

'Sleep badly?' Malin asks.

'No.'

They start walking towards the station in silence.

Malin can tell that Elin wants her to ask her why she's so tired, how she's feeling, something like that, can tell she wants a pat on the shoulder, but Malin doesn't say anything.

They walk past the old entrance to the University Hospital. There's no one sitting under the protruding green canopy.

With each step their silence becomes more complex, and the air between them denser. Something is being teased out, aired, leaving a feeling of pure loneliness, a companionable loneliness that they can both accept.

They walk across the large car park, cross the road, and carry on towards the old barracks where the police station is based. It's a warm day. Almost warm enough to be summer. And they know that a lot's going to happen today, and that they can bide their time until those events are a fact.

They walk down the narrow tarmac road in the shade of the birch trees, still in silence.

They reach the sliding doors of the police station. As they glide open, Malin says: 'You don't look as tired now, compared to the way you did back in the park.'

Elin Sand smiles at her.

Says nothing.

Malin switches on her computer.

Ten emails in her inbox.

She freezes when she sees the third from the bottom, sent an hour ago from the same address as the email about Stenkullamotet.

No heading in the subject line.

A short message:

**She's breathing and she's screaming, can you save her?**

Malin reads the sentence over and over again. Breathes in, breathes out.

If he or she is serious, this means Nadja is still alive.

Nadja.

We can still rescue you.

*Do not reply to this email*, the disclaimer at the bottom says.

The others have also arrived for work early. They're all there now, and she's about to call them over when she changes her mind.

Can you save her?

There's nothing in the email that can help them make any progress. What am I supposed to do with this?

Is this how you play?

And Malin feels like smashing her computer.

Damn.

She calls Johan over, lets him read the email, asks if Forensics have managed to trace the email address.

'No, it's basically impossible,' Johan says. 'The last email was sent from a subserver in China, and God knows where it came from before that. It could just as easily have been sent from here in the station as from a mountaintop in the Himalayas.'

Johan pauses.

Malin asks: 'Security cameras? I want to see if this person actually exists.'

Johan shakes his head.

'Still nothing. But we've got a list of cameras from the council, and have started pulling in the recordings.'

The others have come over to them now. Börje, Elin, Waldemar, Zeke. They stare at Malin's computer.

'So she's alive,' Waldemar says.

'Good news,' Börje says.

'Unless he's just messing with us,' Zeke says, and the others fall silent. Don't want to think that thought.

'What does he want from me, from us, now?' Malin goes on.

'We don't know it's a he,' Elin says.

'We don't know a bloody thing,' Malin snaps.

Göran Möller comes over to join them.

'I think she's alive,' he says. 'Does anyone have any fresh ideas about this? Now that we've all had a chance to sleep on it?' He goes on: 'I should let you know that I've called off the dog patrols. There was no point carrying on. They've covered ten kilometres of forest around the house, so the search area was starting to look ridiculous. I don't believe they would have missed anything.'

As suddenly as the group gathered around Malin's computer it disperses. As if the absence of any real leads, of any definite lines of inquiry had embarrassed the detectives. As if they're ashamed at not knowing what to say or do.

Instead they each go back to their own desk. Drink coffee. Pretend to be busy.

Waiting for something else to happen.

For the evil of love to show itself.

# 44

Douglas Harrysson gets up at six o'clock every morning, drives down to the ICA supermarket chain's warehouse in Tornby, gets in his truck, and sets off on his rounds. First out to Ljungsbro, then Vreta Kloster and out onto the plain in a wide arc to the little shop in Klockrike, and on to Malmslätt.

The stores receive deliveries every day, and he stops ten minutes, fifteen at the most, at each one. He knows the shopkeepers and their staff, but he doesn't want them to get too close. He's never wanted anyone to do that, except his mother.

He's thirty-eight years old, and likes living alone, has done so ever since his mum died, and he drives the truck five days a week, does his rounds, and at weekends he watches television when he's not out on his motorcycle riding through the forests on his own.

He doesn't need anyone else, and sometimes he feels strangely proud of the fact, just as he sometimes feels proud of being really good at delivering goods to different ICA stores.

His work seems insignificant in most people's eyes. But not his. What would happen if the shelves were empty? If the bread and milk ran out?

There'd be a hell of a fuss.

He's a good driver, too, has never even come close to causing an accident.

Now he's heading out towards Lambohov. The shop

there is well-run, and the owner often sees him himself, tries hard to make small talk, but that doesn't work with Douglas Harrysson.

He takes the shortcut from Malmslätt instead of following the motorway from Ryd. He can save five minutes by taking the little-known forest road that runs behind the old airbase, the one the council want to turn into an immigration centre.

He likes this stretch of road.

The birches and pines grow in harmony here, none of the trees looks cramped, and on either side of the road runs a neatly dug ditch, as if the landowner genuinely cared about his land.

Douglas never encounters any other vehicles, and the road is more than wide enough for the truck, so he puts his foot down, and the treetops are transformed into different shades of green as his speed increases, as if he were travelling along a tunnel of green light.

He never has the radio on.

Likes the silence.

Doesn't give a shit about what's going on in the world, or even the local area. Other people can do as they like, and I'll do what I like.

He slows down again. Something is telling him to drive slowly, and he looks around at the forest, along the road ahead of him, and he has to admit to himself that the forest is beautiful at this time of year.

He focuses his gaze.

Something's wrong. He can tell that at once.

He sees something that shouldn't be there.

A naked body lying in the ditch five four three two one metres ahead of him, and he puts his foot on the brake and the truck stops.

I'll keep going, he thinks.

Doesn't want to get out. Doesn't want this to happen.

No one knows he comes this way, no one would know he's seen what he can see right now.

A male body. Contorted arms. But no head.

He knows he ought to be afraid, but his heart isn't racing, his pulse is calm, and Douglas Harrysson wonders what's wrong with him. Why can't he feel anything? Except when he goes to his mum's grave and tries to talk to her.

He starts the truck again.

Drives a short way. Then he stops and turns the engine off once more. Gets out. Walks back to the ditch where the body is lying.

Blood.

Blood everywhere.

The head is lying a short distance inside the forest.

Then he feels all the strength go out of his legs and has to sit down on the edge of the road.

Dead black eyes stare at him.

He fumbles for his mobile. Calls 112.

# 45

Suliman Hajif's head has been severed from his body. It's lying fully visible on a thin layer of moss, five metres into the forest from the ditch where the body is glinting in the sun, surrounded by small, buzzing flies.

A fairly neat cut, Malin thinks as she looks at the neck. Probably not carried out by an expert, but cutting someone's head off isn't actually that hard. There are instructions on how to do it on the Internet.

She's trying to stay cool, not react emotionally to what she can see.

His face is thinner than when he was alive, the nose seems sharper, the cheeks more sunken, the beard more unkempt, and his dark eyes are open wide with astonishment and horror that will last for ever.

His mouth is full of earth, as if to make all words impossible.

Malin, Zeke, Elin, and Karin Johannison are at the scene. Three patrol cars. The uniforms have cordoned off a large area to keep reporters and the public at a distance. The white and blue tape moves hesitantly in the wind.

Karin is inspecting the grass around the body.

Malin walks towards her, looking at the skin. Scratched, lacerated, peeled off in several places, but there aren't any symbols carved into it. There are holes in the shins and lower arms.

A naked body. Mutilated, of course.

The same murderer.

That much is obvious. Two such similar murders don't happen independently of each other. Anyone could reach that conclusion.

Elin is standing just behind her, and Malin can hear that she's hyperventilating.

Zeke is walking up and down some way inside the forest, glancing at the head. Seems to be wondering what chain of events brought Suliman Hajif to this place.

In one of the patrol cars Malin can make out the back of poor Douglas Harrysson's head. He was calm when they arrived, apologised for being so calm, said he didn't know why he wasn't 'as upset as you're supposed to be'.

There's no standard response, Malin thinks. Then she jumps across the ditch and walks towards the car, opens one of the back doors and gets in next to Douglas Harrysson.

He looks perfectly normal.

Normal height, normal weight, an ordinary face. Nothing remarkable at all about him.

She gets him to tell her, slowly and carefully, about his day. About the shortcut, and how he found the body, called the police. He talks about the previous evening, and the ones before that. He was alone at home, watching football. Pay-per-view matches. They'll be able to check.

Malin knows Douglas Harrysson has nothing to do with the murders. If he had, why would he have phoned them? And he doesn't look like a serial killer, Malin thinks, before realising that no one ever does. Men like Jeffrey Dahmer and Ted Bundy seemed perfectly ordinary too.

'We can arrange for you to see a psychologist if you like,' she says.

Douglas Harrysson shakes his head.

'I didn't think so,' Malin says. 'I don't like talking to them either.'

'Can I go now? They're waiting for their delivery in Lambohov.'

'Soon,' Malin says. 'In a little while.'

She goes back to Karin Johannison, who's crouching in the ditch and putting fragments of skin in a small bag. Malin resists the urge to turn away and forces herself to look at the dead body. At the victim on whose behalf she needs to find justice and truth.

'He's been dead four hours at the most,' Karin says. 'Whoever tortured him did it recently, last night.'

'Here?'

'No. Then there'd be much more dirt in the wounds. They're clean, as if the whole thing took place in a clinical environment. And I'm almost certain those tyre tracks up by the side of the road are the same ones we've seen before.'

'Anything else?'

'I've only just got here, Malin.'

At first Karin's sour comment annoys her, but she lets it go. Karin is under just as much pressure as she and the others are. Possibly even more.

She leaves Karin in peace. Goes and stands a few metres away from Suliman Hajif's head.

Tries to come to terms with the grimace on what used to be his face, thinks that perhaps there's some sort of divine justice in this. If it was true that Hajif recruited suicide bombers, then some of their victims must have had their heads torn off in the explosions, one form of violence matching the other, perhaps just the same when it came down to it.

The wind is moving gently through the foliage. And once again Malin feels that there's some sort of lack inside her, a silence she can't explain. That she's standing here looking at the fruits of extreme violence, yet missing something.

The *Correspondent*'s car in the distance.

Daniel.

TV4's local news team. *Aftonbladet. Expressen.* They're all here now.

Malin wonders if they consider the fact that someone like Suliman Hajif has family. He has relatives, parents brothers sisters cousins friends, who will all be told about the death, who will all grieve, yet Malin can't help thinking: I see justice here.

Zeke approaches her.

'First a right-wing extremist, then a missing left-wing girl, and now a suspected Islamist. What next?'

Malin doesn't know where the words come from, but they pop out of her mouth: 'A television presenter? A producer for TV3? If the killer wants to silence someone responsible for some real crap.'

Zeke doesn't answer. He gives her a searching look as Elin Sand walks over to them.

Malin feels Elin's hand on her shoulder. Warm and soft, and she likes it being there.

'We won't understand this by ordinary deduction,' Elin says.

'You're right. What are the rules of this game?'

'There aren't any rules in games except the ones you make up yourself,' Zeke says. 'I've learned that much.'

'Tess?'

'And all other children.'

'So you're saying we shouldn't be looking for straight-forward connections,' Malin says. 'That we should be looking for things that seem insignificant and irregular?'

'Not look for them,' Elin Sand says, 'because that would be impossible. But be open to them.'

Malin moves away along the road, towards the cordon, not in Daniel's direction, but away from him.

★

Daniel takes in the scene. He knows that the mutilated body lying over in the forest is Suliman Hajif. He's found that much out from the uniforms. Karin is poking at something else in the forest now. What could that be?

He knows more than any of his colleagues here. But he can't write about what he knows, because Malin would go mad, and would probably dump him instantly.

So what should he do?

He calls the thickset uniform over to him. The one who told him the victim's name, and said the word 'mutilated'.

'How has he been mutilated?'

'I'm not at liberty to say, you know that as well as me, Högfeldt.'

'Come on, there must be something you could let me have?'

'He's been decapitated. And his mouth is full of earth. But that's all you're getting.'

'Thanks,' Daniel says, thinking that Karin must be looking at the head at the moment.

He walks over to his car, gets out his laptop, and starts writing an article, taking as his starting point the fact that the latest victim is Suliman Hajif. And that someone has filled his mouth with earth and cut his head off his body. He writes – without mentioning anything Malin told him, as if the conclusion is all his own – that the murders are probably connected. Naked bodies found out in the countryside. There must be a connection. That the perpetrator could be someone who wants to silence people who have been outspoken in their opinions. People who are making too much noise. That these murders and the disappearance are all about freedom of speech, and perhaps also about how we choose to use it. He speculates about what he knows, goes on writing.

Divides the text in two.

One news article, with some loose speculation, and then

a more pronounced opinion piece in which he condemns the murders and the brutality, emphasising the connections he can see.

Twenty minutes.

Then the two articles are done.

He reads them through quickly.

There's nothing that could upset Malin. He could have reached the same conclusions even without what she told him last night. He sends the articles to the newsroom and just five minutes later they're online.

The murderer will see his texts. Read the opinion piece in which he or she is labelled 'calculating and sick' and 'an enemy of free speech'.

Will the articles make the killer angry? Furious?

Daniel looks along the road.

Malin.

Standing some thirty metres away.

He sees her take out her phone and answer a call she seems to have been waiting for.

## 46

The aid agency. Everything, all at once. But at least they're calling back.

Why isn't Tove herself calling?

Daniel's standing over there. He's spent a long time sitting in his car, presumably writing an article. She can take a look at it online later.

Karin called her over just now. She'd removed the earth from Suliman Hajif's mouth, revealing an empty space. His tongue has been cut out and removed, and so far they haven't found it.

Göran Möller has arrived at the scene now.

They've let Douglas Harrysson go. The bread and milk can't wait.

She clicks to take the call.

'Malin Fors.'

The body in the ditch is covered in yellow plastic now, an ambulance has turned up, and Malin recognises the two paramedics, friends of Janne's, they nodded at her when they arrived.

'Yes, hello. My name is Lisa Jansson. I'm calling from the aid agency.'

'Did you get my message?'

Silence on the line. Lisa Jansson evidently doesn't know about any message, and nausea starts to rise from Malin's stomach.

Then Lisa Jansson starts talking, and Malin wishes she could vanish from this moment, but the voice goes on relentlessly, rasping out its fucking noise: 'I'm afraid I have to tell you that Tove's missing. She was travelling with a shipment from Kigai to Bale, and somewhere along the way we lost contact with the vehicle.'

Words.

They make their way inside her, then escape, and she doesn't want to let them back in again. But she knows what they said.

'What the fuck are you saying?'

The words are repeated.

'What the . . . ?'

I'm getting angry, Malin thinks. Is that what's supposed to happen?

Tove, missing in the Democratic Republic of Congo. And she sees the faces of rapists, snakes, spiders, amoebas, forcing their way inside Tove, rotting her body.

'The Foreign Office has been informed.'

And Malin realises that there's going to be a lot of media coverage. There always is with disappearances of this sort.

Why the hell am I thinking about that?

I don't want to think about that now.

'Your daughter has been officially reported missing,' Lisa Jansson says. 'I can assure you that we're using all the resources at our disposal to locate her and the two other girls who were with her. The most likely explanation is that the vehicle has broken down and they're stranded in the jungle. Machinery isn't very reliable down there in the heat and humidity.'

'What about me?' Malin shouts. 'What can I do? What the fuck can I do?'

Daniel.

He's dodged beneath the cordon and is rushing towards her.

'There's nothing you can do.'

'You fucking idiot,' Malin roars. 'Why did you send them there?'

'They're volunteers,' Lisa Jansson says. 'And I don't think that tone of voice . . .'

One of the uniforms is chasing after Daniel. Tries to stop him, but he slips away, he's only five metres away from her.

'Are you going to find her?'

Silence on the line.

'Are you going to find her?'

'I can't . . .'

'You can go to hell,' Malin screams, and then she feels Daniel's arms around her, he takes the phone off her and clicks to end the call, and moves with her as she sinks onto the rough surface of the road.

He realises what's happened, Malin thinks. He always understands everything.

'She's gone,' she whispers. 'Tove's missing,' she goes on, and starts to cry.

## 47

They're sitting in the back seat of the *Correspondent*'s car.
Malin is leaning against Daniel and looking out at the forest
road. The leaves seem to want to pull her into their vanishing
perspective, and she feels like throwing the door open and
running away, running all the fucking way to Arlanda and
catching the first plane to the Democratic Republic of Congo.

How do you get to the Democratic Republic of Congo?

Tove travelled from Kigali to Nairobi, then on to
Kinshasa.

And now she's missing.

In a country where rape, murder, and lethal diseases
are everyday occurrences.

Fucking bloody hell.

'Try not to worry,' Daniel says. 'Their vehicle's probably
just broken down in the jungle. She'll turn up again before
tonight.'

'Don't worry?' she yells. 'What a stupid thing to say!
Of course I'm worried.'

'What do you want me to say, Malin?'

'Sometimes it's best to keep your mouth shut.'

'OK.'

They sit beside one another in silence. Malin lets her
anger settle in as her panic fades.

'There's nothing I can do,' she says. 'But I have to phone
Janne.'

'You can keep up the pressure on them,' Daniel says.
'Both of you.'

Malin nods.

'You won't write about this, will you?'

'Someone else can do that if the news gets out, if things don't get sorted out quickly.'

She takes some deep breaths, and he kisses her on the forehead. His lips feel soft and warm.

Then her phone rings.

Janne's number.

'Have you heard?'

His voice is weak, frightened.

'They just called.'

A panicky conversation follows, in which they speak without really hearing, and Malin feels like blaming Janne for encouraging Tove to go, but holds back, because no one would have been able to stop their daughter.

In the end the line falls silent. Malin looks at Daniel, who's staring out of the window and doesn't seem to want to intrude.

'I'll fly down,' Janne says.

'Don't be stupid.'

She hears him take a deep breath.

'We'll speak again when we know more,' he says, and hangs up.

Daniel strokes her cheek, and she takes hold of his hand.

Work, Malin thinks. She knows that's the only thing that can keep her together now.

She gets out of the car. Daniel makes no attempt to hold her back, and as she heads towards the other detectives, all gathered around Suliman Hajif's plastic-covered body, the feeling of unreality becomes almost overwhelming. It feels as if she's moving through a film of her own life, as if the trees, the ground beneath her feet, are merely artfully constructed pieces of scenery, as if the people up ahead of her are actors, and that she is going to have to play herself rather than actually be herself, because how, how on earth am I going to be truly present in a moment like this?

She forces herself to focus.

Where are you, Tove?

Nadja?

Where are the girls? If I find you alive, Nadja, Tove will be OK. That's right, isn't it?

I have to find you now.

Zeke, Elin, and Göran Möller are standing close together a few metres away from Karin Johannison. The treetops are moving above them, shading their faces in turn. The shifting light gives them a speckled appearance, and Malin can't help thinking that they look overwhelmed, that they don't seem to have any idea of where to start.

'I'm so sorry, Malin,' Elin says.

But Malin cuts her off.

'It's a private matter.'

'Calm down,' Göran says. 'Are you in a fit state to work, Malin?'

She looks at him. With her very darkest stare.

'OK,' Göran Möller says. 'Your decision.'

'Where do we go from here?' she asks.


In a small, cramped, third-floor flat in Berga, Suliman Hajif's parents are informed of his death a few hours later.

They scream out loud in the mint-scented living room. They insisted on offering the detectives tea before letting them explain why they were there.

Unsuspecting, hospitable.

Now that they have been told, Suliman's mother is howling, and Elin Sand knows that the howl will haunt her dreams for months to come.

The grief at its core.

She has Waldemar Ekenberg with her, and all he wants is to get out of the flat, leave this meagre dwelling, these alien people whose thoughts and grief he doesn't believe himself capable of or willing to understand.

He gives in to the impulse and leaves Elin alone with Hajif's parents, leaves her there with the crying and the panic, the questions she has to ask. When she emerges ten minutes later to find him standing in front of the block of flats, she marches over to him and says: 'You bloody coward.'

'Is that it?'

'That's it.'

And they set off, back into the May day, back into their investigative work, which – for everyone apart from Johan Jakobsson – means fruitless interviews with people close to Suliman Hajif, with his friends, with his presumed enemies. One of them is sitting in a cell in the custody unit in the bowels of the old barracks, wondering: Will it be my turn next?

The custody officer has told her about the latest murder, and Julianna Raad is suddenly pleased that she's where she is. At least I'm safe here, she thinks, because she knows it could easily be her next time.

She makes herself comfortable on her bunk. Pulls her knees up under her chin. Suliman Hajif.

I knew what he was up to.

Saying one thing in public whilst doing something completely different in private.

I hated him. I hate everything he stood for. But at least he stood for something real. However stupid it may have been, at least he took it seriously.

And soon he'll be buried. When his relatives are allowed to have the body.

I didn't want him to come to this sort of an end. No matter what he'd done. Human beings have to be better than that. Because what's to become of us otherwise?

★

Malin leans her head against the car window. Sees Linköping pass by outside. The uneven grey and white façade of Folkungavallen sports ground, the blocks of flats by the river, the former St Lars school, even greyer, and the petrol station at Braskens bridge.

She and Zeke are on their way to the mosque, to talk to the imam again. Malin called him a short while ago, and he told her he'd left Suliman in the mosque around ten o'clock, that Suliman used to lock up sometimes, that he'd been happy to trust him to do that.

So the imam could well be one of the last people to see Suliman Hajif alive.

He might know something.

But what?

She's just checked Max Friman's Twitter feed. Johan texted to tell her about it. At the top was a new post from Friman: *Hajif. Hard to say the world is a poorer place.*

They need to talk to him again. He's not telling us all he knows. Did he know that Peder Åkerlund's opinions hadn't really changed? Probably.

Waldemar can deal with him. They need his bluntness now, if they're to make any progress with this.

They drive past Johannelund.

Children are running to and fro in the playgrounds, sitting on swings or digging in sandpits, and the football pitches down by the Stångå River are busy, there must be some sort of tournament today.

Life goes on, in spite of everything that's happening.

She's trying not to think about Tove, but fails. She takes her mobile out and thinks about calling the aid agency, that Lisa Jansson woman, then wonders if she might hear something from the Foreign Office. Could things be that bad?

Because if they do contact her, things would have to be bad.

But the Foreign Office are completely useless, aren't they? They haven't managed to do a thing for Dawit Isaak. Now he's rotting in a stinking prison, and no doubt there are plenty of civil servants in the FO who think he's only got his big mouth to blame.

Good, Malin.

Let your mind wander.

She knows how Nadja's parents must feel. They're probably sitting at home now, frightened, worried, impotent. She feels like calling them, but what could she say?

She calls Göran Möller instead.

He answers.

'Have you seen Max Friman's latest tweet?' she asks.

'I've seen it.'

'Perhaps Waldemar should have a word with him?'

'He's on his way,' Göran Möller says. 'He might already be there.'

# 48

Waldemar Ekenberg parks outside the block of flats on Ladugatan.

The pale beige stucco is coming loose from the corners.

He hopes Max Friman is at home.

He can write whatever the hell he likes about Suliman Hajif, Waldemar thinks. And it's not as if what he's written isn't true. But that's not the point.

What does he know, and how can we find out?

Waldemar has found his way back to brutality. It livens him up again now. A year or so ago he felt tired of his own violent tendencies, but not any more. He skipped lunch today so his blood sugar should be low, just right for a job like this.

The flat is on the second floor. So this is where Peder Åkerlund spent his last evening alive, drinking beer and vodka.

Fair enough.

He rings the bell. Hears footsteps inside the flat.

Then silence.

And he shouts: 'Police. Open up.'

'What do you want?'

'To talk to you. Open up. Otherwise I'll break the door in.'

Scare the bastard, Waldemar thinks. And the door opens a crack, revealing Max Friman's face, and a pair of frightened eyes.

The security chain is still on.

'Can I see some ID?'

Waldemar shows his ID.

The chain comes off. The door opens fully.

'You can't be too careful,' Max Friman says, and Waldemar closes the door behind him. Then he clenches one fist, swings, and feels a crunch under his knuckles as his fist connects with Max Friman's nose.

The imam, Samid Samudra, is sitting with his legs crossed on the floor of the large prayer room. He's wearing a white kaftan, and Malin can't help finding the contrast of the white fabric against the patterned carpet beautiful.

Malin and Zeke are each sitting on a low stool. The imam looks at them, waiting for their questions, doesn't seem to want to say anything.

'Did you notice anything unusual when you went home last night?' Malin asks.

'Nothing at all. He said he was going to stay for a while. Look at the Internet.'

'And you went straight home?'

'I live just around the corner. I didn't see anything odd on my way home either.'

'Did Suliman have any enemies? Any that you were aware of?'

'No. He was very well-liked here. He was good for the younger boys.'

'Had anyone threatened him?'

The imam holds his arms out.

'He wouldn't have told me if they had.'

Malin looks for grief in Samudra's eyes, and believes she can see it. This was an older man trying to help a younger one find his way in life. That's all it was, isn't it?

'Can you think of anything we should know that might help our investigation?'

'No.'

'What about the recruitment of terrorists that he's said to have organised?' Zeke suggests.

'Those were just malicious rumours.'

'The recruitment of fighters and suicide bombers? Could there have been any truth in that at all?'

'Lies. As far as I'm aware,' Samid Samudra says, and the look in his eyes changes. Becomes defensive, almost aggressive. 'Anyway, what does that have to do with anything?'

Zeke, irritated: 'Let us be the judge of that.'

And now Malin leans forward and says: 'Two young men have been murdered, one of them Suliman. A young girl is missing. We don't yet know what might be relevant or not, but we're trying to find out. We want to catch whoever murdered Suliman. So please, tell us what you know. Is it true that he was recruiting suicide bombers? Was that newspaper right?'

'I don't know,' the imam says. 'If he was, they would never have told me. They understand that I have to remain absolutely neutral on any issue that isn't strictly in accordance with Swedish law.'

'They?' Malin asks. 'So he was involved in something, along with a number of others?'

The imam smiles. And holds his mouth in that stiff smile.

'You were supposed to give them your tacit blessing?'

'I wouldn't have been able to do anything.'

'So it did really happen? What about those terrorism-motivated trips?'

'I know that Suliman went to Yemen once. Some sort of training camp.'

'Tell us,' Zeke says.

'That's all I know.'

Malin looks around the room. It must have once been the storeroom of the business that used to occupy the premises. It's well-maintained, the white walls look freshly painted. She can feel that they're fumbling for clues: what would terrorism-inspired travel have to do with the murderer's game? Or should that be murderers? She has no idea, but everything is connected to everything else somehow or other. One connection could lead to another, and they have to take whatever they can find in the deepest wells of emotion.

That's always where the truth is hiding.

The imam scratches his beard as Malin changes position on her stool.

'Did he travel alone?' she asks.

The imam sits silently.

'There was someone with him, wasn't there?'

The imam stands up and leaves the large prayer room. A couple of minutes later he returns.

He hands Malin a note.

'I never gave you this,' he says, and walks out again.

Waldemar Ekenberg prefers to pay his violent visits on his own.

That way there aren't any witnesses.

And his 'victims' are always more scared when he's alone, when they realise that they're on their own with a man who loves violence.

He's dragged Max Friman into the living room, and has given the cry-baby a towel to staunch his nosebleed. He chose a white one so the blood would show up nicely. Feeble bastards like Max Friman can never handle the sight of their own blood.

'Did you know that Peder Åkerlund's opinions never really changed?'

'What do you think?'

'That you did.'

Max Friman nods.

Smirks.

'This is serious,' Waldemar yells. 'Who the fuck do you think you are? Huh? A man gets killed and you tweet about it like it's a good thing. And you know what? That makes us think you know something. That you might have some idea of who could have killed him.'

Max Friman looks up from the sofa with a stubborn expression on his face.

Maybe he's not so feeble after all.

'Why would I know that? Suliman Hajif was just a fucking Islamist moron when it came down to it. They've got no business being in our country, and that's what I wrote. Everyone knew he wasn't remotely moderate.'

'How did you know that?'

Max Friman doesn't answer.

'You wrote that the world isn't a poorer place.'

Max Friman looks down at the floor, appears to think, then turns his head towards Waldemar.

'And I don't think it is, either.'

Hatred in his eyes now.

He definitely isn't the joker I thought he was, Waldemar thinks. There's more to him than fear and cowardice.

'What were you doing last night?'

'My girlfriend was here. You can ask her. But watch out. What she'll tell you will make you doubt your own masculinity.'

Waldemar laughs.

What a little shit.

'I will,' he says.

'You don't imagine I've got anything to do with the murder?'

Waldemar ignores the question.

Maybe you killed Hajif, but aren't guilty of the other crimes. Maybe you knew enough to mislead us?

No, that's hardly likely.

Waldemar's own confusion starts to make him angry.

I want to get something out of you, anything at all. Let's see how cocky you really are.

So he takes a few steps towards the sofa and raises his fist once again towards Max Friman, who jerks back instinctively.

'I'll report you, you bastard!' he yells.

Waldemar sticks his fingers in his nostrils and jerks him to his feet, then stares deep into his eyes. Breathing coffee breath on him.

'Do that and you can join your friend Peder in hell.'

'I'll tell you something if you let me go,' Max Friman whimpers.

Waldemar lets him fall back to the sofa, and watches him take several deep breaths before he starts to talk.

Malin and Zeke are standing outside the mosque. Zeke has the mosque's laptop under his arm. The sky is clear, and the sun's rays are reflecting off the windows of the block of flats behind them.

They look at each other.

The note they were given by Samid Samudra. They'll look into it, but their intuition is telling them to pause here.

'Where do you think he went after he left here last night?' Malin says.

'Probably down to those houses, then off towards the road.'

'Or else he went through the woods and headed home that way. That's the shortest route.'

'It must have been dark.'

'He might have had a light on his mobile. I'm going to take a look.'

She heads up into the trees. The ground is dry as she scans it. She sees nothing, and after a hundred metres or so she reaches a narrow paved footpath.

She closes her eyes.

Tries to hear something, feel something, anything at all. But nothing happens.

She goes back to Zeke. The neutral expression on his face can't hide his uncertainty.

'How does this all fit together?' he says.

A name on a piece of paper. An address in Ryd.

'Peder used the party's money to pay Suliman Hajif,' Max Friman whispers. 'He paid for plane tickets for six guys from Ryd who wanted to go to Syria. He thought it was a good way to get rid of the bastards. The end justified the means. He said it didn't matter who blew who up down there. At least we'd be shot of them up here.'

'How did it happen?' Waldemar asks, tapping his fingers together.

'Easy. He transferred the money to an account at a Saudi bank. And from there the plane tickets were paid for via a travel agent in Germany, I think.'

Pragmatic. Sophisticated, Waldemar thinks. Like some latter-day ruddy CIA.

'So you're saying Suliman and Peder were allies?'

'Yes.'

'And they joined forces to send fighters and suicide bombers to Syria?'

'Yes.'

All of a sudden they have a wealth of new suspects who can be connected to the two murders. Relatives of the six Linköping boys who went off to war and may have blown themselves to pieces. Relatives of their victims in Syria who happen to be living in Sweden.

But where does Nadja Lundin fit into the picture?

Is she a smokescreen? What if she actually has nothing to do with this? Was that little coffin containing the tongue merely a game designed to confuse us? And, if so, is the game over now?

*You can play for a while.*

'Did anyone apart from you know that Peder was mixed up in this?'

'No, not as far as I know.'

'Sorry about your nose,' Waldemar says, and turns to leave. Before he opens the front door he says: 'But you'd probably agree that it was necessary?'

# 49

The yellow brick buildings seem to be sagging under the invisible weight of the blue sky. The white panelled balconies are stained with rust, laundry jostling for space with all manner of clutter.

Malin pulls open the door to the block of flats on Rydsvägen, hears Zeke's breathing behind her.

The imam gave them this address, gave them the name Mehmet Khoni.

Waldemar has just phoned to tell them the results of his interrogation of Max Friman.

We're definitely going to have to ask this Khoni guy about that, Malin thinks as she climbs the speckled stone steps to the first floor.

She rings the bell.

No response.

Silence inside the flat.

Where are you, Mehmet? Are you lying somewhere with your tongue cut out?

'He's not here,' Zeke says. 'Let's go back to the station.'

It's already half past eight in the evening by the time they all gather in the meeting room. Göran Möller has written the murder victims' names on the whiteboard in large letters:

*Peder Åkerlund*
*Suliman Hajif*
*Mutual interests. Both liars.*

A bit further down, Nadja Lundin's name, followed by a question mark.

Göran Möller is sitting at the end of the table. He looks around at the detectives he's been put in charge of. Waldemar Ekenberg seems to have perked up, but Börje Svärd looks like he mostly just wants to get away. Johan is alert, Elin Sand looks tired, lets out a big yawn, and in both Malin and Zeke he detects a deep frustration, as if they're both wearing blinkers that they're trying to pull off.

Malin. He doesn't know if she's heard any more about Tove.

But he can't think about that now. She's chosen to work, even though the worry must be driving her mad. She seems to be focused, she's looking at me as if she wants me to help her. But how? I can only be her boss. Nothing else. Whatever Sven Sjöman meant to her, I'm neither willing nor capable of filling that role.

Malin's phone rings. She yanks it out and clicks to take the call, gets quickly to her feet and says: 'It's OK, it's fine, I can talk now,' and leaves the room.

Malin hears the voice at the other end of the line. Some civil servant at the Foreign Office, a Kent Persson, who's apologising for calling so late. He asks her to hear him out.

I don't have any other choice, Malin thinks, looking off towards the end of the brown-painted corridor. She asks: 'Has she been found?'

Kent Persson says: 'No. We haven't yet been able to localise our missing citizens.'

'So what are you doing, then? In order to localise them?'

'We're deploying our resources as best we can.'

'What resources?'

'I'm afraid I can't reveal that. I understand your

anxiety, but the most important thing right now is that this doesn't get out, that it's withheld from the media so that we can get on with our work undisturbed.'

'Do you know what's happened?'

'I'll be honest with you,' Kent Persson says. 'We don't have any idea. Their truck was found abandoned three hours ago. Unfortunately there was no sign of our missing citizens by the vehicle.'

'Is that all you've got?'

Silence on the line. Kent Persson, a young man, judging by his voice, has no answer.

Malin feels like screaming at him, but knows that anger would do nothing but harm at this point. And then there's Janne, the idiot, who wants to go down there. Has he set off? But not even he would do something like that. He ought to go. Should I call him?

'Let me know if anything changes,' she says, and ends the call.

She stands motionless in the corridor outside the meeting room. Doesn't feel up to calling Janne.

Tries to hear what they're talking about in there now.

Can't hear anything.

So she puts her ear to the door and hears her colleagues' voices as if from a great distance.

'Can we get hold of the names of the victims of any suicide bombers?'

'Impossible. That would take months.'

'What does the link between Hajif and Åkerlund really mean?'

'It makes it less likely that the murders are the result of any disagreement between them. Seeing as they were using each other.'

'That could have gone bad.'

Johan: 'We need to check out the parents and relatives of the men who've gone to Syria, either to blow themselves to pieces or get killed by jihadists. They had plenty of reasons to hate both Hajif and Åkerlund if they knew about the way they were working together.'

'I'll get hold of the names,' Göran Möller says, and Malin knows why she was looking at him a few minutes ago. For the paternal look Sven used to give her when things were rough. She'll never have anything like that from Göran Möller, but that's fine.

'The fact that they both presented a particular public image of themselves whilst thinking and acting in a completely contradictory way – what does that mean?' Göran Möller throws the question out into the room.

'That the murderer doesn't like hypocrites,' Johan Jakobsson says. 'He wrote about masks, after all.'

Then silence.

Who likes hypocrites? Malin thinks. Again.

'What about Nadja Lundin, then?' Göran asks.

Silence inside the room.

Even more silent within Malin.

Is this about vengeance? she wonders.

It could be. But what sort? The sort of vengeance I can recognise and understand, or some other sort of vengeance?

The calf's tongue with the message, the amputated tongue, acid in the Broca's area. The emails. If a relative wanted to avenge the death of a son or other family member, why all these crazy theatricals?

Vengeance and love belong together. Both are coloured red.

If Tove doesn't turn up, I shall search for her to the ends of the earth, and I'll rip the heart out of anyone who's harmed her.

Voices. Quiet, only just audible: 'The recordings from the security cameras are on their way.'

'We didn't get anything from Peder Åkerlund's call

history. And Forensics have looked at Max Friman's computer now – nothing there either.'

'Suliman Hajif's mobile?' Waldemar wonders.

'He didn't make any calls from his mobile at all yesterday,' Göran Möller says. 'We already know that much. And evidently he didn't have a computer of his own. But Forensics are going to examine the mosque's computer as soon as they have time.'

'Any ideas where Mehmet Khoni might be? What could he know?'

'We're knocking on doors in the area around the mosque. There aren't any doors to knock on close to where the body was found.'

'The man in the hoodie?'

'Damn it! We need to make some progress. Nadja could still be alive.'

Malin opens the door.

'They haven't found Tove,' she says, and sits down at her place, and looks out at the pre-school's empty playground, the little playhouse where the children love to hide, before coming out after a while as apparently completely different people.

## 50

Mehmet Khoni pulls up his jeans, adjusts his Metallica T-shirt, then walks into the police station, goes up to the reception desk, and gives his name.

Samudra called him. Said the police would be paying him a visit, that they wanted to talk to him, told him what had happened to Suliman.

Madness, he thought then. Madness, he thinks now. It feels good to be inside the station, he kept looking over his shoulder the whole way here, wondering what was going on behind him.

At first he thought about leaving town, going to stay with relatives in Malmö, but then he realised it made more sense to talk to the police. He hasn't done anything illegal, and if he can help them catch Suliman's killer, so much the better.

The woman in reception smiles at him.

'I'll call Malin Fors.'

He knows who she is. Has read about her in the paper.

Mehmet Khoni turns around.

Looks out across the car park. The reporters hanging about outside look bored. The light from the street lamps makes the cars shimmer in the twilight. White, red, and silver, and the darkest, sparkling black.

So he came, Malin thinks as she walks towards the entrance through the open-plan office. She'd had a feeling he might, had been hoping he would. She knows he must be feeling frightened if he didn't have anything to do with the murders.

She's expecting a replica of Suliman Hajif, a long beard and a kaftan. Instead she finds a handsome young man in perfectly ordinary clothes.

He's smiling at me. And what a fucking smile.

Doesn't look like he's carrying a weapon.

'Mehmet Khoni?'

Khoni nods.

'Malin Fors.'

She holds out her hand and he shakes it.

Should I search him?

No.

'You wanted to talk to me?'

'Yes. Let's go and sit down,' Malin says, and leads him through the office and into one of the small interview rooms at the back of the building.

They sit down, and Malin tells him what they know about the link between Hajif and Åkerlund, about the payments and plane tickets. Mehmet Khoni leans back.

'I helped with recruitment,' he says. 'Organised their travel, made sure the money transfers worked.'

'I don't even know if that's illegal,' Malin says, 'what you did.'

'It isn't. People are free to travel wherever they like. I had nothing to do with the purpose of the trips. And what they got up to once they got there doesn't come under Swedish jurisdiction, does it?'

'Why did you do it?'

'Money. No other reason. I've got an aunt back home in Lebanon who needs an expensive operation.'

He seems likeable, Malin thinks. Charming, even, and that charm has driven young men to their deaths.

'How did they come into contact with each other, Hajif and Åkerlund?'

'Åkerlund had received some threatening letters that he

thought had come from Suliman, but they hadn't. He suggested that we work together instead of fighting. We all wanted to get these guys down to Syria. And he had the money.'

Smart, Malin thinks. Creative, in an extremely warped way.

'I can give you a list,' Mehmet Khoni says. 'Of the people we sent. I don't know what's happened to them, but they're unlikely to be coming back. Maybe you ought to talk to their families?'

Malin pushes a sheet of paper across the table.

Mehmet Khoni writes down six names.

How much death and destruction can these people have spread? Mehmet Khoni's actions? Suliman's? Peder Åkerlund's confused contribution?

All the same: while Hajif made me absolutely furious, I'm being charmed by Khoni. He's using all his techniques on me, I know that, but even so, I can't resist.

She asks him about his alibis for the nights of the murders, and whether he knows Nadja Lundin. He has alibis, says he was at home with his uncle, gives her the number, encourages her to check. He had never heard of Nadja before seeing her in the paper over the past few days.

'Did Suliman ever receive any threats from anyone related to the men you sent to Syria?'

'Not that I know of.'

'Did any of them know about the connection between you and Åkerlund?'

'I don't think anyone knew apart from us and him. You can appreciate how sensitive it is.'

'The imam?'

Mehmet smiles but doesn't answer.

'What did you think about the fact that he was presenting an entirely different public image?'

'He was smart. That's all. I think he genuinely thought

it made sense to become integrated here. And then shift society onto a more Muslim direction from within.'

'Anything else?'

Mehmet thinks. Then he says: 'He said he'd seen a black van. He thought it was following him. I remembered that when I heard he was dead.'

'When was this?'

'Six months ago, maybe. He never mentioned it again after that.'

'What make of van was it?'

'No idea.'

The tyre tracks Karin found were probably left by a van. We ought to check out everyone in Linköping who owns a black van. But the database doesn't allow you to search by colour. Which means we'll end up with a list of thousands of van owners.

'How about you? Any threats? Strange vehicles?'

Mehmet Khoni gives a wry smile and shakes his head.

He can see straight through me, Malin thinks. He seems to know how her mind works, and says: 'I've never been as devout as Suliman. I don't care about what's happening in Syria. If you ask me, misogyny and all that other crap is just stupid. Anyone can see things are a fuck of a lot better here than they are in the Arabic world.'

They stand up and leave the room, and she guides Mehmet Khoni back towards reception. It's time for him to go home.

When he realises what she's going to do, he stops abruptly.

'You don't think I'm going to walk away from here now? With a madman like that on the loose out there? He snatched Åkerlund and Suliman, and now he's going to get me. There's no way I'm walking out of here.'

'You can't stay here,' Malin says. 'That's not how it works.'

'How does it work, then?'

She looks out at the car park, and at the impenetrable darkness beyond it.

'I haven't got anywhere else to go.'

'Your uncle?'

'I'd be found there.'

'OK,' she says. 'Follow me.'

She takes him downstairs to the passageway that leads to the custody unit. She explains the situation to the weary custody office, who mutters something in response, something about it being against the rules, but OK, just for tonight.

Soon they're standing outside a cell. The guard fumbles with the key, opens the door, and then walks away.

'Here you are,' Malin says. 'Leave the door ajar, because if you lock yourself in, only the guard can let you out.'

'Thanks,' Mehmet Khoni says.

Then he disappears into the cell and closes the door behind him, and Malin hears the lock click.

Malin walks slowly through the corridor past the other cells. The time is now half past eleven, and she's tired, but doesn't want to go home yet.

There's still something she hasn't done, and outside one of the cells she sees the name *Raad, Julianna.*

She stops. Opens the hatch, and sees the young woman sitting on her bunk, wide awake, and staring defiantly back at her.

'You,' she says.

'Can I come in?'

'Sure. Like you have to ask permission.'

A few moments later the custody officer has opened the door to let Malin in, and now the two women are sitting side by side in the cell.

'Did you know about Hajif and Åkerlund's dealings with each other? And the fact that they weren't who they were pretending to be?'

Julianna nods.

'Why didn't you say anything? Hajif might still be alive if you had.'

She shrugs her shoulders.

'Perhaps that's why.'

To you this is a war, isn't it? Malin thinks.

'You don't remember anything else that might be important?' Malin asks. 'I mean, you've had plenty of time to think down here.'

Julianna Raad takes a deep breath.

'This is something, actually,' she says. 'I saw a man staring at me several times last autumn. Like he was following me.'

'Do you remember what he looked like?'

'He was in his forties, maybe, average looks, brown hair down to here.'

Julianna holds one hand up to her shoulders.

'There was something weird about him.'

'Was he wearing a hoodie?'

'No.'

'Where did this happen?'

'I don't remember. The Gyllen Café, maybe. Or the café at the library? I was spending a lot of time there back then. It could well have been the library café.'

'Are you sure?'

Julianna Raad leans forward, turns her head to the side, and looks Malin in the eye.

'I'm not sure of anything. Maybe this man only exists in my imagination. Maybe my subconscious is inventing things to help me get out of here?'

'You mean you're saying things you think we want to hear?'

'Have you ever been shut in one of these cells? For several days?'

Malin doesn't answer.

She remembers the room at the treatment centre. The cramped little room where she had to spend the first few days all on her own, with just her thoughts for company. Her angst and anger. She spent the time talking to herself, but the words were meaningless because no one was listening. That room will be with her for ever.

What are you saying, Julianna? Malin thinks.

What is this one of the investigation's voices saying?

What lonely, dark rooms will it lead to?

Svartmåla.

Where Nadja disappeared from.

Viveca Crafoord has a house there. I'll talk to her.

Hear what she has to say about a person like the one I'm trying to find.

# 51

*Thursday, 18 May*

The forest lights up in the beam of the car's headlamps. The trunks and darkness between them, the moss and undergrowth, the soil they're growing in.

The coffin containing the tongue.

Are you in a coffin, Nadja?

Where does that image come from? Malin wonders, as she squeezes the wheel more tightly and forces herself to stay awake: she mustn't fall asleep while she's driving.

I want to see you come running out of the forest, Nadja. Not like Maria Murvall, naked and raped and covered in sores, but in one piece, intact, both physically and mentally. Promise me that's how you'll come to me.

You're not dead.

I know that.

Neither are you, Tove.

Janne phoned a short while ago. But she didn't take the call. She knows she's on her own with this. As is he. If he's decided to go down to Africa she can't stop him, and wouldn't want to either. Perhaps he can find Tove. Good luck, off you go.

She looks along the forest road.

Suliman Hajif saw a black van six months ago.

Julianna Raad saw a weird man at roughly the same time.

The person in the hoodie outside the school.

Are they one and the same man? If so, who?

Malin called Viveca as soon as she got back to the police station from the custody unit.

'Where are you?'

'Out in the country.'

'Can I come over?'

It's been several years since they were last in touch, when the brilliant psychologist helped her with a case. Viveca must have been able to hear the seriousness in Malin's voice.

'Of course you can. I'm on my own out here, my husband's in the city.'

'I need your help.'

'I do read the papers, Malin. So I can understand that.'

'I'll be there in half an hour.'

'You remember where the house is?'

'How could I forget?'

She drives into Svartmåla, past Nadja's family's summer cottage, the house from which she went missing. It's dark and deserted now, and there are lights on in just a couple of the houses in the area. No one noticed anything the night Nadja disappeared.

She carries on past the dark gardens for three hundred metres, some of them wild, some neatly maintained, until she reaches Viveca Crafoord's architect-designed wood-and-concrete box.

The front door opens, and there's Viveca, standing in the light of the headlamps.

The wrinkles on her face are a bit deeper, her shoulder-length hair a bit greyer, but the energy and nobility in her bearing are the same.


'You don't mind if I have a drink?' Viveca asks. She doesn't bother to wait for an answer, and pours herself a whisky from the decanter on the sideboard.

'No problem,' Malin says. 'Have you got a glass of water?'

Viveca disappears into the kitchen and comes back with an espresso and a glass of cold mineral water.

'You might need this,' she says, smiling at the espresso.

They sit down on the comfy white sofas, and Malin notices that the art has changed since last time, it's more contemporary now, must have cost a fortune from the fancy galleries in Stockholm.

Viveca leans forward and takes a sip of her whisky.

'How can I help you?'

Malin explains about the case they're working on, the murders, the abduction, the messages, the brutality, the links to Syria, and the feeling of utter confusion, the fact that they don't know where to start looking, which threads they should follow, and that nothing is getting any clearer, either to her or the other detectives.

'What sort of person are we looking for? Who would be capable of something like this? A parent exacting revenge for the loss of their child?'

There's a noise from the forest outside the house. Malin thinks she can hear scratching, but knows it's just her imagination.

'Parents don't usually take revenge like that,' Viveca says. 'That stems from a much simpler type of rage. I'd imagine that you'd want a less ambiguous course of action if you were taking revenge for your child.'

'So what do you think, then?'

Malin can feel how tired she is. She wants Viveca to reveal the truth to her, here and now, give her the name of the murderer, and tell her where they can find Nadja Lundin.

'I think you should be looking for someone who felt very exposed as a child,' Viveca says. 'These games could be a way of establishing control, power. The violence seems to be closely connected to the underlying motivation, and could be a way of looking for love, even if that sounds very odd. He might be re-enacting things he himself has experienced. In some ways he sees no difference between violence and love. Perhaps the violence also gives him a degree of sexual satisfaction.'

'A sexually-motivated lunatic?'

Viveca shrugs.

'That's probably not all that likely, really. If that were the case, the corpses would show signs of sexual assault. Another thought that occurred to me is that he might have been beaten to make him be quiet.'

'And now he wants to make himself heard.'

'Something like that. I'm just speculating, Malin. And the question is, what does he want to say? I've got no idea about how he chooses his victims.'

'You keep saying "he"?'

'I'd be very surprised if it was a woman.'

'How old do you think he is?'

'Somewhere between eighteen and forty-five, but obviously that's a guess.'

'Marital status?'

'Single. Incapable of an intimate relationship with another person.'

'Where should we look?'

'Go back in time. Look at old cases of abused children. Talk to Social Services.'

'And Nadja?'

'I've met her,' Viveca says. 'She had coffee here once. Smart girl. Full of life, plenty of opinions about the world.'

Malin smiles.

'What do you think about her?'

'I think she's alive. At least, I want to think she is.'

Malin takes a sip of the espresso. The bitter liquid tastes perfect at this moment of exhaustion.

'The same man?'

'It looks like it.'

'Why would he keep her alive?'

Viveca shuts her eyes, nods to herself.

'To demonstrate his power. To give the game another dimension. But there's a risk that he'll kill her as soon as he gets fed up. Maybe he saw her being mean when she was playing with someone else, and wants to give her a taste of her own medicine.'

'You think it's urgent?'

'You know it is.'

'The two victims presented one image of their ideologies in public whilst actually believing the exact opposite. What does that mean?'

'If the murderer knows about that, he may have experienced something similar. Perhaps he's been misled, profoundly let down. And he probably has a dual personality himself, of course, someone who appears to be perfectly ordinary in many ways. Serial killers usually are.'

The whisky on the table. The amber-coloured liquid. Shimmering, and Malin wants to reach her hand out, grab the glass, and down it in one.

'Is it hard?'

'Yes.'

'I can see that.'

'Every day.'

And Malin comes close to telling her about Tove, can feel anxiety tearing her apart, but she says nothing, wants to keep this discussion clear and defined.

'What could he have done with Nadja? Raped her? Locked her up somewhere? Buried her alive in the forest? We did find that buried coffin with a calf's tongue in it, after all.'

Viveca appears to ponder this, but Malin knows she's had the answer ready since the start of the conversation.

'Like I said, I think he's keeping her alive somehow. And that he's enjoying the fact that no one can hear her scream for help.'

# 52

I can hear her scream. Inside me, at least.

What would be the point of this game otherwise?

I'm the only one who can hear her voice, the sense of impotence it conveys. I can recognise myself in that feeling. In the tone of voice rather than the pointless words.

And that feeling, I can use it. I can take it by the hand, go back in time to that room, and there I can take my own hand and say: Everything's going to be OK.

Everything's OK.

I tried to wake Mum up, but it was impossible. I whispered in her ear that she could say whatever she wanted, as long as she woke up.

I understood who Dad was. How he had misused words. What falseness was.

Nadja Lundin.

Not as lovely as everyone seems to think. I saw her behaving stupidly, making fun of people. And that's when I had the idea. Of playing a game with her and the police, the way the police played with you, Mum.

I hear Nadja, and believe the lies. I fall silent and play, and write a new message. Destroying the hypocrites.

That way I can give you your words back, Mum. And if I do that, all the words will have their right meanings again.

I read what I've written.

Words are like worms crawling out of the ground after heavy rain. They think they've reached salvation, only to be crushed beneath a little boy's boots.

I love hearing her scream.
The warm hand in mine.
Mum's hand, before it grew cold.

## 53

Let me out. I don't want to die here. I want to be able to move again, I don't want to lie here in my own excrement, howling, and you hear me, through the earth.

It feels damp now. Has it been raining? Or am I in the jungle?

But I have to get out. Otherwise I'll die.

I'm dying, Mum.

And Malin imagines she can hear the words as a whisper in her third dream that night. She thinks it's Tove who's whispering, and Malin is running through a dark jungle where snakes snap at her legs and leeches want to penetrate her body, and unknown predators from long ago call after her: 'She's dying, Malin.'

'She's dying, and it's your fault.'

Then she reaches a clearing.

Nothing growing on the ground, just earth, wet earth, dry earth, and she kneels down in the middle of the clearing and starts digging with her hands. Her nails are torn off, blood pours from her fingertips down into the earth, and she digs and digs, and in the end she is standing in what will one day be her grave.

She tries to climb out. But the edges are slippery, because the rain has reached the jungle. She can't get a grip, and now wet earth is being shovelled over her, and she screams, falls to the bottom of the grave, feels the earth fill her mouth, and she screams, everything turns black, and she screams, and hears Daniel's voice: 'Wake up, Malin. Wake up, for God's sake!'

His arm around her.

Sweat. Mine or his? Mine.

'I'm sorry, I'm sorry, I'm sorry.'

He holds me.

He holds me tightly, and I want him to go on doing that.

I couldn't manage without you, Daniel. Nothing bad must ever happen to you.

Two kilometres away the doorbell rings in Börje Svärd's villa.

Kristina Nederdahl called him in the middle of the night, said she couldn't hold back any longer, wanted to see him, said yes when he asked.

He opens the door.

Sees her smiling face.

Her whole being is beautiful and expectant, and he lets her in, takes hold of her shoulders while they're still in the hall, and she turns around and her lips meet his, and he feels something burst inside him, feels that something about this moment is right, right in a way it hasn't been since Anna died.

## 54

Malin reads the online newspapers on her laptop as she stands at the kitchen worktop. She's just sent an email to the others, telling them what Viveca said about their potential perpetrator.

She drinks coffee. Feels how tired she is. It's just past six o'clock, she's slept for four hours. That will have to do.

She reads the updated version of Daniel's article, the one she knows he wrote at the scene where they found Suliman Hajif.

The conclusions he draws are fairly detailed, and Malin wonders if they seem far-fetched given the information he had. Does it look as if he knows anything he shouldn't?

She feels like going into the bedroom and waking him up. He's betrayed a confidence.

Then she reads the article again. Calms down. I'm just being paranoid, she thinks. Then she reads his opinion piece. It's bold, almost to the point of being foolhardy. What if the murderer reads it? Gets it into his head to silence Daniel? But it needed to be written. We can't let ourselves be frightened into tolerating violence without a fight.

She closes the laptop and drinks the last of her coffee.

She goes out into the hall. Looks for her keys in her jacket, and finds a piece of paper that wasn't there before.

She takes the note out. Unfolds it.

Daniel's handwriting.

'You're the best.'

Damn.

Now I've started to cry.

She holds the note tightly in her hand, forces back her tears, and leaves the flat. Fifteen minutes later she reaches the station after a brisk walk during which she does everything she can not to think about Tove.

Instead she soaks up the spring morning.

Nothing new from the aid agency. Nor from the Foreign Office, and she's doing her best to turn Tove's disappearance into a dream, a non-fact, and as her heart begins to beat faster in time with her rapid pace, she can feel that she's almost succeeding. She can hear nothing but birds. Their heartfelt song.

Only Zeke and Johan are there before her when she walks through the door, then she hears her mobile buzz.

She stops on the way to her desk, takes out her phone, clicks to open the text.

A sudden chill runs through her body.

Geographical coordinates.

Then a poem:

You might find beneath the earth
Something hidden inside a curse.
Don't pause to worry,
You need to hurry.

Malin calls the others over.

'I've just had a new message.'

She shows them her mobile. The message is from a concealed number.

'Pull up those coordinates, Johan,' Zeke says. 'Malin and I will head out there at once.'

From the corner of her eye Malin sees Elin Sand arrive at the station.

'We'll take her along,' Malin says. 'There might be a lot of digging.'

She raises her voice: 'You're coming with us, Elin. Hurry up.'

Johan taps at his computer and brings up the coordinates on his screen, then a picture.

It shows a location just south of Linköping.

Grävlingskorset, outside Bankekind.

Is there any folklore connected to this place like there was with Stenkullamotet? Is there another enchanted oak tree? Malin wonders. She isn't aware of anything, nor are the others.

The game goes on.

Someone who seems to be able to do anything, to be everywhere.

'Come on, we're going,' she calls out.

Perhaps they can still save Nadja?

'Johan,' Malin says calmly. 'I want you to look through old cases of child abuse that might have been reported by Social Services. Specifically the sort where it looks like someone has tried to keep a child quiet. A child that would now be somewhere between eighteen and forty-five.'

'You mean shutting a child in a cupboard, that sort of thing?'

'Something like that. But broader than that, slaps across the mouth, muzzles, things like that.'

'OK.'

'And see if you can find out where that text came from.'

Zeke and Elin are standing by their desks gathering their things, strapping on their service weapons.

'Hurry up!'

A few minutes later the three of them are sitting in a police car, and Malin calls Karin to tell her to meet them at Grävlingskorset.

*

It takes them a few minutes to identify where the ground has recently been disturbed. It's an area of bare earth approximately one square metre in size, in the shade of a large birch tree, hidden behind a clump of trees some distance from one of the three roads that meet at Grävlingskorset.

It takes them half an hour to dig down one metre, and they're sweating in the heat and sunlight, cursing the dust that swirls up from the dry earth. But they go on digging.

Because they know there's something here.

Nadja.

Perhaps the answer to our questions is hiding underground.

Perhaps you're here.

Zeke's spade is the first to hit something hard.

Should we be more careful? Malin thinks, wiping the sweat from her brow. He could have left a bomb here. Some other sort of trap. Who knows what a mind like that could come up with?

'It's a coffin,' Karin says. 'Like the last one.'

Carefully they clear around the coffin. Karin finishes the job. Using a brush she removes the last of the soil before lifting the coffin out of the grave with gloved hands.

'I'm going to open it right away. The rest of you get back. At least twenty metres.'

'You're mad,' Malin says. 'I'll do it.'

'My turn to risk my life,' Karin says.

'Not a chance.'

'Let her do it,' Elin says, and Zeke looks as if he's going to protest, but stops himself.

'OK,' Malin says.

She, Zeke, and Elin go and stand on the other side of the road, taking cover behind a stone wall.

'Heads down,' Karin calls. 'And keep them down.'

Malin crouches down beside Zeke. He rubs the top of

his shaved head. Clenches his jaw. But there's no trace of fear in his eyes.

No anxiety.

This needs to be done.

'You can come out now,' Karin cries. 'Be careful. Try not to disturb the ground any more than we already have.'

They walk back to her, and she points down at the open coffin on the ground beneath the birch tree.

Blue and grey flesh.

The sight is easier now, the second time.

'It's a human tongue,' Karin says. 'My guess is that it's Suliman Hajif's. The cut seems to match.'

As if this were the most normal situation in the world, Malin asks: 'Any message?'

'Not in the coffin, but possibly inside the tongue,' Karin replies, and Elin Sand says: 'I never want to get used to this.'

'You won't need to,' Zeke says. 'We've got to put a stop to this madness.'

Karin is now crouched down beside the coffin, pulling at the tongue with a pair of tweezers.

Then she takes a scalpel from a pink case Malin hasn't seen before and carefully cuts the blue-grey flesh, into what seems to be a cavity.

She puts the scalpel back in the case. Picks up the tweezers again, and pulls out a damp, bloody piece of paper. She puts it down on the lid of the coffin, unfolds it using the tweezers, as casually as if she'd never done anything else, as if this was what she was born to do.

*Is it lonelier to be with people who ought to love you, or to be buried alive?*

A car drives past behind them. A black van, Malin thinks before turning around.

But it's a white Mazda. A woman at the wheel. Malin makes a mental note of the registration number.

She reads the message again.

So you've buried her alive.

Which means you're alive, Nadja. Alive, and the very loneliest of people.

## 55

A thousand things to look for, check, work through.

What's most urgent?

He doesn't know why, but Johan Jakobsson puts everything else to one side and starts searching through the old files that have been digitised in recent years. He loses himself in his work, oblivious to the other people in the open-plan office.

He tries search-words: *child, abuse, social services, cupboard, muzzle*. All of them at the same time: no matches.

He removes cupboard and muzzle.

Hundreds of matches.

He adds broken teeth.

Five matches.

He opens the files, reads through them. The first concerns a small girl who was assaulted by her father in Ljungsbro twenty years ago. She had been given a recorder by her grandmother, and her father got fed up with the noise when he was drunk, and hit the girl in the mouth several times with the recorder.

A case that's over thirty years old catches Johan's attention. A seven-year-old boy whose parents thought he talked too much.

'He never shut up.'

Eventually they started to hit him every time he spoke without permission. First on his body, then on his face as well. When the school reported his parents to Social Services, a medical examination found more than seventy bruises on the boy's body. And he'd had a number of teeth knocked out. He ended up being placed in a foster home.

A punch for a word, a word for a punch.

Johan rests his head in his hands and feels the warmth of his own cheeks, thinks of his children, and how they've never come close to anything worse than a sharp reprimand, and how bad he feels on those occasions. He thinks of his daughter, it could be her who's missing, and he feels grateful that they only have an illness to deal with, a terrible illness, but a manageable one.

I need to show this case to Göran Möller, Johan thinks. We might be able to check the boy out. It's a long shot, but it could be worth it. And it fits in with what that psychologist said.

Göran Möller makes himself more comfortable in the chair that once belonged to Sven Sjöman. The white façade of the hospital is visible through the window behind him, people in the car park.

Johan Jakobsson is sitting on the other side of the desk looking at Göran Möller's strangely comforting face. He actually succeeds in spreading calm in spite of the pervading chaos, and Johan realises that he's struck lucky with his new boss, that what drove him out of Helsingborg was just an unfortunate accident.

Göran Möller is no racist.

He's a very capable police officer.

'It might be worth looking into,' he says. 'But tread carefully. He's probably living a perfectly ordinary life somewhere.'

'I'll be careful,' Johan says.

'Malin's called,' Göran says. 'They've found what looks like Hajif's tongue.'

'Another message?'

Göran Möller nods, and tells him what the note said.

'That doesn't leave us any the wiser,' Johan says.

'Malin's sure he's buried Nadja alive somewhere.'

Johan Jakobsson says nothing for a few seconds. The thought of the girl lying shut inside a coffin is unbearable, the self-preservation instinct kicks in and the images of the inside of a dark box gain no purchase.

What can I say?

Johan looks at his boss. A decent man.

'Have you had time to visit the regional museum yet?' he asks.

'No,' Göran Möller replies.

'They've got a famous painting by Böcklin. "Isle of the Dead".'

'I'd like to see that. It feels a bit like we're stuck on that island now.'

Johan smiles.

'Do you like it here?' he asks.

'This is a good team,' Göran Möller says, and smiles back.

Göran Möller looks around his office.

He's got some Goya reproductions on the walls. None of the difficult ones, just "The Nude Maja" and "The Clothed Maja". He's been to Madrid, where he was particularly struck by the brushwork in the painting of the naked woman. Two paintings of the same subject, different yet the same.

Which is best?

Loneliness, or being buried alive?

Malin sounded agitated when she called. The new message doesn't get them anywhere, and what have they actually got to go on?

She was right.

He suggested that she and Zeke go and see some of the parents of the men whose names Mehmet Khoni gave them. Perhaps that could help them make some progress.

Malin sounded dubious, and repeated what her friend the psychologist had said.

But psychologists are often wrong.

Göran Möller closes his eyes. Feels something nagging at him from his memory, something just out of reach.

He gets to his feet and leaves the station.

## 56

Malin watches Zeke talk to a woman in her mid-forties dressed in a black skirt and flowery red blouse. She sees them standing in a neat living room in a ground-floor flat in Ryd.

She hears what they are saying, but can't process the words. She's completely absorbed by the dark rings below the woman's eyes. The sorrow in her eyes when she opened the door to them just now. The way her whole being seems to have fled her body, or rather condensed into one single, immense emotion.

Don't let that be me, Malin thinks.

Naturally, the woman doesn't know anything that could help them with their case. She hadn't even had any idea that her son was on his way to Syria. She knows nothing about Suliman Hajif. Malin can see that.

Have there been any bitter recriminations against the people who were recruiting fighters?

Grief.

No one has the strength to feel anything but grief. He died for nothing. There's nothing good down there. Just different types of bad.

Zeke is still talking to the woman.

We can't waste any more time here, Malin thinks. We have to find Nadja, and she isn't here, and Malin feels like a jumping jack that can't control its own movements.

In her mind's eye she sees Peder Åkerlund's mother in her wheelchair. Her useless legs. Fettered to a body she can't escape.

Broken bodies everywhere.

Malin walks out of the flat and stands in the sunlight, trying her very best not to go mad.

Göran Möller has found his way to the regional museum, and now he's standing on the second floor of the yellow brick building, staring intently at the painting in front of him. It seems incredible that it's here right now, Böcklin's painting of a white figure approaching a rocky island.

He doesn't know why he's come here. He felt an acute longing to see the masterpiece that is on loan for the museum's exhibition of symbolist art.

He spends a long time standing in front of the painting. Feels his knees begging him to change position, but he doesn't move.

The isle of the dead is remarkably empty.

There are no dead there. Only their invisible souls.

Unless the figure approaching the island is death?

He thinks of their murderer as someone leaving the island to come back to life. Perhaps his actions are an attempt to bring himself to life?

In which case, presumably he's been trying for a long time?

Göran Möller walks on. In one room he finds some old hunting scenes. Game being pursued by frothing dogs whose tongues loll out of their mouths.

And suddenly Göran Möller remembers what it was he couldn't grasp earlier, a conversation with a colleague a long time ago, ten years or more. The colleague had been telling him about a case he had worked on where they had found dogs that had been tortured. Kenneth Johansson in Karlstad, that was who it was. They sat next to each other at a Police Association dinner, and Kenneth had been upset about the dogs.

Hadn't one of the dogs had its tongue cut out?

Göran Möller goes back to the "Isle of the Dead".

He knows that serial killers often start with animals, and move onto people later.

Were you on the island? Göran thinks. Did you start on dogs there, and now you're heading back across the water with people?

Kenneth Johansson must have retired by now. But it might be worth contacting him.

Malin asked Zeke to drop her off at the library after they'd seen the last of the parents. They can finally drop that line of investigation.

The conversations were quite fruitless, and Malin had to struggle to pay attention.

Now she's sitting by the huge windows looking out on the Castle Park, sunk deep into one of the egg-shaped chairs she knows Tove loves sitting in.

It's not far from here to Folkunga School, just a hundred metres or so. Perhaps the man in the hoodie came past here on his way to loiter outside the school. It strikes her that the library keeps cropping up. Nadja spent a lot of time here. And Peder Åkerlund's ex-girlfriend. The man that Julianna may have seen. And its proximity to Folkunga School.

A game of coincidences.

And she spins her chair around.

Looks at the rows of books.

She can feel Tove here, wishes she was with her. But that's impossible.

She stands up and goes over to the information desk. Behind the gleaming, curved wooden desk sits a red-haired woman the same age as her. Malin introduces herself, and the woman looks at her curiously.

'I have to ask,' Malin says. 'Have you noticed any peculiar visitors in the past six months?'

The woman smiles.

'We have our fair share of oddballs, like all libraries.'

'I'm thinking in particular about a man who usually goes around in a black hoodie. In his forties.'

'Sorry,' the woman says. 'I haven't noticed anyone matching that description.'

'Not in the café either?'

'No.'

She pauses.

'Your daughter was often here last summer,' she goes on. 'We discussed Jane Austen. She had some great things to say about her books. How is she these days?'

And that's when Malin snaps.

She marches determinedly out of the library, heading in completely the wrong direction.

# 57

Malin is standing in front of the mirror in the toilets in the Hamlet bar. Can feel the beer and tequila coursing through her body.

Hates her own weakness. But if she can't give in now, when will she ever?

Never.

That's the only answer.

There's nothing useful she can do with her anxiety, her fear. Nothing to be gained by meeting either grief or relief halfway.

Better to suppress everything.

That's my duty.

Not drinking.

And she adjusts her clothes, kicks the toilet door several times, hard, breaking the veneer, until in the end there's a hole right through it.

Damn.

Hope there's no one standing outside.

She opens the door, and the cloakroom outside the toilet is empty.

She goes back to her booth in the restaurant. Looks over at the bar. She's been drunk hundreds of times. She's fallen off her chair, onto the floor, she's made a fool of herself, and if she went over there now she'd feel ashamed. And she knows that shame is one of the feelings that keeps her away from alcohol.

That she herself has two sides.

If not more.

The good police officer. The weak alcoholic.

The loving mother.

The mother who doesn't take any responsibility at all.

Tove must hate me, deep down. For everything I did and didn't do when she was growing up.

Malin sits back in her secluded wooden booth. Another beer and a fresh shot of tequila are standing in front of her.

No. I can't resist.

This isn't good enough. I'm through with shame. If anyone ever can be.

But I can't stand myself, the boring person I really am.

Her mobile rings. Daniel.

'Ten minutes,' he says, and as he slides into the booth opposite her seven minutes later he points at the glasses.

'The first ones?'

There's no trace of reproach in his voice, no anxiety, merely a statement of the facts.

'No.'

'How many?'

'One beer and one tequila before you got here. And I want to drink those so fucking badly, but I'm not going to.'

'Good.'

'It won't make anything better.'

Daniel smiles, and in the dim light his face looks almost perfect. His features take on a sharpness that isn't really there in daylight.

Everything's better with a bit of darkness, Malin thinks. And she wants to tell him that she loves him, but can't bring herself to say the words.

The waitress comes over.

'Is there something wrong?'

'Nothing wrong at all,' Daniel says, and takes a swig of the beer.

They each order steak and eat it in silence, and Malin washes hers down with plenty of water. She's afraid Daniel is going to ask about Tove, and he knows that. And stays silent, because when things look hopeless, soothing words are often superfluous.

Nor does he ask about the investigation, seems to appreciate that she needs silence, that he clearly needs it as well.

When the waitress has cleared their plates Malin says: 'That was a good article.'

'Thanks.'

'You managed to manoeuvre around what I told you very neatly.'

'So you thought it was OK?'

'I can hardly put a muzzle on you.'

'You probably can, actually.'

They pay the bill and go out into St Larsgatan, walk down towards Hamngatan, and in the main square the pavement bars are full of people making the most of the mild May evening.

It isn't that long since I was sitting here with Tove, Malin thinks, and you have to come back, because otherwise I'll have to live the rest of my life in a world of ghosts. I'd move away from here, but my world would forever be suffused with your spirit.

Will I hear your voice? Sense it?

She feels Daniel's arm around her, pulls him closer to her, and he says: 'She'll turn up OK. I can feel it.'

They go their separate ways up on Hamngatan. Daniel has to be at the newsroom at four o'clock in the morning and wants to sleep alone, and Malin wants to be on her own too.

She hesitates outside the Pull & Bear. Wants to go into the pub and drink herself stupid.

Instead she walks to the car park. Sits in her old white Golf.

The alcohol's out of my system, she thinks, and takes her phone out.

Calls Janne. He answers at once.

'Have you heard anything?'

'No.'

'This is terrible,' Janne says.

'I know. Are you going to go?'

'No. Not yet.'

'I can help with the flight.'

'You haven't changed.'

'This is driving me mad with worry.'

'Do you want to meet up?'

Malin can hear Janne's voice at the other end of the line. His question is considerate, but he doesn't really want to meet. And neither does she. Because what would they do? Sit and hold each other's hands? Reflect each other's anxiety?

Not a chance.

'Let's talk again when there's any news,' she says, and ends the call.

She starts the car and drives through the city and out onto the plain. The water of Lake Roxen has tiger stripes in the moonlight, and a flock of broad-winged birds is flying low over the muddy fields closest to the lake. The farms are all dark, and she wonders where she's going.

She drives up into the forests near Stjärnorp.

Thinks about all the evil that has existed there, all the violence, thinks that it never ends. The only thing that changes is that the evil changes tone, colour, or smell, and the only thing we can do is protest against it with our words and deeds.

If we can see it, of course.

Evil often exists without us suspecting anything. Sometimes disguised as love, bewilderingly similar. Multifaceted, elusive, contradictory.

You hate, she thinks. Because you want to love. Want to be loved.

Did Nadja do something to you?

Is she less than perfect, as her friends and mother have implied?

Did your paths cross somewhere?

She's driven deep into the forest on a narrow unpaved track. Somewhere around here is where Maria Murvall wandered through the forest with her body shattered and her genitals mutilated.

She stops the car. Switches the engine and the headlights off, and the moonlight can't reach down to where she is.

Everything is dark.

She jumps across the ditch, heading into a forest that's darker than her soul, darker than her life will ever be.

Feels alien hands on her body.

Trying to get inside. Wanting to destroy her. Own her. Take her life.

She screams: 'TOVE TOVE TOVE. NADJA NADJA NADJA.'

And whispers: 'I'm coming, I'm coming now.'

# 58

*Friday, 19 May*

Göran Möller called the Karlstad Police early that morning from his flat. It was a bit of a long shot, after all, and he hesitated before phoning.

He was told that Kenneth Johansson, lead detective on the case involving the dogs, was on holiday.

They gave him Kenneth's mobile number, and he's waited until now to phone. It's eight o'clock, and he's sitting at his desk in his office, looking down towards the hospital on the other side of the road.

The phone rings five times before Kenneth Johansson answers, having obviously just woken up. His voice sounds rough, with a tone only strong spirits and tobacco can create.

'Kenneth.'

'I don't know if you remember me?' Göran Möller says, and introduces himself.

'I remember that dinner. A long time ago now.'

Slowly and methodically Göran Möller explains his reason for phoning, and he hears his fellow detective sigh at the other end of the line, and wonders where he is. Mallorca? Egypt? Bulgaria? Somewhere cheap, probably, or at home in Karlstad? But Göran Möller doesn't ask, he merely listens.

'We never got anywhere with those dogs. It was a bloody horrible case . . . They were greyhounds, and, let me tell you, they don't look too great when they've been cut up. They must have been alive when he did it, because they'd run around that clearing out in the forest. There was blood everywhere, and their coats were more red than white. Don't ask me how it happened.'

'I seem to remember you mentioning something about a tongue being cut out?'

'One of the dogs was missing its tongue, that's right.'

'Was there anything special about the location?'

'How do you mean?'

'Did it have any particular relevance to local history, were there any stories about it?'

'Now you come to mention it, someone from the local history association did call us. Apparently a witch was supposed to have been burned on that site in the forest back in the seventeenth century. But what was I supposed to do with that sort of information?'

Göran Möller gazes out of the window, down at the steady stream of people heading into the hospital at that time of the morning.

'Did you identify any suspects?'

'No. A few other greyhound owners got in touch. They thought they were being stalked by some bloke. They didn't have much of a description, and it was supposed to have happened several months earlier.'

Göran Möller takes a deep breath. His next question is a serious long shot, given the amount of time that has elapsed.

'Was there a van involved? Did a black van ever crop up in the investigation?'

'No.'

'I gather you're on holiday. Whereabouts are you?'

'Canary Islands. Playa del Inglés. My other half likes it here. I bloody don't. But it's my last holiday before I retire. So what the hell.'

'At least you can have a drink.'

His colleague laughs.

'I've had one or two.'

Malin is sitting at her desk in the open-plan office. Looking down at her beige trousers.

That hour she spent in the forest last night feels unreal, as if it never happened, but the livid scratches on her ankles are proof of her foolishness.

She forces herself to think of her peculiar behaviour that way.

As temporary madness. Impulses she has to follow to stop herself giving in to the really dangerous impulses, so as not to go properly insane.

The phone on her desk rings.

Göran Möller, asking her to come up to his office, and a minute later she opens the door to find him sitting with his back to the sun shining through the window.

'Have a seat,' he says.

She sits down.

Then Göran Möller tells her about the other case he's found out about. The dogs in Karlstad, and what Kenneth Johansson told him.

'There could be a link,' Göran Möller says. 'Now this person has crossed the boundary, for some reason, and has started attacking other people instead of animals.'

'Unless it's just coincidence,' Malin says, nodding thoughtfully. She goes on: 'But we still don't have a name, or anything, really.'

'Have you got any ideas?'

Malin thinks. She likes the fact that Göran Möller's question indicates that he's treating her as an equal. No father/daughter relationship here, and not boss/subordinate either. Just two police officers who are trying to make progress with an investigation.

'We could issue a request to every district in the country to see if they've had any similar cases of animal torture. If they have, we might be able to discern a pattern. A timeline. If it's the same person moving from place to place.'

Göran Möller lets out a whistle.

'You mean, if he's moved from place to place, we ought to be able to track him from the population register? Get the name of anyone who was in those places around the time of the attacks?'

'Yes,' Malin says.

'Is it even possible to run that sort of search?'

'Johan will know,' Malin says, and Göran goes on to give her a quick update on the old case Johan found. He's looked into it, and things seem to have turned out OK for the boy. He's an engineer in Uppsala these days, with a wife and three children.

'I'll send out the request to the other districts,' Malin says. 'We can start with that.'

'Your interviews with the families of the young men who went to Syria, did they provide anything useful?' Göran asks.

'Nothing.'

'And Nadja?'

'We're doing everything we can,' Malin says. 'We're in the murderer's hands here. She could be anywhere, and we've got nothing to go on. He'll contact us again, though, don't you think?'

'He will,' Göran Möller says, sounding mostly as if he's trying to convince himself.

# 59

I'm so thirsty. I'm shrinking. My muscles need water.
   This is my grave.
   I'm going to die here, dissolve into the earth, eaten by worms.
   There's no hope for me.
   I'm giving up now. It hurts too much.
   I shall stop breathing.
   Damn you all.
   You're all going to die.
   All of you.
   I'm no longer in your world.
   But the clock is ticking, and in my mind's eye I see a bomb, close by in the ground next to the coffin.
   I don't want to be blown to pieces.
   So hurry up.

# 60

Malin composes an email and sends it to every police district in the country.

Asks about cases of abused, lacerated animals, dogs, perhaps a case in which one of their tongues has been cut out. She could do her own search of the shared database, but the digitised records are still less than comprehensive. There could be cases where details have been missed from the official reports, or incidents the police are aware of, but which never led to an official investigation.

She knows the email will be forwarded to every police station in the various districts.

The whole country will see it, and if anyone can help, they will.

She leans back in her chair.

She might get an answer immediately, or it might take time. Or she might not get any response at all.

Nothing happens for the first ten minutes.

She stands up. Fetches a cup of coffee.

Then she looks over towards the entrance. Karim's face. He's let his beard grow since she last saw him, it's now perfect hipster-length. He's pushing a pram ahead of him through the office, and the members of the investigative team gather around the pram to look inside it.

The pram is decorated with Burberry fabric this time. Genuine, no doubt, Malin thinks, and can't help smiling. She remembers Tove's pram. A battered old Brio.

Tove.

No.

Karim. There you are.

Impeccably dressed, as always. A patterned brown tie that looks as if it could cope with a few baby-food stains.

Malin goes over to join the others. Looks down into the pram at the sleeping child, and feels invisible hands clutch at her ribcage, feels her eyes grow moist. She can't escape this grief over what never was and never will be, but she holds it back.

'He's beautiful,' she says to Karim. 'Just like you, apart from the beard.'

Karim laughs.

'He takes after his mum, thank goodness.'

Malin realises that she's missed Karim. He always does his bit when they have a difficult case, and the station feels poorer without his elegant presence. A colourless prosecutor is standing in as chief of police, and hardly ever shows his face.

'When are you coming back?' she asks.

'In two months,' Karim says.

'Are you looking forward to it?'

He nods, looks down at the pram, and says: 'He's wonderful. Fun to play with.'

By the time Malin gets back to her computer she's received two new emails.

One from Umeå, one from Örebro.

In Örebro they had a case in which two cats were found in a park. They'd been cut using a knife, the police officer writing the email is sure of that. But there was no investigation because their boss thought the cats could have inflicted the wounds on each other with their claws.

'But they were obviously knife wounds. And one of the cats had had its tongue lacerated.'

The case in Umeå was just one year ago. A greyhound

had been found, alive, down by the river. At first there didn't seem to be anything wrong with it. Then the vet at the kennels where the police had taken it called to say that someone had severed the dog's larynx.

There was no investigation that time either.

After all, it was only a dog.

Malin writes back to thank the senders. Thinks that none of the incidents has coincided. They've taken place in different places at different times, forming an arc that stretches across ten years.

She goes over to Johan, hoping that he might be able to make something of this.

'It ought to be possible to conduct a search,' Johan says without looking up from his computer.

He seems brighter today than he has for a long time.

He must have got a good night's sleep. Perhaps because his daughter wasn't in pain? Or did his wife decide to give him a treat last night? Either way, some sort of burden has lifted from his heart.

Malin pulls over a chair and sits down, crosses her legs, and leans forward towards Johan.

'It won't be a particularly exact search. But by defining the parameters I ought to be able to get a rough list of people currently living in Linköping who've lived in Karlstad, Umeå, and Örebro during the past ten years.'

'All of those places?' Malin asks.

'At least one,' Johan says. 'Sometimes two or three.'

'That's going to be a lot of names. People move to Linköping all the time. The university.'

'And work,' Johan says. 'There are a lot of companies here that act as a useful rung for people on the career ladder.'

'Can you give it a try, then?' Malin says. 'How long will it take?'

'Give me an hour or so,' Johan says.

'You can't do it any faster?'

Johan looks up from the screen. Stares at her as if she is an idiot.

'You know me, Malin. I take great pride in working as slowly as possible.'

## 61

A thousand names. Give or take.

A thousand men aged between eighteen and sixty-five, any one of whom could be the man they're looking for. Johan has printed out the list, and it lies like a snake across the table in the meeting room.

The preschool children are out playing.

She goes and opens a window. Lets in their laughter and cries and all the emotions carried by their voices, all their expectations of life, moment by moment.

Johan pins the list up on the wall, and Malin, Zeke, Elin, and Göran take their seats. So many names, and so little time.

'Can you refine the search so we only get the ones aged between thirty and forty-five now?' Göran Möller asks. 'The likely age of our murderer, in other words.'

Johan shakes his head.

'This is as close as I could get. Between voting age and retirement. We'll have to do the rest manually.'

They stand up, pens at the ready, and divide the names between them. They cross out anyone whose age doesn't match what Viveca deemed plausible.

That leaves them with four hundred names.

'Still far too many,' Malin says. 'How can we narrow it down further?'

'Marital status? Didn't Viveca Crafoord tell you he probably lives alone?' Zeke suggests.

'We'll try that,' Göran Möller says.

It takes them half an hour to identify the single men on the list.

Around one hundred and fifty names left.

'We can get passport photographs of them,' Göran Möller says. 'Show them to Mehmet Khoni, Julianna Raad, and anyone else who might have seen the man in the hoodie, anyone who might remember something if they're shown a picture. Check them against the register of car owners too. We might get something that way, find one of these men who has a van.'

Johan gets up and leaves the room. Malin and the others stay where they are.

'At last, something to work with,' Malin says.

'If we don't get anywhere with the passport photos and vehicle register, we'll have to start checking them out one at a time. Looking at their online activities, or anything that could be connected to our case,' Elin says.

'We can see if they've got a criminal record too,' Göran says. 'And if they've ever been linked to any old cases of child abuse.'

There's a knock on the door.

Ebba, the receptionist, comes in without waiting for an answer. She's holding a video cassette in her hand.

'This just arrived from Forensics. They got it from the council yesterday. They wanted you to look at it at once. They've made a note of the section they want you to see.'

Thirty-five minutes and forty seconds into the recording, a black van stops on a dark street.

A clock at the bottom left of the screen says 01.53. The date is 15 May.

The vehicle's number plate is impossible to see.

The front windscreen is tinted, and the figure behind the wheel only just visible.

The van's engine stops, the lights go out, and the figure seems to disappear from behind the wheel. Then nothing happens.

Followed by more nothing.

At 02.02, one of the side doors opens, and a few seconds later a young, clearly intoxicated man stumbles into shot and walks over to the open door of the van. He looks inside, apparently curious, then climbs in, and the door quickly closes, and Malin sees the van shake slightly. Thirty seconds later the engine starts and the van drives off.

'That's a Volkswagen Transporter,' Zeke says matter-of-factly.

Malin feels her heart pounding inside her chest.

Was that where and when Peder Åkerlund was killed, at 02.02, or did he die later, somewhere else? Or was the hydrochloric acid injected into his brain inside the van?

Because that was, is, Peder Åkerlund on the video.

They watch the clip again.

And again.

'It's not often you see something like this,' Göran Möller says eventually.

'Thank God,' Elin says.

The door to the meeting room opens again.

'I've run a check on the database of registered vehicles,' Johan says. 'Eleven people on our list own a van.'

'How many have a Volkswagen Transporter?' Malin asks. 'Why?'

They show Johan the recording, and in the meantime Malin looks through the eleven names on the list.

'Five of them,' she says, and stands up.

'Bloody hell,' Johan says.

First everything happens, then nothing. And now everything again. Malin goes over to the whiteboard and writes the men's names on it.

*Johan Skogdahl*
*Jonas Ahl*
*Wilmer Gregory*
*Gustav Friberg*
*Stefan Ingvarsson*

There's another knock on the door.

A young woman in uniform holds out a bundle of print-outs of passport photographs.

'None of them has a criminal record,' she says.

'These are the eleven men who own a van,' Johan says, thanking the uniform before she disappears.

He pulls out the pictures of the five Volkswagen owners and lays them down on the table.

'I've never seen any of them before,' Malin says, even if there's something vaguely familiar about a bearded man named Jonas Ahl.

'Nor me,' Elin Sand says, and both Göran Möller and Zeke shake their heads.

'But one of them could be our man,' Göran Möller says, and Malin can't help feeling pleased that he's taking charge, even though this is probably just another dead end. It helps fend off her own doubts.

'What do we know about them?' Malin asks.

'Nothing,' Johan says. 'Apart from the fact that they don't have criminal records.'

Malin gathers the photographs together, picks them up and says: 'Zeke and I will go and show these to Julianna. And Mehmet Khoni. Is he still here?'

The others look at her in surprise.

'He's down in the custody unit. Long story.'

'You'll have to check,' Göran Möller says.

'See if you can get a bit of background on them,' Malin says, turning to Johan. 'Elin, you help him,' then she sees

Göran Möller smile before saying: 'Then that's what we'll do, Malin.'

As she leaves the room her phone rings. The aid agency that sent Tove to hell.

Damn them.

She answers and talks to Lisa Jansson while she and Zeke head down to the custody unit.

The wretched woman says that they now believe that Tove and the other two girls may be in another, more remote mountain village, where some businessmen may have taken them after their vehicle broke down.

'That's what we're hoping,' Lisa Jansson says. 'We're trying to get hold of a helicopter to get out there as soon as possible.'

'OK.'

Malin ends the call. Good news. That has to be counted as good news, surely?

They reach the custody unit, and the guard lets them inside. The door to Mehmet Khoni's cell is open.

## 62

Mehmet Khoni frowns and says: 'I've never seen any of these men before.'

He smells of sweat, and his breath seems to come from deep down in his guts.

Couldn't someone have given you a toothbrush? Malin thinks. Then she realises that until a few minutes ago, she and the guards were the only people who knew that Mehmet was here.

'OK,' Zeke says.

'How long are you planning to stay here?'

'Until you've caught the lunatic, or until you throw me out. I'm not in any hurry. It's better to be here than dead, I reckon.'

'Only the dead can know that,' Malin says.

Mehmet smiles, and she hears Zeke chuckle behind her. The two men evidently share the same sense of humour.

They leave Mehmet and move on to Julianna's cell.

The guard turns the lock, and Julianna flies up, she must have been asleep and now they've woken her from a dream.

Harsh.

But not brutal.

Malin lays the pictures out on the floor of the cell.

Julianna sits back down on the bunk and looks at them carefully.

Shakes her head.

'I don't recognise any of them.'

'You're sure?' Malin asks.

Julianna leans forward, rubbing her eyes.

'I'm still a bit groggy.'

'So you've never seen any of them before?' Zeke asks.

'If I had, what would I stand to gain? Can you get me out of here?'

'It doesn't work like that in Sweden, and you know it,' Malin says. 'What's done is done, but I daresay I could ask the prosecutor to request a more lenient sentence if I say you helped us.'

'Promise?'

'I promise to do what I can,' Malin says, feeling a tingle in her stomach that quickly turns to anger.

Two brutal murders, and she's sitting here trying to cut deals with us. And after taking potshots at me as well.

She ought to be glad I don't give her a beating.

'Have you found Nadja?' Julianna asks.

Malin shakes her head.

'Do what you like with the prosecutor,' Julianna says, 'but I recognise that one.'

Julianna Raad points at the man in the middle photograph. Commonplace appearance, straight nose, full beard, and dark brown hair. One of hundreds of thousands of men in Sweden who could be described with exactly the same words.

'Who is he?' Zeke asks.

'I don't know his name,' Julianna says.

But we do, Malin thinks.

'It could have been him staring at me. In the library café. I remember now. It was him.'

Malin looks at the photograph.

*Jonas Ahl.*

Could you be our man?

Nadja spent a lot of time at the library. Could you have seen her there?

And then Malin realises who he is. The man she bumped

into by chance, pushing a book trolley on the lower floor at the library. They exchanged a few words. He worked there. His hair was cut differently and the beard was gone. But it was the same man.

And she remembers the message hidden inside the calf's tongue: *I shall burn these words to secure them.*

Could that have been a reference to his work?

'Thanks,' Malin says. 'We'll see where that gets us.'

They hurry back upstairs to the office and over to Johan's desk. Elin joins them when she sees them rush past.

A quick report.

'Jonas Ahl. I haven't got to him yet,' Johan says.

'Me neither,' Elin adds, then Johan taps rapidly at his keyboard with the others standing behind him.

'Who is he?' Malin asks. 'And get an alert issued on that van of his.'

'Will do,' Elin says.

'He lives at Piongatan 16,' Johan says. 'In the middle of the city. He works as a book restorer at the library.'

Johan goes on typing.

'He went to university in Gothenburg, and has lived in Malmö, Karlstad, and Örebro.'

A pause.

'And Umeå.'

Then another pause.

'Looks like he moved here just over six months ago.'

'Which is when he's first supposed to have been seen,' Malin says.

'His time in Karlstad matches the case with the animals. The same with Umeå.'

Malin looks at his picture again.

How do they proceed from here?

Bring him in and try to force him to say where Nadja is? Or shadow him, see what he reveals?

Play with him for a little while?

But there's no time for games. Malin can feel it.

If anything has ever been urgent, this is it.

At the same time she gets a feeling that she, they, are still being directed by someone else's will. Jonas Ahl, if he's the man they're looking for, must have worked out that sooner or later they would start to get closer to him. Perhaps he knows more about what we're doing than we realise?

But there's no way he can know about this.

And something else is bound to happen if we don't stop him now.

'Like I said before, no criminal record. He was born in Växjö. I can see if Social Services there have anything on him, but that could take a while.'

'Anything else?' Zeke says, just as Malin's phone starts to ring.

Unknown number.

Something new about Tove?

Malin clicks to take the call before she has time for any more thoughts about her daughter.

A woman introduces herself.

Petra Stålek.

'We met at the library yesterday. You asked me if I'd ever seen a man in a black hoodie here, and I couldn't think of anyone. But it's just occurred to me that our restorer, Jonas Ahl, actually wears a black hooded jacket. Even when it's really cold he sometimes just wears that.'

'Thanks,' Malin says. 'If Jonas is there, try to keep him there until we arrive.'

'What for?'

'We need to talk to him. Don't mention the police. It makes people nervous. Just try to keep him there.'

'I don't think he's even here at the moment.'

'We're on our way,' Malin says.

# 63

As a book restorer, Jonas Ahl would have access to chemicals, Malin thinks as she and Zeke stride through the entrance to the library.

The large space is hot. The sun is shining on the windows that stretch ten metres from the stone floor to the ceiling.

Presumably he can get hold of whatever chemicals he wants much more easily than other people.

Hydrochloric acid.

Chemicals that can be used to knock people out.

They go straight to the information desk. A short, skinny woman with her mousy hair cut in a bob stares up at them.

'We're looking for Jonas Ahl,' Malin says. 'I spoke to Petra Stålek a little while ago.'

'Jonas is off today. Was it important? I recognise you. You're from the police.'

'We should have said so,' Zeke says. 'Sorry.'

Petra Stålek approaches from deeper inside the main hall of the library. She's wearing a green corduroy dress that complements her red hair.

They shake hands.

'He isn't here,' she says. 'Apparently he's taken some time off this week.'

Malin nods.

'Is your boss here? I mean, the head of the library?'

'I can give her a call.'

Five minutes later Malin and Zeke are standing outside

a bright red door in the administrative part of the library. They knock, and from inside the room a brusque female voice calls: 'Come in!'

They go in.

Behind a clinically clean desk sits a woman in her mid-forties in a grey dress. Her face is dominated by a pointed nose, and her brown hair is pulled up into a tight bun.

She looks like a bank manager, Malin thinks as the woman introduces herself as Sigrid Trulsson and invites them to sit down.

'You wanted to talk about Jonas?' she says, switching her phone off. 'Has he got himself mixed up in something?'

We don't know, Malin thinks.

'We're not at liberty to say,' Zeke replies.

'What do you want to know about him?'

'When did he start working here?' Malin asks.

'Six months ago. Before that he was at the regional museum in Örebro, and before that at Västerbotten Museum. He had good references from both places. What's he done? I find it very hard to imagine he's done anything silly. He's not the type.'

'He might not have done anything,' Malin replies. 'What type would you say he is?'

'The strong, silent type,' Sigrid Trulsson says, and laughs. 'But, joking aside, I don't really know him that well. He's a very good restorer, though. We have some priceless old books in our collections, and he looks after them like they were his children. And he's not afraid to muck in elsewhere if necessary. Some of the books are so heavy, and he helps carry them. He's strong. And that can actually be very useful in a library.'

'Have there ever been any problems with him?' Malin asks.

Sigrid Trulsson looks surprised.

'What sort of problems?'

'Anything,' Zeke says. 'Anything at all.'

'Nothing, I'd have to say.'

'He's never threatened anyone? Been violent?'

'Violent? No, thank God.'

'Or expressed any strong political views?' Zeke asks.

'No, not that either. Now that I think about it, he's probably a bit of a lone wolf. Seems happiest on his own.'

Malin can't help thinking that the conversation isn't going anywhere.

'Does he have his own room?' she asks.

Sigrid Trulsson nods.

'Can we see it?'

'Of course.'


The laboratory-like room is located in the basement, and has no windows. A number of old, handwritten books lie open on easels. There's a collection of small brushes on a side table. A white medicine cabinet contains glass bottles of chemicals. The chemical symbols don't mean much to Malin, but she does recognise one of them.

Hydrochloric acid.

'Can he get hold of whatever chemicals he needs as part of his job?'

'He has my permission to do that, yes,' Sigrid Trulsson says. 'He mixes them himself to get what he needs. He's very knowledgeable.'

'Can we see the lists of his purchases?'

'Yes, but it might take a little while.'

'The sooner the better.'

'Does he have a computer?' Zeke asks.

'He does, but he takes it home with him when he's not here.'

'Yes, the woman at the desk said he was off today. Do you know where he is?'

'No idea.'

Malin walks up and down the room. Looks through the papers on the desk, the folders in the bookcase, looking for any sign that Jonas Ahl is the person they're after, but she doesn't find anything out of the ordinary. On another side table there's an open book, *Forgotten Swedish Places*.

'Well, thanks for taking the time to see us,' Malin says. They head back upstairs and out into the May sunshine.

'Time to pay him a visit,' she says, and sees that she's missed a call from Göran Möller.

Elin Sand is waiting while Börje Svärd inserts the lock-pick into the door to the flat on Piongatan where Jonas Ahl is supposed to live.

Göran Möller has sent them here. Told them to be careful, and now they're standing in the neat stairwell with their guns drawn.

They've already rung the bell, but there was no answer. No sounds from inside the flat.

Börje is working the pick with one hand as he holds his pistol in the other. He mutters a curse, and Elin can see that he's sweating.

He seemed happy, really cheerful in the car on the way here just now. The head teacher of Folkunga School had called him, and they'd met up. And Börje let on that she spent the night with him. He was as proud as any teenager over his latest conquest, which amused Elin. There was nothing stupidly macho about his joy, more bemusement that his own curiosity about women never seems to run out.

And perhaps he genuinely feels something for this teacher?

Elin doesn't know why, but she changes position, goes to stand beside Börje instead of right behind him. She feels her heart start to thud in her chest, feels fear and nervousness propel adrenaline out into her body.

The lock clicks twice in quick succession.

'That's got it,' Börje says.

He puts the pick back in his jacket pocket, and Elin sees him push the handle down, the door opens outwards, then all she is aware of is a sudden intense burst of light and a sense of the world being compressed, of someone pressing her eardrums and eyes deep into her brain.

Then heat.

A heat that can destroy everything in its path.


'I've sent Elin and Börje to his flat,' Göran Möller says, as Zeke and Malin are passing the Konsert & Kongress entertainment venue. 'I didn't want to wait.'

Zeke at the wheel, Malin sitting back in the passenger seat.

'What did they find?' Malin asks. She would rather have got there first, and Göran Möller knows it.

'They've probably only just got there.'

'OK. We're on our way.'

'I didn't want to wait because of what Johan found out from Social Services in Växjö, where Jonas Ahl grew up.'

'He was in their records?'

'It made me feel sick when I heard,' Göran Möller says.

'For God's sake, just tell me, then!'

Malin puts her phone on speaker, and Göran Möller's words fill the car, oozing like yellow-brown pus, dripping from the roof.

'Jonas's father killed his mother when Jonas was nine years old. He's supposed to have filled her mouth with soil, then left his son alone in the flat with her. They were found by relatives four days later. Jonas Ahl, just a young lad at the time, was sitting beside his mother's body picking at the soil in her mouth. He didn't say a word for several years after that. He lived with various foster families, but none of them seemed able to cope with his silence.'

Can a child be lonelier than that?

The loneliest in the whole world.

'His dad was a popular local politician. A high-profile Social Democrat who specialised in legal matters. He was very active in the fight for disabled rights. Jonas's mother kept a diary that showed that he had abused both her and their son. He was extremely strict and controlling, whilst simultaneously working publically for a gentler society.'

'A domestic devil.'

'Yes, like that police chief who was convicted of multiple rapes despite campaigning for gender equality.'

It all fits.

With Suliman and Peder. Their loud professions of goodness hiding terrible attitudes and behaviour. You're killing your father, aren't you, Jonas?

What about Nadja, though? Why her? She must have done something that made you think she had a dual personality as well.

'Hang on!' Göran Möller suddenly yells. 'Just hold on, for God's sake. We've just had an emergency call. An explosion, on Piongatan. Shit!'

'We're already on our way,' Malin says.

'Christ. I told them to be careful.'

Elin.

Börje.

She ends the call. Feels Zeke put his foot down on the accelerator as her mobile buzzes.

A text.

Can you save what I can't?

You bastard, Malin thinks. But Nadja is alive, that's what you're trying to say, isn't it?

Or are you trying to tell me something else?

## 64

After a long shift in the newsroom, Daniel Högfeldt feels exhausted as he hurries the five hundred metres between the paper's office and his flat, eager to get home as quickly as possible.

He heard an explosion a short while ago, in the distance, and assumed that the noise came from Saab, and that they were testing one of the many weapons systems they manufacture.

He puts his key in the door to his flat. He slept badly last night, wished Malin had been with him, but she wasn't there, and the bed felt way too big, cold and lonely in a way that it had never been before.

He wanted to call her just now, but knows she's busy.

His trousers come off, then his top.

Down with the venetian blind, then the roller blind, and now the white room is dark enough. He wonders if he ought to dig out the sleep mask he bought for a trip to New York that never actually happened. But he's tired enough to fall asleep without it.

He curls up and pulls the covers over him, and detects his own smell on the cotton, Malin hasn't slept here since he changed the sheets.

He closes his eyes. Breathes out and in, trying not to think of anything, but his mind wanders to the comments left beneath his opinion piece, particularly one that the editor deleted.

The one written by someone using the alias Mandela,

in which he expressed his hatred of Daniel for having an opinion about the murders, and said he ought to shut up if he didn't want to end up like Hajif and Åkerlund.

Lunatics.

The Internet's full of them.

It's far too easy to press send.

And people are only too happy to do so.

He doesn't remember the other comments, and instead loses himself in images of Malin, and Tove, and he sees her in his mind's eye in the Congo, somewhere in the jungle, in good health, and with that image in mind, Daniel Högfeldt falls asleep.

He doesn't notice the door of the flat being opened five minutes later, or the man creeping towards his bed holding a large, damp rag in his hand before he presses it against Daniel's nose and mouth.

His sleep changes, becomes dreamless, and deeper than ever before.

A pale darkness with red edges.

From inside it he fails to notice the man wresting his body into a large bag and leaving the flat. And the bag being placed in the back of a van. A van that then drives off towards an unknown destination.

## 65

What's happening? Malin throws herself out of the car and runs towards the ambulance parked on the street outside the ochre-coloured *fin de siècle* building.

Who are they lifting into the ambulance on a stretcher? Who is it?

Börje. That's Börje's soot-smeared red face under the oxygen mask.

She recognises one of the paramedics.

How bad? she asks with her eyes.

The man shakes his head, and she looks over towards the door and the fire engine, as firemen rush into the stairwell, and uniformed police officers try to keep curious onlookers back.

She just manages to take hold of Börje's hand and squeeze it before the ambulance doors close and the vehicle drives off.

She turns around.

Elin Sand is sitting on the grass outside the building, wrapped in a yellow blanket. Her face is black with soot, but she seems unharmed. Malin goes over to her, kneels down, and puts one hand on her shoulder.

'Are you OK?'

Elin Sand looks at her, then points at her ears.

'I can't hear anything.'

And Malin repeats, this time articulating clearly: 'Are you OK?'

Elin nods.

'We were about to enter the flat. Börje had picked the lock, and that's when it went off.'

'Was Jonas Ahl there?'

'It was empty, as far as I know.'

Malin strokes Elin's cheek before getting to her feet. She sees Göran Möller, Zeke, and Waldemar standing under a tree, staring at their mobiles.

Perhaps they're reading the text message? She forwarded it to all of them.

Can you save what I can't?

Göran and Zeke's expressions are full of fear, fear that stems from a realisation that you don't have control of anything. That life is a never-ending earthquake.

They're trying to work out what's happening, but can't, and Malin has the feeling that the ground Linköping stands on, perfectly stable until very recently, is in the process of being ripped open and destroyed, and that one man – his rage and confusion and hatred and love – is capable of bringing down a whole city.

Then her mobile buzzes once more.

Two precise coordinates, down to the last decimetre.

She rushes over to Zeke, Göran, and Waldemar at the same time as she calls Johan. She gives him the coordinates. She could probably work out the location on her phone, but how the hell do you do that?

'I've had another text. Nothing but coordinates.'

'He may have set another trap,' Göran Möller says. 'From now on we have to be even more careful.'

'Is there enough time for that?'

'There has to be.'

'I doubt it,' Waldemar coughs.

'The girl's still alive,' Malin says.

In her mind's eye she can see a helicopter hovering above dense jungle. Tove, standing on a rock in a clearing, waving.

Her phone rings.

Johan, calling back.

'It's an abandoned lot in Ljungsbro, in an old residential area. If the coordinates are accurate, they lead to a well behind a derelict house.'

He gives her the address, and Malin grabs Zeke's arm. 'Let's go.'

'Where the hell are you going?' Göran Möller says, trying to stop them.

'Where he wants us to go. What do you think?'

'You're not going anywhere without the bomb squad.'

'They're too slow,' Malin says. 'It could be too late by then.'

She looks over at the gathering of reporters. Daniel isn't there. He must be at home sleeping, she thinks.

Her phone buzzes once more:

Hurry, hurry, the clock is ticking.

'You can't stop me,' Malin says, then turns and hurries to the car. She wonders if Zeke is following her, and as she opens the driver's door she hears his voice right behind her: 'That's my seat.'

She runs around to the passenger side, looks over at Göran Möller, and Waldemar, who are waving them off, saying: 'Go, go, go!' without actually saying it.

The mass-housing project of Skäggetorp, Ikea's even more depressing retail barn, the fertile land of the plain, the brown ploughed fields. The water of Lake Roxen looks dull beneath the sunlight from a hazy sky, and the little red soldiers' cottages that are now modest summer houses seem to vanish into the evening, swallowed up by an invisible giant.

The spire of Vreta Kloster.

They drive past the first crime scene, from the road they can make out the locks and the tall trees surrounding them.

Peder Åkerlund's corroded brain.

Suliman Hajif's amputated tongue.

Jonas Ahl's mother's mouth, full of earth.

They drive into Ljungsbro, under the viaduct, past the former site of Wester's fruit farm, and into the district of Källhemmet. They turn into Bohagsvägen and pull up outside number 57.

The old house is falling down.

The garden overgrown.

They stop.

Get out.

Am I going to be blown up? Malin thinks. Is there another bomb here?

She looks at Zeke. He radiates concentration. Nothing else. It is in situations like this when he shows his true self. He won't back down one millimetre.

They go around to the back of the house. The garden is protected by a tall, dense hedge. Jonas Ahl could do anything he wanted here without fear of being seen.

The stone wall of the well is covered by grey-green moss.

A well, Malin thinks. Deep in the ground. Just like the coffins.

They look down into the darkness, and Malin wonders: Are you down there, Nadja?

She drops a stone in.

There's no splash, just a gentle thud. Three seconds. Something like ten metres to the bottom.

This must be where he was leading us.

'Have we got any rope in the car?'

'We have,' Zeke replies, and runs off.

Malin stands alone by the well. Calls down into it: 'Nadja, Nadja, we're coming. Don't give up.'

I'm going down there, Malin thinks. Down into the darkness to get you. Maybe we'll both be blown up?

Zeke comes back with the rope. They fasten it to a sturdy apple tree, and Zeke takes hold of it, saying: 'I'll go.'

'Never,' Malin says. 'You've got Tess, she's only little. Tove's older. She'd manage.'

Malin doesn't let herself think further than that. She grabs the rope from Zeke and goes over to the well, climbs over the edge and starts to bounce her way down the dry, brick-lined walls.

Zeke shines his torch down.

Can you see us now?

Malin can hear sirens. Police cars arriving. Fellow officers who can't help her. She has to do this on her own. The walls of the well squeeze her like the muscles of a boa constrictor, and she wants to get out, but knows she has to carry on.

Damn, it's deep.

Zeke's torch can't reach all the way down here.

She bounces her way down in the darkness, feels spiders' webs catch in her hair, as tentacles seem to feel their way across her cheeks.

Am I ever going to get back out again?

Then she feels firm ground beneath her feet.

She's there.

Completely dark now. But the walls have widened into a small cave. She takes out her mobile, switches the little torch on, and looks up. The sky is a circle, as if in another world. She shines the torch around her, turns around and around.

What can I see?

There. There, behind a rock, something is sticking out.

A white-painted corner, and she kneels down and crawls over to the rock and drags it aside.

A small coffin.

But big enough for human remains.

And a ticking sound.

A note on the coffin:

*Dare you open it, because it might save her?*

Tove, Nadja.

I'm going to save them, Malin thinks. That's all I'm good for. And that's what I'm doing. Yet even so her hands tremble as she reaches for the little coffin with the ticking sound. She tries to hold them still, but they refuse to obey her, and she swears, curses this dark hole, brushes a spider from her hair, feels more of them crawling up her ankles, and she hates the arachnids as much as she hates this moment, and that hatred makes her hands steady, and they approach the coffin, and she knows she has to open it, even if it might lead to her death.

She takes hold of the lid, hesitates for a second, hears Zeke's voice: 'How's it going down there?'

She doesn't reply, just yells: 'Get away from the opening!' and then lifts the lid of the coffin straight up, feeling herself breathe hard as sweat breaks out right across her scalp.

The feeling of being in her own grave.

The lid in one hand.

No explosion.

Malin looks down into the coffin. A clock, an old-fashioned stopwatch. Counting down. Twenty-nine minutes left.

What happens then?

In twenty-nine minutes?

A note beside the stopwatch.

New coordinates.
A short message.

*Ha, ha, boom, boom.*

You sadist.
But you reap what you sow.
She grabs the note and the timer, puts them and her mobile in her pockets. She fumbles for the rope in the darkness, ties it around her waist, and takes a firm grip of it with both hands.
She calls up: 'Pull me up, now!'
And she is drawn towards the light.
Slowly, slowly.
The light. Close now.
And she sees their faces.
Zeke, Nadja, Tove.
They're all there.
Daniel.
Did I get blown up after all?
She's up.
Clambers over the edge. The light must have been playing tricks on her, on her eyes, the feeling of seeing her deathbed.
Zeke's there. Some muscular uniforms. None of the people she loves most.
And no Nadja.
But we're coming now, we're going to make it.
The clock is counting down.
Twenty-six minutes and twenty seconds left.

# 66

Save me. I can't breathe any more.

The air has run out completely, one breath is like a hundredth of a breath, and I try to hold my breath, counting. Slowly, slowly, slower than the seconds.

One hundred and ninety-nine, two hundred, two hundred and one . . .

The ticking stops, and then I hear a whistling sound, a mad whistle that makes my whole body shake, and I shake with cramp from the whistle, my body hits the wood on all sides and the whistling goes on and on until suddenly it stops.

I become still.

And the ticking is back.

Louder and louder and LOUDER.

It's too late.

You can't save me.

Mum, Dad, all the rest of you.

You won't be in time.

## 67

They throw themselves into the car once more.

Zeke starts the engine, looks at Malin.

'Where to?'

'Head out towards the plain, it ought to be in that direction,' and soon they're racing through the sleepy residential area at over a hundred kilometres an hour.

A risk in itself.

A danger to others.

Malin calls Johan, gives him the new coordinates, and this time she waits as she hears him tap frantically at a keyboard.

'It's in the middle of the plain. Towards Klockrike. A few kilometres from Stenkullamotet.'

Johan is talking calmly, and Malin knows he doesn't want to stress her.

The game goes on, she thinks as she ends the call.

Here is there.

Here is there, wherever they aren't.

You probably killed her long ago.

She takes out the stopwatch.

Eighteen minutes left.

A message arrives. Johan has sent a picture of the location, and road directions.

She reads them out to Zeke.

'Drive as fast as you can.'

'Can we get there in time?'

'Yes. We can get to the location, anyway. What happens when we get there is another matter.'

She closes her eyes, feels the car accelerate, hears the engine roar with joy at the chance to unleash its potential. If they went off the road now, or hit another car, it would mean certain death.

She counts the seconds, minutes, gets annoyed every time Zeke has to slow down for a bend or a junction. But there's no better driver than him.

She opens her eyes again.

Fields of yellow rape, and Zeke turns off onto a gravel track that leads off between the fields, and a minute or so later they reach one that's been left fallow. There are just a few thin remnants of the previous year's crop left.

Zeke stops the car.

'It should be here,' he says. 'In the middle of this field.'

Malin opens her door and leaps out. She runs off across the field, looking for anything that catches her eye. Some difference in the colour of the earth, and off in the distance she sees something blue. A pipe, a plastic tube, that must be it.

Zeke is running beside her now, heading towards the tube. The ground there has been dug up, an area large enough to contain a human body. A grave, Malin thinks.

They crouch down.

Malin takes the stopwatch out and puts it down beside her.

Barely ten minutes left.

'The spades!' she yells.

Zeke rushes back to the car as Malin begins to dig. She tears at the ground with her fingers, feeling her nails give way as blood seeps from her fingertips.

No pain.

How deep down are you, Nadja?

Just below the surface they find a large container with

a few drops of water at the bottom. Another tube leads down from it.

Are you alive, Nadja?

You're coming now, aren't you? You're digging. Mum and Dad, you're digging.

You're hurrying.

Hurry up.

Unless it's a badger?

Someone who wants to be dead along with me.

Malin is shovelling the earth over her shoulder. Zeke is doing the same.

Sweat is pouring off her now, and it feels like the lactic acid is going to beat the adrenaline, but at this moment the will to live is stronger, so they keep digging as the clock counts down.

They follow the tubes down into the earth.

Three minutes now.

Two minutes and fifty seconds.

Faster now, Malin.

Then her spade hits something hard. We're never going to have time.

And they free part of what they've found.

Part of a coffin, where the tubes stick through the lid, and Malin can hear ticking now, two clocks ticking, and they beat their spades on the lid of the coffin, aware that they're never going to uncover the whole lid in time.

They beat and hammer and bang, and Malin screams: 'We're coming, Nadja, we're coming!'

Göran Möller puts his foot down on the accelerator after turning onto the gravel track leading through the fields of rape. The siren of a patrol car is wailing behind him.

I'm responsible for them, he thinks. I should have stopped them. This is too dangerous.

But sometimes the world is dangerous.

And we're the ones standing in the front line.

Will they make it in time? he wonders, as his car lurches along the track.

There can't be many seconds left now.

The wood gives way. First a small hole, then gradually larger.

Fifty-five seconds now.

A face.

Eyes staring out of darkness.

A mouth opening, forming itself into a scream, but nothing comes out. Just the angry ticking sound, and Zeke swearing at the splinters he gets as he tries to make the hole in the coffin large enough to pull the girl out.

A face.

It's you, Nadja, we're here now, and Malin can smell the stench of excrement and urine, but she can also see the life in Nadja Lundin's eyes. The hope.

Thirty seconds.

Malin reaches down into the hole alongside Zeke.

Then the ticking stops and is replaced by a loud whistling sound that cuts through Malin's eardrums, and she tears at the wood, reaches her arms in towards Nadja Lundin, puts her hands under her armpits and then pulls.

She's never pulled so hard in her entire life.

You're coming with us.

Up.

And Zeke breaks more of the wood.

Nadja's body moves. She's helping now. Kicking with her legs. Malin can feel it as half of her upper body comes free.

Her skin is more like dirty, torn fabric than skin.

Fifteen seconds.

Twelve.

The whistling becomes a ringing sound.

Dust everywhere.

Her entire upper body now.

Up, up.

Zeke stops tugging at the wood, grabs hold of Nadja and helps to pull.

She stares at them.

Who are you?

Who am I? Where am I?

Up, out of the coffin.

She tries to stand, but her legs won't bear her weight, so Zeke picks her up, and Malin helps him, and quickly, quickly, they scramble out of the shallow grave.

Three seconds.

The ringing sound ebbs away.

And everything goes silent apart from the approaching sirens.

Göran Möller arrives just as the explosion rips the air apart and shakes the windscreen of his car.

One hundred metres out across the field he sees a cloud of dust rise towards the sky, and little lumps of earth rain down on his car.

He punches the steering wheel, and goes on hitting it.

They didn't get there in time.

It's all too late now.

## 68

Daniel Högfeldt's arms are stretched out, and the man in the room has driven nails through his wrists.

He used the nail-gun on his calves as well.

Daniel feels the pain through the veil of drugs, but adrenaline makes it vague and diffuse, bearable in the midst of all that is unbearable.

The room is dark and damp. He can see water running down bare stone walls, and a red lamp is shining right in his face.

The man in black is moving at the edge of the room, seems almost to blend into the rock wall.

Faced with the fact that anything at all could happen, your reaction ends up being almost indifference, Daniel thinks.

Then fear takes hold of him and he wants to scream. But his mouth is full of earth, unless it's sand, and he's thirsty.

Have I still got my tongue?

There.

There's my tongue.

It would make sense to think of myself as dead, Daniel thinks. But he doesn't want to stay calm, because if the adrenaline stops pumping, he'll end up screaming with pain.

Can I meet death halfway?

He glances down.

His chest is bare.

Completely exposed to the figure at the edge of the room.

Helpless.

Like a corpse that's about to undergo an autopsy. That's about to witness the cause of its own death.

# 69

Dust swirls through the air as Göran Möller runs out across the field.

Fog.

The dust is like fog, and he races through the earth-red veils.

It can't have happened again.

Where are they? Let them be here somewhere.

Then he catches sight of Zeke.

He's getting to his feet, and he coughs, stumbles towards Göran. Holds up his hand. Gives him the thumbs-up, and points behind him.

Göran Möller rushes past Zeke, deeper into an increasingly murky world.

Malin.

There she is. She's kneeling beside a body that looks naked and clothed at the same time. She's waving her hand in front of the figure's face. It's a girl, and as Göran Möller gets closer he sees that the girl's chest is rising and falling, rising and falling.

She's alive.

Malin's alive.

She turns her filthy face towards him, smiles.

The look in her eyes says: We made it, we made it.

But did we? This isn't over yet. We haven't caught him. The game isn't over.

Göran Möller crouches down beside her, asks: 'Are you hurt?'

Malin shakes her head.

'We managed to get far enough away. There were a few extra seconds before the bomb went off.'

Göran looks over towards the five-metre-wide crater beyond them. He can't see how deep it is, but it was a powerful explosion.

'What about her?'

'She's going to be OK,' Malin coughs. 'But we need an ambulance.'

While they wait for the ambulance they try to get some sort of response from Nadja Lundin, but she just stares up at the sky, doesn't seem to hear what they say, or want to drink the water they offer her. Göran Möller calls her parents, tells them she's alive, that she's going to be OK, but that she isn't able to talk for the time being.

Fifteen minutes later the ambulance arrives and she is put inside.

One of the paramedics sits down beside her.

Malin's ears are ringing, but she can hear again. Zeke seems to be similarly unharmed: shaken, but not hurt.

The ambulance drives off, and Malin thinks: We made it.

Then she thinks of Tove.

Why haven't I heard anything more?

Has the helicopter crashed? Or was there never another village, still less a helicopter?

Her stomach feels like a lump of rock and stagnant water at the same time.

'How's Börje?' she asks.

'He's in intensive care. Internal bleeding and burns.'

'Is he going to be OK?' Zeke asks.

Göran Möller hesitates before replying.

'He's not?' Malin says.

'It's fifty–fifty.'

The bastard, Malin thinks. What's he going to come up with next?

'Where could he be?' Göran Möller asks.

They're avoiding saying his name, unwilling to humanise him like that, it's better to keep him as a nameless creature.

'In his van?' Zeke says.

'Not impossible. There's been no sight of it since the alert was issued,' Göran Möller says.

'We need a wash,' Zeke says. 'And a change of clothes.'

'Get back to the station.'

Uniforms are milling about around them, don't seem to know what to do with themselves. Music is coming from one of the patrol cars, one of that spring's big hits, but Malin has no idea who the artist is.

Then her phone buzzes again.

Another text.

Maybe you could save her, but can you save your love?

Before she has time to show the others, another message arrives.

A YouTube link.

Malin clicks on it as Göran and Zeke lean closer to her. They watch the video together in silence.

Daniel naked, nailed to a piece of plywood in a room with stone walls.

The room is bathed in a red light.

Daniel.

I can't manage without you.

He's groaning. His mouth is covered by tape.

The look in his eyes is pure fear.

Then a man in a hood comes into shot. His face is just vague shapes, and it's impossible to say if it's Jonas Ahl.

He says, in a voice that's so cold that it seems to be

made from some unknown metal: 'I'm going to silence him. The game is over now. I'm going to silence everyone, so that you realise the importance of watching your words. Of being honest.'

The man moves away from the camera. To the left of the picture they see him do something at a table. In the background Daniel appears to have lost consciousness, his head is hanging limply to one side.

The man with the hood comes back into shot.

Eyeballs in an otherwise featureless blackness.

Then a long, echoing laugh.

'Can you save your beloved?'

The video ends.

Malin throws her phone on the ground and rushes out into the field, screaming as loudly as her lungs are capable of, and she hears the scream make its way out across the plain, slowly dissolving into its constituent parts and falling to the ground.

She screams again.

Realises that what's coming from her lungs is death, that the scream is just disappearing into nothingness, and then she feels Zeke's hand on her shoulder.

'Come here, Malin.'

She follows him back across the field towards the car, and Göran Möller holds her phone out to her.

'Take this call.'

She takes the phone.

'Mum? Is that you? It's me, Tove.'

## 70

The truck had broken down. They were helped by people from a mountain tribe. Spent two days walking to their village, where there was a radio. Then a helicopter picked them up.

'Everyone was so kind, Mum. They wanted ten dollars to let us use the radio, but then they realised we didn't have any money. The aid agency sent some cash with the helicopter.'

Malin feels the phone shake in her hand. Tears are streaming down her cheeks.

'Where are you now?'

'In Kinshasa. They flew us straight here.'

'Are you coming home now?'

'What do you mean?'

'Don't you realise how worried I've been?'

'This was nothing, though.'

Malin feels anger crowding in: NOTHING? But she holds back.

'I love you,' she says instead. 'You know that, don't you?'

'I love you too, Mum. But I'm doing important work here.'

'Come home.'

'This is home now. Is everything OK with you?'

'Everything's fine,' Malin says. 'Just as it should be.'

'OK. They want me to hang up now. The satellite link costs a fortune.'

'Bye.'

'Bye, Mum. Say hi to Daniel.'

★

They decide to hold an improvised meeting by the car.

Questions fly between Malin, Zeke, and Göran Möller.

'Where could he be?'

'Has Johan found out anything else?'

'Where was that video filmed? Can we trace where it was uploaded from?'

Their questions remain unanswered, and their frustration is growing.

'Fuck!' Malin eventually shouts. 'Fucking bloody hell!'

So much has happened, yet they still know hardly anything.

Zeke tries to calm her.

One of the uniforms, a heavily built man is his mid-twenties, Malin remembers that his name is Andreas Gran, approaches them. He holds up his phone.

'I've watched the video.'

Don't bother us now, Malin thinks.

'Get lost,' Zeke says. 'We're busy.'

'Wait, you have to listen to me.'

We don't have to do anything, Malin thinks.

'You heard what Zeke said,' Göran Möller says. 'Bad timing.'

'But . . .'

'Leave it,' Malin snarls.

The thickset cop, Andreas, looks upset, almost tearful, then he gets angry instead: 'I know where the video was filmed. Do you hear? I'm quite certain.'

They stop, stand motionless. Feel the words they were about to utter catch in their throats.

Göran Möller recovers first.

'OK. Let's hear it.'

Andreas clicks to start the clip, then pauses it at a point where you can see most of the room.

'Bare rock walls,' he says. 'Ventilation pipes in the ceiling. And you see that wall over there, those hooks? The way they look sort of double? They were made specially for that site. I recognise them because my grandfather designed them. That's the big bomb shelter up in Kvarn. You know, the abandoned military area up towards Tjällmo. That's where he is.'

Malin sees Daniel in the background of the picture.

His body hanging lifeless.

Her whole being is a mass of contradictions now: relieved and angry, full of anxiety and exhaustion.

'You're quite sure?'

'Hundred and ten per cent,' Andreas says. 'You can hang your helmet and rucksack on those hooks at the same time. They were only ever installed there. I went there once when I was little, thought it was a really cool place.'

'Hundred and ten per cent certain?' Zeke says.

'Definitely.'

You don't even realise how stupid that sounds, Malin thinks.

Then she slaps his shoulder a couple of times. Hard and laddish.

'Fucking well spotted,' she says. 'Thank you.'

He's there, Malin thinks. Daniel is there.

A silent room.

And he must be terrified.

As terrified as I am.

I have to reach you in time. I can't start all over again.

That's enough now.

You mustn't die, Daniel.

If you do, I'll die too.

And she thinks of a child, playing restlessly, certain that each moment is both the last and the first.

## 71

That's the end, hanging there. When I'm done with him, it's over.

Then you'll be able to talk, Mum. Say whatever you want. Then the whole world will hear what you say.

He wrote about me as if I were the devil. And got people to believe it. All to make himself look good, when in fact he's the evil one.

Black plus white equals grey.

Everything is grey.

But I'm turning it red.

I shall cut off the hands he uses to write with.

Or shall I burn out the lungs that give your words the air they need?

Lungs, hands. Hands, lungs.

Eeny, meeny, miny, mo.

Hands it is.

Or tongue?

What do you think, Mum?

I wish you could see me play. The way you thought the police played with you when you went to see them.

The laughter behind your back.

The animals weren't enough in the end. I came to this city, saw these false, arrogant people, and felt I had to act. Something snapped.

Animals weren't enough. It was time for people.

Cut Hajif's head off, crucify you, render the first one mute.

I walk towards him now.

To silence the person I became when you disappeared. Mum.

I'm doing this for your sake.


This is the end. Daniel sees the man as if through an unfocused pair of binoculars with red lenses.

He's got a knife in his hand, or is it a syringe? It makes a noise. A blowtorch?

The man takes his hand. Gently. Why gently? Then he lets go of it.

It's hot now.

The sound.

The blowtorch.

The pain. It forces through all the walls his body has built up, and he screams, even though he can't.

## 72

Malin, Zeke, Göran Möller, and Andreas Gran are moving through the dense Östergötland forest.

The undergrowth crunches and snaps as their shoes break through the vegetation, as if the earth were protesting against their arrival in this forgotten place.

They're going as fast as they can.

Stumbling. Feel the lingering smells of the previous autumn's decay. Last year's dead plants try to cling to their legs and drag them down to the ground.

Stop them.

They're cursing.

And Malin feels the undergrowth scratch at her ankles.

Daniel.

I'm on my way.

I'm coming as fast as I can.

They left their car over by the old barracks. There was a white Skoda parked there already. A hire car. The windows of the old buildings are covered with plywood on which someone has drawn stylised screaming faces.

Jonas Ahl, or someone else.

The way Zeke was driving it's a wonder we got here at all, Malin thinks. Then tries not to think at all.

The bomb shelter is supposed to be four hundred metres to the north, straight through the forest, with no approach road so that the enemy wouldn't be able to find it. Blasted out of the ancient bedrock.

'It should be here,' Göran Möller says after they've been running for a while.

'We're close,' Andreas says.

He's out of breath, as is Zeke. None of them has anything like Malin's stamina.

Andreas stumbles.

Malin doesn't wait. But he soon catches up with her.

They look around. The forest seems to live its own life here, and only a few stray rays of light pierce the canopy of trees.

A little further on the ground starts to rise, it looks fairly natural, but there's still some sort of elevation ahead.

They move forward, weapons drawn.

'We're standing on top of something now,' Zeke says, and Malin wonders what might be going on below them.


'Don't you want me to do it, Mum?'

The man turns his back on Daniel as he turns the blowtorch up to maximum.

'Don't say that. I want to do this. It's so nice. Please, Mum.'

Daniel looks at him. Tries to move his hands, but it's hopeless.

He's held tight.

The man hadn't started to burn him. He paused, apparently unable to make up his mind, then started babbling one nursery rhyme after the other, and now he seems to be talking to his mother.

What about my mother? Daniel thinks.

She died fifteen years ago. I buried her, and I haven't really thought about her much since then.

'So I can do it, then?'

The blowtorch.

It's howling. Its blue flame looks even bluer in the red light.

'I'm going to do it.'

Daniel sees him come closer and closer.

Goodbye, Malin. I hope you can hear this. I love you.


'Over here! There's a hatch.'

Göran Möller is standing ten metres away, pointing at the ground with his pistol. Malin and Zeke run over to him, and Malin grabs hold of the handle of the hatch, pulls it towards her, and Göran Möller seems to want to object, but stops himself.

'He must have closed it after him,' Göran Möller says. 'Unless there's another way down.'

'There must be,' Andreas Gran says. 'To get all the essentials and equipment in.'

'We haven't got time to look for it now.'

'You stay up here,' Malin says to Andreas. 'Unless you know your way around down there?'

A fixed ladder leads downwards.

Down into unknown darkness.

Malin takes the lead and they start to descend. The walls of the tunnel shimmer with damp, and the stench of mould makes it hard to breathe. The rungs are rusty and sharp, yet simultaneously slippery with some sort of algal growth.

Am I going to fall? Malin thinks. What if one of the rungs gives way?

Down, down.

Into the darkness. They can't switch on the lights of their mobiles because they need to hold on to the ladder with both hands.

The air feels stuffier with each rung.

Her heart is pounding in her chest. Sweat is running down her cheeks from her scalp.

Hurry.

Daniel.

You can't die.

I might only have a few minutes.

If that.

Ten rungs, twenty, fifty, seventy-three.

Malin counts them all, and once she is down in the passageway she switches on the torch on her mobile and looks around her.

The tunnel reaches off in two directions, like an endless catacomb. She listens for sounds in the rock. Can't hear anything. She moves to make space for Zeke and Göran, and soon the three of them are standing there together.

'Right or left?' Zeke asks.

'We're not splitting up,' Göran Möller says. 'We stick together.'

'Is he here?' Malin asks. 'Are they here?'

And she sees Daniel in her mind's eye, alone with the evil, and she walks off to the right, quickly, holding her pistol out in front of her in one hand, and her illuminated mobile in the other.

Then she hears a scream. Unless it's just her imagination?

'He's here,' Göran Möller says. 'Somewhere.'


Did I just hear something? Is someone coming?

Did she manage to rescue the frightened girl? The one with the big ego?

The one I saw hounding the staff at the library? The one who asked me to fetch a book from the archive, and then laughed and said she didn't need it?

That's what she was like.

But she's learned her lesson.

And I've been able to play, Mum, you've watched me play from up in heaven.

I'm going to burn him now.

But first I remove the earth from his mouth.

LISTEN TO HIM SCREAM.

HA HA.

It's great fun, isn't it?

Malin hears the scream.

She's sure now.

Recognises Daniel's voice somewhere inside it.

Where's the scream coming from? Further on? Or behind them?

She runs, hears the others' footsteps behind her, and Daniel screams again.

Closer now.

The others must have heard it too, and with every step they get closer to his screams.

Another junction. Straight on, right or left?

Which is life, which is death?

Where's the big room? The heart of the shelter?

They carry straight on. Reach an opening blocked by two black, rusting doors.

Screaming.

Daniel.

I'm here.

Close.

What's he doing to you?

Göran and Zeke each drag one side of the door open.

A huge room comes into view, a church hall of a space, with a tarmac floor, but no windows or benches. Fifty metres by thirty, and at least twenty metres up to the gently arched stone roof. Water drips down onto the floor, trickling down the walls and out through tiny drainage holes.

The rock is weeping, Malin thinks. The earth.

But the room is empty, and she hears more screaming.

Sorry, Daniel, I haven't reached you yet.

It can't be too late.

\*

The heat on his chest is unbearable. He wishes he would pass out, but his consciousness refuses to loosen its grip.

His entire being is heat, and in that heat is the smell of his burning hair, skin, and flesh, and he screams as his nipple burns to charcoal. As if from a distance he can hear the laughter of evil and insanity.

The heat cuts into his bone.

Then the world finally disappears from Daniel Högfeldt.

They run on, and now they're standing in front of another iron door, the door that seemed to conceal the scream that's just fallen silent.

Red light is seeping out beneath it.

There is a barely audible sound, roaring and hissing in turn.

We have to get in, Malin thinks.

She imagines she can hear more screaming.

Even louder.

Howls of pain.

All three of them grab hold of the handle, try to pull the door open, but it's locked.

'Fuck!' Malin screams, knowing that the man inside can hear her.

They're coming to rescue you now.

So absurd.

Nothing can save you.

They'll never be able to force the lock, and I am holding the blowtorch like a pistol.

I can make out your ribs now.

Soon I'll uncover your lungs. And will see to it that they never give air to your ramblings again.

You lasted a long time. Your consciousness didn't want to release you from the pain.

'What do you say, Mum? Shall I let them in?'

'Never, never.'
I turn around. Ready to go on.

Göran Möller has inserted his lock-pick into the door, and
is moving it frantically up and down.
'The keyhole's too rusty,' he says.
'Keep going,' Zeke hisses.
Malin is stamping her feet, eager to get inside the room,
Daniel could still be alive. Must be, I couldn't bear it if
you died.
I want our love.
There's a click and the door opens, and they're struck
by bright red light. Through her blurred vision Malin can
make out a spotlight, then Daniel, naked and strung up,
and in front of him a man who must be Jonas Ahl.
Or is it someone else?
A blowtorch.
He is pointing it at Daniel's heart, and Malin raises her
pistol, takes aim at the black outline of the man's back,
and shoots him.
Hands steady. Not frightened of hitting her beloved.
She shoots the man first in the heart, then in the spine,
up towards his neck, and he collapses onto the concrete floor.
The blowtorch falls from his hand and rolls towards
the spotlight, towards what appears to be advanced broad-
casting equipment, where it goes on hissing angrily.
The air reeks of charred human flesh and blood.
Daniel.
His chest is an open wound, and she can see several
ribs. His body is hanging limply from the nails.
Blood is trickling onto the floor.
She takes his head in her hands. Strokes his cheeks.
Sees her fingers turn red.
'I'm here now. Hold on. You're going to make it. I've
saved you. Tell me I've saved you, Daniel.'

You're coming home, she thinks. To our home. The one we're going to make together.

Far away from all suffering.

A place of safety, one that feels impregnable.

Free from this fake red light.

There's no such thing as safety. I know that.

Maybe not even when our ashes are deposited in the earth.

Daniel coughs. Spits up blood.

They're trying to get him down, but are having to be careful. The nails through his arms and legs are fixed firmly enough to hold his weight.

'Malin?'

She puts her face close to his.

'I'm here.'

He spits out more blood. A thin stream is trickling from his chest, colouring Malin's blouse red. She puts her finger on it, trying to stem the flow.

What sort of world is this? she thinks.

'Malin.'

'I can hear you, Daniel.'

And somewhere close to her a thousand voices are singing again. Peder Åkerlund, Suliman Hajif, and Jonas Ahl, whose lifeless face is staring up at Göran Möller.

They're singing from hell. From a realm deep below the earth.

Where is your voice coming from, Daniel?

'I love you,' she says.

We're going to carry on breathing, together, you and I. We shall breathe together for ever.

# Epilogue

*We are the dead.*
   *Hear us.*
   *Wherever our voices are coming from.*
   *We're in the earth, we're in the air you breathe, in fire.*
*Perhaps we're in fire most of all.*
   *For me and Peder and Suliman there is no forgiveness.*
   *For Nadja Lundin there are no longer any words.*
   *She is sitting mute and silent in a hospital on the shore of*
*Lake Vättern, refusing to acknowledge that the world exists.*

For the three of us there is nothing but pain and loneliness. And perhaps we deserve that. But what does this
world really do to us? We just tried to make sense of it in
our words and deeds.

The clear light of early summer is streaming in through
a closed window.

Malin is sitting beside Daniel's hospital bed.

He's being kept sedated to stop the pain from overwhelming him. He's going to make it, as long as he doesn't
suffer any severe infections, without any long-term damage
beyond the scars that will never fade.

Börje Svärd is lying in a different department. By his
side sits a woman who barely knows him, but who still
insists on being there.

He too is going to be all right. The doctors managed
to stop the internal bleeding, and his face didn't suffer
any burns because he had already lowered his head when
the explosion happened.

She squeezes Daniel's hand and thinks about Tove, about

love. How it exists everywhere and can take so many forms, and how confusing and scary it can seem. Because at the heart of all violence is a love that has taken the wrong path.

Malin leans her head against the white sheet.

Falls asleep.

And she dreams about Tove.

In her dream Tove is running across a burning field. Flames the height of a man are chasing her, driving her on and consuming everything in their path.

But Tove isn't frightened.

There's happiness in her face.

She's running ahead of the fire, singing and dancing, and Malin hears her words: 'See me run across the earth, see me vanquish fire.'

In the best books, the ending often comes as a shock.
Not just because of that one last twist in the tale,
but because you have been so absorbed in their world,
that coming back to the harsh light of reality is a jolt.

If that describes you now, then perhaps you should track down
some new leads, and find new suspense in other worlds.

Join us at www.hodder.co.uk, or follow us on
Twitter @hodderbooks, and you can tap in to a
community of fellow thrill-seekers.

Whether you want to find out more about this book,
or a particular author, watch trailers and interviews, have
the chance to win early limited editions, or simply browse
our expert readers' selection of the very best books,
we think you'll find what you're looking for.

And if you don't, that's the place to tell us what's missing.

**We love what we do, and we'd love you to be part of it.**

www.hodder.co.uk

 @hodderbooks

HodderBooks

 HodderBooks